PERIL IN PAPERBACK

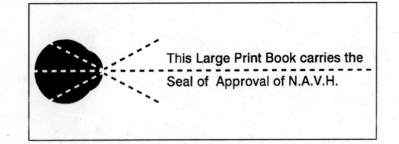

This Large Print Book carries the
Seal of Approval of N.A.V.H.

A BIBLIOPHILE MYSTERY

PERIL IN PAPERBACK

KATE CARLISLE

WHEELER PUBLISHING
A part of Gale, Cengage Learning

GALE
CENGAGE Learning·

Detroit • New York • San Francisco • New Haven, Conn • Waterville, Maine • London

GALE
CENGAGE Learning·

Wheeler Publishing Large Print Cozy Mystery.
The text of this Large Print edition is unabridged.
Other aspects of the book may vary from the original edition.
Set in 16 pt. Plantin.

LIBRARY OF CONGRESS CATALOGING-IN-PUBLICATION DATA

Carlisle, Kate, 1951–
    Peril in Paperback : a Bibliophile Mystery / by Kate Carlisle. — Large Print edition.
        pages cm. — (Wheeler Publishing Large Print Cozy Mystery)
    ISBN-13: 978-1-4104-5426-3 (softcover)
    ISBN-10: 1-4104-5426-6 (softcover)
    1. Books—Conservation and restoration—Fiction. 2. Rare books—Fiction.
3. Murder—Investigation—Fiction. 4. Large type books. I. Title.
PS3603.A7527P47 2013
813'.6—dc23   2012044654

Published in 2013 by arrangement with NAL Signet, a member of Penguin Group (USA) Inc.

Printed in the United States of America
1 2 3 4 5   17 16 15 14 13

This one's for you, Jane, with all my love and gratitude. Thanks for being there for me when I was overwhelmed by a desperate desire to explore that cheesy haunted house and when I insisted on driving hundreds of miles to find a goat farm. Thanks for your steadfast insistence that I sample every champagne in the world — all in the name of art and research, of course. And thanks for everything else, too. Love you!

CHAPTER 1

"We call it the Library Suite," my hostess said, beaming with pride as she led me into the spacious bedroom that would be all mine for the next six days.

"I can see why." As I looked around the room, I hoped my expression remained calm despite the volatile mix of shock, fascination, and trepidation coursing through me as I took in the mad proliferation of books.

I love books, but this is crazy, I thought. That funny old cliché about the walls closing in on you? It wasn't so funny anymore. On the other hand, there were so many books, I wouldn't be able to see if the walls were getting closer or not.

"Isn't it marvelous?" Grace said, tugging to smooth out the pale sage duvet cover on the king-sized bed. "Ruth teases me about my book obsession, but I have a good time with it."

"I'm stunned," I muttered. It was the truth. The number of books she'd managed to cram into this spacious bedroom/sitting room was astounding.

I'm Brooklyn Wainwright, book-restoration expert and lover of books, good food, and wine, and lately, doughnuts. I had driven up to Lake Tahoe that morning with my two favorite neighbors, Suzie Stein and Vinnie Patel, to spend the week at the home of Suzie's wealthy, eccentric aunt Grace Crawford. We were here to celebrate Grace's birthday. It was the Big 5-0, and Grace wanted to do it up in style.

Grace's good friend, Ruth Kinsley, had convinced Grace to celebrate her fiftieth birthday with an old-fashioned house party on the lake. In her engraved invitation, Grace had promised her guests that this weeklong party would be the most delightful, most fabulous shindig ever, the sort of party we'd all still be talking about for the next fifty years.

I was looking forward to the party atmosphere, but I also hoped I might get some quiet relaxation time. After all, I was about to spend seven long days in a gorgeous home with little else to do all day but sit around and enjoy the beauty of its idyllic lakefront setting. Sounded good to me. I'd been working too hard lately and the long hours were starting to catch up with me. In fact, watching Grace refold the cashmere throw at the end of the bed made me want to lie down and take a nap.

"I looked over my list of guests," Grace said, fluffing one of the pillows. "And I couldn't think of anyone who would appreciate this room more than you."

"That's sweet, Grace," I said, hoping she could hear the sincerity in my voice as I parked my rolling suitcase near the foot of the bed. "You know how much I love books."

"You and me both," she said, laughing as she glanced around. "I guess that's pretty obvious."

I laughed with her. It would be rude not to, right? I continued my slow turn, gazing at the four walls that were covered in bookshelves crammed with books. There was the occasional window, thank goodness, and a few pieces of necessary bedroom furniture: an elegant dresser and mirror; a small but comfortable love seat that faced two matching chairs at one end of the large room; and a sumptuous bed with an ornate paneled headboard filled with — you guessed it — more books. Other than those items of furniture and the windows, it was bookshelves that occupied every inch of wall space. Even the dresser held a row of books lined up beneath the matching mirror.

"I had no idea you had so many," I said.

She lifted her shoulder in a shrug. "I can't seem to quit collecting."

Time to seek professional help, I thought, not unkindly, as I continued to survey the room. I knew Grace was a book lover. That was how we'd met. About a year ago, Grace had mentioned to her niece, Suzie, that she wanted some of her favorite books rebound, so Suzie had recommended me. Since then Grace and I had done business several times. I'd visited her home once before and we'd had afternoon tea in her grand salon.

Grace Crawford was nothing like what I'd expected. I had imagined a genteel, gray-haired granny type who knitted quietly, surrounded by her twelve cats. For excitement, she might play a mean game of canasta.

Instead, Grace was down-to-earth and fun. A ball of energy, she was petite, like Suzie, and wore her dark brown hair cut in a sassy bob. She favored bright, loose clothing, long dresses and flowing tops that billowed dramatically when she walked into a room. The first time I met her, I'd had the instant impression of a colorful tropical bird in perpetual motion. I liked her.

Except for this massive home perched on twenty private acres overlooking Lake Tahoe — well, and the gazillions of valuable books and all the lovely, expensive furniture and furnishings and artwork inside the house — you would never know that Grace Crawford was a self-made billionaire. She had amassed a fortune in the computer games industry and was recognized among her family and friends and most of the world at large as the original geeky game girl. In personality and demeanor, she was the oddest blend of Old World elegance, laid-back sixties cool, and nerdy earnestness. I liked all those aspects of her. And Grace's quirky sensibilities — such as putting a suit of armor in the powder room, or serving bite-sized Twinkies next to the delicate cucumber sandwiches at afternoon tea — never failed to make me smile.

Plus, she'd given me a lot of business lately. I liked that about her, too, naturally.

Vinnie had often referred to Grace as a book hoarder, but I'd dealt with a true hoarder recently and couldn't agree with Vinnie's assessment. When I walked through the rooms of Grace's home, I didn't get the same closed-in, claustrophobic, unstable feeling that I'd felt inside the hoarder's house. Grace was an unconventional collector, for sure, but a hoarder? I didn't think so. But now, seeing this room, this Library Suite in which I would be living for the next seven days, I was beginning to think twice.

Still, the room was beautifully furnished, large, and, most of all, clean. There was no scent of mustiness, either. A hint of mustiness could be charming in a hole-in-the-wall used bookstore on Green Street in San Francisco, but not in a bedroom in which I would be sleeping for a week.

So here I was in a clean, charming bedroom with lots of books and even a small couch on which I could relax in quiet comfort. *Why am I complaining?* I wondered. And right then and there I made a decision to be grateful and enjoy this room with all its books and nooks and crannies and quirkiness.

When Grace had called to invite me to her birthday party, she'd asked if I wouldn't mind doing some bookbinding work while I was here. I had immediately agreed and had packed my travel set of tools and repair supplies. I was always happier when I was busy with books. Grace not only wanted some repairs made but had also asked me to check out and oversee the library archivist she'd hired recently to catalog her extensive collection of books.

12

Glancing around the room now, I realized what a huge job it would be. Heck, it would take more than a week to catalog this one bedroom alone. The archivist and I had our work cut out for us.

Grace was watching me, so I flashed her a genuine smile as I gave the walls one more glance. "Thank you so much. I know I'll have a wonderful time here."

She seemed pleased as she nudged her glasses up her nose. "Now, the library is just down the hall, so you can come and go without disturbing anyone else in the house. Most of the other guests are in the second- and third-floor bedrooms, but I didn't think you'd mind being on the first floor."

I was determined to ease her worries. "I don't mind at all. This couldn't be better. You know me. Can't get enough books, right?"

She laughed, a sweet trilling sound completely incongruous with her geek-dynamo personality, but charming. "I'll let you get settled. And I'll tell you what I've told everyone else. I want you to feel free to explore the whole house. I know you've been here before, but you've never had the full tour. You've got to see some of the other rooms. There are many surprises."

"I can't wait. I've heard about some of

them," I said. On the drive earlier, Vinnie had given me a hint of some of the more bizarre features of this gigantic fun house.

"Oh, good." She rubbed her hands together gleefully. "If I were you, I would start with the conservatory. We have a marvelous collection of exotic flora and it's such a soothing, pretty space. But when you get tired of all that peace and quiet, the game room is not to be missed. It's so much fun."

"That's what Suzie said."

"Suzie loves the game room. And the music room is pretty special if you're into musical instruments. We have a three-hundred-year-old harpsichord that still sounds beautiful. And we can supply a complete wind and brass section for anyone who's in the mood to jam. And percussion, of course. Every noisemaker you can think of." She laughed, then added, "Or you can just have a seat and watch things happen. There's a player piano, but I've also rigged some puppets to play saxophone and guitar. It's a total blast."

She had morphed into an excited young gamer. "It sounds awesome," I said. "I can't wait to do some exploring."

"It's an adventure, for sure." She took a breath and appeared to remember she was a grown-up. Grabbing my arm, she strolled with me to the bedroom door. "We're all meeting for cocktails at five o'clock in the Gold Salon. That's up the grand stairway. Turn left and go halfway down the hall. It's on the north side of the house, overlooking the lake. I drew a map for everyone and left one on your nightstand."

"Oh, thanks. I think I remember how to find the grand staircase, but after that I'm lost."

She chuckled. "Ruth dubbed it the grand stairway when she first saw it and we've called it that ever since. It's just the main staircase off the front door."

"I remember. It is pretty grand, now that you mention it."

She smiled. "If you get lost, just look out any window. If you can see the lake, you're looking north. We have two main hallways running the length of the house: one in the front of the house and one in the back. Two side halls, the east and the west. If you can remember that your room is off the back hall, closest to the lake, you'll always find your way."

"I think I've got it," I said, utterly confused.

She laughed again. "Oh, you'll get lost once or twice, but that just makes it all the more fun. Now, don't be late for cocktails. I can't wait for all my favorite people to meet and mingle."

"I'll be there," I assured her as we waved good-bye to each other. I stood at the doorway and watched her walk down the wide, wood-paneled hall and turn a corner. Grace didn't know me very well yet, but suffice to say I wouldn't miss a cocktail party for the world. I decided I would scout out the Gold Salon on my tour this afternoon. That way I wouldn't get lost and be late for cocktails. That would be rude.

Twenty minutes later my suitcase was emptied and stowed in a corner of the walk-in closet. I had hung up my dressy clothes and folded everything else in the dresser drawers. All my toiletries were arranged along the counter in my private bathroom, and I'd placed the books I'd brought with me on the table next to the love seat under the pretty bay window. As it turned out, bringing a few books along wasn't quite as necessary as I'd thought when I packed them. But how was I to know Grace Crawford owned every book ever written?

"Are you all settled?"

I glanced up and saw Vinnie standing in the open doorway. Suzie stood behind her, wearing a curious grin as her gaze swept my room. "Wow."

"Tell me about it."

"Holy kebabs, Brooklyn," Vinnie whispered, her voice tight with alarm as her eyes goggled at the sight of all those books. Abruptly, she whipped around and wagged her finger at Suzie. "This is exactly what I was afraid of." Then she whirled back to me, wearing a look of regret. "I'm sorry. Why don't we try to find you another room?"

"I'm okay here," I insisted. "I like it."

She turned back to Suzie. "You must apologize to Brooklyn for your aunt's crazitude."

"I'm not sure that's a word, babe," Suzie said.

"It should be," Vinnie said darkly. "It describes Grace perfectly."

"I think this is cool," Suzie said, walking into my room and looking around. "Besides, Brooklyn's met Aunt Grace before and knows she's a book nut. And she's been to the house before, too. So what's the big deal?"

"I never saw this room before," I muttered. "If Derek were here, he'd laugh his ass off. Me, entrapped by books. Obviously, my book-obsessed karma has come back to bite me on the butt."

"Wow, two butt mentions in less than ten seconds." Suzie gazed at me. "You must miss him a lot."

"I do, but I didn't know there was a correlation between Derek and, you know, butt references."

"Derek has a very attractive backside," Vinnie said. The words were even more humorous when said in her lilting Indian accent.

Suzie waggled her eyebrows. "Guess you can tell we take the subject of Derek's bum very seriously at our house."

"I appreciate that," I said, smiling. "I do, too. And I do miss him. But I'm happy to be here with you guys. And I know Derek would be happy to hear I was here with you guys for the week."

"He doesn't know you're here?" Vinnie asked.

I shrugged. "He left on assignment three weeks ago and I didn't have a chance to remind him."

"Can you call him?" Vinnie asked.

"I suppose I could if it were an emergency," I said. "But I'd rather not bother him otherwise."

"Don't worry. I'm sure he'd approve," Suzie said, and chuckled. "There's a lot less chance of you getting into trouble if you're with us."

"Not that we believe there will be any trouble," Vinnie said quickly, rapping her knuckles against the smooth wood top of the dresser. "But I'll knock wood just in case."

"Good thinking," I said, and tapped the wood frame of the bathroom door. I can use all the good-luck rituals and charms I can get.

It had been only a few months since trouble had last found me. I'd been at the mercy of someone who wanted to kill me, and that wasn't the first time it had happened. I'd tried to make light of it, but the jokes were losing steam. The fact was, I had an alarming tendency to find dead people, followed by an ineffable need to see that justice prevailed on their behalf. Invariably, I would end up in a face-to-face confrontation with the dead person's killer.

It had gotten so bad that I'd finally sought spiritual guidance from Guru Bob, otherwise known as Avatar Robson Benedict, the leader of my parents' commune and an all-around remarkable guy.

Guru Bob had suggested that the universe might have cast me in the role of nemesis for the dead. Seriously.

19

I still wasn't sure what I thought about that.

But it had been eight long weeks since I'd had any run-ins with dead people or the killers who made them that way, so I was hoping all that was behind me.

Vinnie stared up in horror. "For the love of Shiva, there are books on the ceiling." She glared at Suzie. "This is beyond peculiar. How can we be sure that Brooklyn won't be smothered in her sleep? You must do something, Suzie."

"I'm fine," I said with a casual air. "It's just a bunch of books up there."

But Vinnie was starting to freak me out. Grace had indeed managed to hang bookshelves from the ceiling. They were unique and beautiful, really. The shelving fanned out from the central chandelier like the petals of a flower. Although you couldn't really call it shelving; these were more like attractively paneled, triangular-shaped boxes that held books. Looking up, you could see that there were books, but you couldn't read the titles unless you lowered the shelf. Or the petal. Whatever it was.

The petals were made from different shades of wood and they spanned to the corners of the room in a pretty swirling pattern. *Almost like a spiderweb,* I realized. I was all operated by remote control. While unpacking, I had discovered the small remote-control module and had pushed the power button, thinking I was turning on the television. Instead, the shelving began to move up and down.

It shocked me, and in my moment of panic I started pushing buttons at random. The shelves moved up and down in no discernible pattern, no rhyme or reason, only movement. I couldn't get them to stop and was getting a little freaked out. I fancied myself going insane, dashing outside, throwing myself into the lake, and drowning.

Not that I was overly dramatic or anything.

After a minute, I figured out the right buttons to push and it all made perfect sense. I took a moment to check that there was nothing but books in the shelves, then resolved to examine them later for cataloging purposes.

I knew Grace was a computer wizard and an engineering genius, but I was still mystified. I'd never seen anything like it. Why had she chosen to build this odd creation? Was it a whim of the moment? Maybe she'd thrown it together on a spare Saturday, just for giggles.

On the positive side, the ceiling was at

least twelve feet high, so I wasn't likely to suffer claustrophobia from the thought of all those moving petals enclosing me in their web. And now I was mixing metaphors again. Never a good sign.

I tried to ignore the shivers that skittered across my shoulders at the thought of being trapped.

"Okay, that's pretty freaking weird," Suzie admitted, staring up at the odd sight. "But you have to admire Grace's ingenuity."

"Ingenuity." Vinnie rolled her eyes at her partner. "Your aunt is crazier than a bagful of monkeys, but your unconditional love for her is admirable, I suppose."

Suzie shoved her hands into her cargo pants pockets. "My unconditional love for you knows no bounds, sugar."

"Ohh." Vinnie slapped her hand over her mouth, overcome with emotion. She flung her arms around Suzie and squeezed. "I love you, too, Suzie. Even if your aunt is a wack-a-doodle."

Suzie winked at me over Vinnie's shoulder and I smiled at the clever way she'd wrapped up that conversation. But their easy affection made me think of Derek again and I was surprised at the depth of my own longing. I missed him more than I ever thought I would and wished he were here with me.

But that was impossible. He was on a monthlong security assignment in Europe, where he was posing as the fiancé of some megabucks socialite who'd been receiving death threats.

I would just have to suck it up for the next few weeks. I was perfectly fine without him. I really was. And I trusted Derek completely so that wasn't an issue, even though I hadn't been able to stop myself from Googling the woman at the center of his assignment. Just as I'd feared, Thomasina Marchand was young and gorgeous and artistically gifted. She dressed impeccably. And did I mention her beauty? And her immense wealth? Not that Derek could ever be swayed by material things, but, nevertheless, I'd been suffering little pangs of jealousy ever since he'd flown off to pretend he was in love with her.

But that was completely normal, right? Anyone would have those little pangs, right? Of course they would. It didn't mean anything. Derek's and my connection was beautifully solid. We had a happy, loving, exciting, and totally trusting relationship. He simply had an assignment to carry out, protecting Thomasina from threats of death until she reached the age of twenty-five, as specified in her father's trust. That would happen in the next few weeks. I knew Derek would perform his job to perfection, and then he would come home to me. That was all there was to it. I wasn't worried. Nope, not me. No way.

But the fact that he hadn't called me in three weeks was starting to bug me. Not in a clinging-girlfriend kind of way, you understand. No, I was beginning to worry that something might be wrong. Could Derek be hurt? In danger?

"Come on, let's check out more of this crazy place," Suzie said, slipping her arm around Vinnie's waist.

"Yeah, okay," I said. "But look. Do you guys mind if I make a quick phone call first?"

"Of course not, Brooklyn," Vinnie said, her smile serene again. "Why don't we meet you in the conservatory in fifteen minutes? Will that give you enough time?"

"More than enough. Thanks."

They reminded me where the conservatory was, then walked out, closing the door behind them. I went to find my cell phone and sat down to make the call to Derek. I listened to the ringing of his phone and felt more connected to him already. I wasn't sure if that made me a lovesick idiot or just a lonely girlfriend. Either way, it was kind of pathetic, but I didn't care.

"Hello?" a woman answered, whispering breathlessly into the phone. *Derek*'s phone. "Who is this, please?"

I had to bite my tongue to keep from saying, "Who the hell is *this*?" Who was this woman and why was she answering my boyfriend's phone? Was this Thomasina? I decided on the spot to make it sound like a business call.

"I must speak to Mr. Stone immediately. This is his office calling." I sounded officious and demanding, which was exactly how I felt.

"Ooh, his office. No, I'm sorry, but Derek cannot come to the phone." Her voice was tinged with a vague but plainly Western European accent. *French? Belgian? Sexy.* She giggled softly. "He's . . . ooh . . . he's . . . ah . . . occupied. Much too . . . busy . . . to speak." Her rapid sighs made it sound as if she were in the throes of rapture. *Seriously? Is she kidding? What the hell is going on?*

Oh, God. Did I really want to know?

"Adieu," she added in that same sultry tone, then disconnected the call, leaving me to blink and stare at my phone in stunned disbelief.

CHAPTER 2

"Well, that sucked big-time," I muttered to myself as I sat and stared at the phone. Feeling a little shaky, I got up and paced the room. And fretted. And wondered. And got a little pissed off at myself for fretting. Then I fretted some more.

I'd already rejected the idea that Derek might be cheating on me. It wasn't in his nature to lie or play games. But it also wasn't like Derek to let someone answer his phone for him. He ran a multinational security firm and was constantly in touch with partners and clients, evaluating problems and working out solutions. Even when he was working undercover, he would make himself available whenever necessary to deal with critical client issues. His phone was rarely out of his sight.

At least, that's what he had always told me.

So what had just happened? Why would

that woman, whoever she was, pull something like that? Had she stolen Derek's phone? Maybe Derek had done something to annoy her and she was striking back the only way she knew how. Or maybe she simply *wanted* him and he wouldn't comply. I preferred that explanation. Thomasina Marchand was wealthy enough that she might feel entitled to have whatever she wanted.

I fretted some more, then got angry. I refused to feel guilty for calling him while he was working. I also refused to let one ounce of jealousy slither into my heart. But, unfortunately, this incident had reminded me once again that Derek and I lived in different worlds.

It also reminded me that my feelings for Derek were completely different from anything I'd ever felt for another man before. And that scared me. I had always been the strong one in the relationship. I never got whiny; I got mad. I didn't agonize; I walked out. I took action. But now I felt frozen; I didn't know what to do. It was Derek's fault. No, it was my fault. I cared too much.

I paced over to the window and stared at the lake. I was back to fretting again. Had I never cared deeply enough about my former boyfriends? Had I been so shallow, so unfeeling, so hard-hearted that I couldn't be hurt by them? Maybe. Did that mean that this phone call had been some kind of karmic vengeance?

Okay, that was stupid. This wasn't about me. This was about some mean-spirited woman who'd decided to screw around with Derek and me.

Maybe I should have resisted calling him while he was on assignment. He hadn't told me not to call him, but I had never done it before.

And now I could feel the guilt seeping in. I shouldn't have called. It was all my fault. That's what I got for poking my nose in Derek's business.

But no. That wasn't right. I shouldn't feel guilty. This was Derek's fault. No, wait. It was *her* fault. *Who the hell is she?* I hated her.

Oh, God, here came the jealousy.

I almost laughed at myself. Why was I jealous? This wasn't about Derek and me. It was about that woman and her malicious attempt to make me feel bad. And how stupid was I that I'd almost bought into it? She had tried to make me believe that Derek was cheating on me.

But Derek wouldn't do that. Would he?

"Oh, hell." I pounded the wall. My

thoughts were dark and spiraling and weaving themselves into sick, twisted desires that included smacking that skinny French — Belgian? — bitch in the face. And maybe giving Derek a light kick in the shins while I was at it. He shouldn't be leaving his cell phone around for some anorexic Euro twit to use for taunting his real girlfriend.

Okay, that made me feel better.

I sank into the comfy chair by the window and decided it was time to —

A piercing scream interrupted my thoughts.

"Thank God!" I jumped up and ran across the room, threw open the door, and looked both ways down the long hall. Fifty feet away at the far end, a thin woman stood silhouetted by a paned floor-to-ceiling window. She turned and I could see that her eyes were squeezed shut. She was holding her hands over her ears as though she was trying to block out some horrible noise.

"Are you all right?" I shouted as I ran toward her.

"No!" she cried irately. "I'm going freaking crazy in this place!"

As I came near, she glared at me, almost as if it were my fault that she was in a panic. I slowed down and took closer notice of her appearance.

Her eyes were wild and out of control. Her pupils moved every which way, first staring at me, then glancing at the walls, the ceiling, the floor. She must have been yanking at her short reddish hair because it spiked out in odd patterns all over her head. I appreciated the spiked look as well as anyone, but this woman was at least fifty years old and wore a vintage Chanel suit with demure heels. Spiky was not working for her.

Up close, her face was that of a woman much younger than fifty. Maybe thirty-five? It was the Chanel suit that threw me off. How old was she, anyway?

"Are you in trouble?" I asked gently. "Are you lost?"

"Of course I'm freaking lost!" she ranted as she swung her skinny arms around madly. "That's what she does! As soon as you figure out where you are in this monstrosity, she changes everything around. It's enough to drive you freaking nuts."

I took a step back, away from the visceral rage she emitted. "Okay," I said slowly, nodding, assuming she was talking about Grace. "I can walk you back to the front door and the grand stairway is right there. Maybe you can find your way from there."

"Oh, shut up," she snarled. "Stop patron-zing me."

Damn. I tried not to stare, but I could see the skin pulled tightly away from her eyes. Her eyebrows were unnaturally arched and her upper lip line was flawless. Not a wrinkle to be seen. I revised my estimate of her age back to fifty-plus. She appeared young until you got up close enough to see that she'd recently had a really radical face-lift. Scary.

So she was angry *and* vain. And she reminded me of someone else in my life. Was I staring into the future? Was this how my worst enemy and true world-class bitch, Minka LaBoeuf, would look at age fifty?

Minka had been a thorn in my side since college. Worse than a thorn; she was a big, ugly spike. Over the years I had tangled with her, even trading punches a few times. Minka was a horrible person, and this woman standing in front of me was chillingly similar to her.

Oh, dear. I couldn't imagine living in the same house with Minka for a whole freaking week, so there was no way in hell I was going to put up with this lady's negative vibe for that long.

"Look, I'm Brooklyn Wainwright," I said patiently. "I'm a friend of —"

She grunted derisively. "I know who you are. Little Suzie's told us all about you."

31

I took a step back. "You have the advantage, then," I said, trying to match her supercilious tone. As I turned to leave, I added, "Sorry I interrupted your dramatic little moment."

"Wait. How the hell do I get out of here?"

"Not my problem."

"No, wait! I really am lost."

"You'll find your way." I kept walking. She wasn't about to apologize for being a haughty cow, so why should I help her? Besides, it was just a long walk down the hall back to the grand stairway. It's not like we were trapped in a cave or anything. She wasn't really *lost*.

"I'm sorry," she whined.

Huh? I took another step but then stopped. It was an apology, albeit a pathetic one. So I faced her and asked, "Where are you trying to get to?"

She fisted her hands against her hips. "There's supposed to be a hallway leading to the back of the house. It was there yesterday. But now it stops right here." She shook her finger at the solid wall; then her shoulders drooped in defeat. "Never mind. I can see you don't believe me. I don't believe it myself."

I shrugged. "I just arrived a little while ago, but I do know that the front door is back that way." I pointed down the hall, then nodded toward a closed door a few yards away in the opposite direction. "And the library is right in there. Maybe there's a door inside that leads out to the hall you're thinking of."

"I doubt it," she said. Her forehead furrowed as she glanced around in several directions. She pursed her lips — which couldn't have been easy with her skin pulled back so tightly — and made a decision. "I'll go to the front door and start over." She walked past me, then sighed and turned. "I'm Madge Crawford. My husband, Harrison, is Grace's older brother."

"Nice to meet you," I lied, and thought to myself, *Poor Harrison.* But then my conscience got to me. Maybe she was just stressed out. Maybe all that tight facial skin had given her a permanent migraine.

"Look, we got off on the wrong foot," I said, seeking peace. "Why don't we —"

"Really?" She rolled her eyes. "We're still chatting? Is this what I'll have to deal with all week?" Then she turned and stalked away down the hall. I sent off a fervent prayer that she would get lost permanently.

"Yoo-hoo. Over here, Brooklyn." Vinnie waved as I walked into the sunny conservatory. "How is Derek?"

"Oh. He's . . . um, fine, I guess," I muttered, my head still swirling with negativity. The only good news about running into nasty Madge was that I'd forgotten all about the ugly phone call with the Belgian bimbo. I'd spent my entire walk to the conservatory mentally grousing about Harrison Crawford's unpleasant wife.

But now I stopped, made a slow circle and took in my surroundings. "What a beautiful room."

Suzie nodded. "Cool, isn't it?"

"It is my favorite place in this monstrous house of tricks," Vinnie said cheerfully.

"I can see why," I said, staring up at the tempered-glass ceiling. "It's wonderful."

"At least there's nothing hanging up there ready to snare you," Vinnie muttered, casting a quick glimpse upward.

It was as magical as any world-class botanical garden I'd ever visited, except smaller. With an iron frame and glass walls, the Victorian-styled structure was about the size of a small gymnasium. A pea-gravel path wound its way around dozens of exotic plants and trees. In front of each flourishing plant was a tasteful bronze plaque identifying it and its country of origin, along with a list of any idiosyncrasies, such as the un

34

usual smell of the bark on one tree or the star-shaped fruit of another. Looking closer, I noticed that if the plaque had a blue triangle in the corner, it indicated that the plant was poisonous.

Small benches and rattan chairs had been placed in carved-out alcoves along the path for guests to sit and read or rest in the quietly verdant environment.

The two-story conservatory had been built alongside the west end of Grace's home to take full advantage of the afternoon sunlight. There were unobstructed views through the glass of the crystal-blue waters of Lake Tahoe and the forest of thick pine and evergreen trees that grew on the steeply rugged mountains surrounding the lake.

The three of us wandered the garden path in silence for a while, stopping now and then to admire a lush flowering plant or read the fascinating history of a rare tree whose branches stretched up to skim the glass ceiling. It was the first time I felt my shoulders relax since I'd arrived at Grace's home.

"I love the vibe of this room," I murmured. My mind was so much calmer than it had been a few minutes ago. I wanted to stay right here. Maybe I could pilfer some blankets and curl up on that bench for the night.

"Feeling better?" Suzie asked.

I smiled. "Yes. Much better."

Vinnie threaded her arm through mine. "Brooklyn, you looked so sad when you walked in. If you are hurting, I hope you know we're here for you."

I leaned against her petite shoulder and sighed. I had intended to dish about Suzie's rude aunt Madge, but instead blurted, "I tried to call Derek, but a woman answered his phone."

"What?" Suzie said, outraged on my behalf.

"I was as surprised as you are." I waved my hand. "Never mind. It's no big deal."

"It's a big deal if she hurt you," Suzie said gruffly.

Vinnie tightened her arm against mine. "You know it means nothing. Don't you, Brooklyn?"

"Of course." But a sudden case of sniffles betrayed me. "I must be catching a cold."

"Someone needs a hug." Suzie came around behind me and the three of us held one another close for a moment. The warm cocoon of friendship touched me profoundly. Naturally, my tears welled over and the sniffling got worse. It was hell being a cheap crier.

"Feeling the love?" Suzie said almost a minute later, grinning as she eased back.

"Yeah." I tried to laugh, but I was sniffling uncontrollably.

"I'll bet you could use a drink," Suzie said.

I nodded, helpless to speak.

Vinnie pulled a clean tissue from her pocket and handed it to me. "Here you go."

I blew my nose and dabbed away my tears. "Thanks. You guys are the best."

"Bet your boots," Suzie said. "Now, if you feel like talking about it . . ."

"I don't, but thanks." I lifted my chin and shook my hair back. "I'm sure there's a simple explanation for what happened, so I refuse to give it one more ounce of energy."

Suzie punched my upper arm lightly, then tugged me toward the open doorway. "Then there's nothing left to do but go have that drink."

The house party was in full swing by the time the three of us walked into the Gold Salon. The room was right where Grace had told me, near the top of the grand stairway on the second floor. Three large bay windows covered the north wall of the salon. Each boasted a spectacular view of Lake Tahoe's shimmering surface that reflected the swirling colors of the dusky sky.

Ho-hum, I thought, smiling. *Another spectacular view of the most beautiful lake in the world.* Grace's home was full of them. If I lived here, I would never get tired of staring out the windows.

Aside from the views, the Gold Salon was magnificent, even if overindulgent brothel styling wasn't one's taste. It wouldn't surprise me to learn that the room had been decorated by a team of eighteenth-century French whores — all with exquisite taste, of course. The walls were lined with glittering gold brocade and the curtains were thick, shimmering burgundy velvet, and pulled back so the view could be appreciated.

Settees and chairs covered in gold-toned tapestry designs were arranged in attractive, comfortable seating groups across the long room. One huge Oriental carpet covered the sleek hardwood floor.

"Champagne, mademoiselle?" a strolling waiter said. He held a tray of delicate fluted glasses filled with bubbly golden liquid. With his free hand, he made a sweeping gesture toward one of the corners of the room. "Or we have your choice of cocktail available at the bar."

"No," I said with a determined smile as reached for a flute. "I'll have champagne."

"Me, too," Suzie said, and grabbed two more glasses. She handed one to Vinnie and we all clicked them in a toast. Suzie said, "Let's celebrate."

"To the settling of scores," Vinnie said, her normally smooth forehead lined in dogged resolution.

I giggled at her vindictive tone. "Thank you, Vinnie. I appreciate that." My friends always made me feel better. Although, truth be told, I rarely giggled. Maybe I'd already gone off the deep end.

"We've got your back, girlfriend," Suzie murmured. "Say the word and we'll take that bitch down."

I laughed. "Thanks, Suzie. If you hadn't —"

"There you are, Brooklyn."

I turned. "Oh, Grace. Your home is magnificent and I've barely begun to explore the place."

"Aren't you sweet?" she said, then winked at Vinnie, who scowled back. "Just take care, watch your step, and nobody will get hurt."

Suzie laughed, but quickly pressed her lips together when Vinnie gave her the stink eye.

I would definitely have to do some exploring later. I wanted to find out why Vinnie so adamantly disapproved of Grace's home. Unless it was simply Grace herself she disapproved of.

Grace smiled as she gently guided me away from my friends. "I have someone I want you to meet."

Tonight Grace had dressed formally in a slim purple toga-style dress that was a lot prettier than it sounded. She'd managed to fluff up her usually straight dark brown hair so that a halo of curls surrounded her pretty face, while a profusion of gold-wired crystals dangled from her ears. She was not a tall woman, but she was slender and had such a command of the room that she appeared positively statuesque. Or maybe it was her immense wealth that made her appear so regal.

Grace led me directly toward the bar, where a tall, broad-shouldered blond man stood alone, sipping a cocktail. He looked to be in his late twenties and wore a white dress shirt tucked into black trousers. Simple, but elegant. If this was Grace's archivist, he didn't look like any librarian I'd ever seen. Instead, he resembled a certain movie star from the sixties who my mother had once confessed to having a huge crush on. Troy Donahue. Thick blond hair, soulful blue eyes. What a cutie.

Grace took hold of the blond man's arm. "Nathan, let me introduce you to Brooklyn.

Wainwright, my favorite bookbinder." Grace turned to me. "Brooklyn, this is Nathan Hayes, my new librarian . . . person. Oh, what do you call yourself, anyway?"

"Librarian is fine." Nathan smiled indulgently at his new employer. "Although my correct title is archivist."

"Yes, that's right," she said, patting my arm as she pulled me closer. "You two will be working together for the next few days and I couldn't be happier about it. Finally my books will have some order to them."

As Grace spoke, I watched Nathan's eyebrows lift ever so slightly in a subtle but clear sign of masculine approval of me. *Isn't that nice?* I reached out and we shook hands. "Hi, Nathan."

"It's a real pleasure to meet you, Brooklyn," he said, his voice just smooth and deep enough to be wildly appealing to ninety-seven percent of the female population. "I've heard a lot about you."

With all the angst and drama I'd been through earlier, I'd forgotten about working with Grace's archivist this week. Now I looked forward to having the distraction of work to keep me from wallowing in anxiety.

The fact that the distraction included a handsome guy wouldn't hurt, either.

After a minute more of small talk, Grace

left us alone to speak to her other guests.

"I've already Googled you," he confessed. "I'm impressed."

"Thank you." I smiled. "And as soon as I return to my room I'm looking you up. I hope you haven't broken any laws lately."

His laugh was spontaneous and hearty. Talk about a distraction. "You won't find anything exciting about me, I'm afraid. I've spent most of my working life sequestered in university libraries."

"Not such a bad place to be sequestered."

"Not bad at all," he said easily. "I love being around books."

I glanced around, then leaned closer. "You've come to the right place."

"I know." He chuckled. "This place is stuffed with books, isn't it? Grace told me she was putting you in her Library Suite. How do you like it?"

My eyes widened. "Oh, my God, you've seen it?"

"Oh yeah."

I shook my head in wonder. "I'm still in shock."

He laughed again, then lowered his voice. "It's like they moved the entire Library of Congress into that room. But I understand the bed is very comfortable. I mean, Grace said she bought a new mattress for the room, so that's how I know the bed is . . . oh, boy. Not that I've . . . I wouldn't . . . I mean . . . I'm going to shut up now."

He was blushing! How adorable and refreshing. And I was laughing. Having fun. I'd forgotten how flirting with a cute boy could change your attitude about life in general.

Not that I'd be running off to marry the guy or anything. I really was devoted to Derek. But after that phone call with Thomasina, I worried that I'd be drowning in melancholy and uncertainty for the next week.

Instead, for a half hour we talked and flirted and sipped champagne. Nathan confessed that he was the world's biggest football fan, and I revealed my predilection for Ghirardelli chocolate with caramel. As we exchanged information and stories, Nathan glanced casually around the room. I didn't take it personally because I was doing the same thing. It was what people did at parties. But as I chuckled over his amusing story about the one and only bookbinding class he'd ever taken, something caught my attention at the far end of the room. Something that didn't belong there. I focused my gaze on it and lost the thread of the conversation.

I held up my hand to interrupt his story. "I'm sorry, but would you excuse me for just a minute?"

"Oh." He was taken aback but recovered quickly. "Sure thing."

But I was already gone, weaving my way through the small groups of partygoers. I tried to nod and smile and say hello as I passed quickly, hoping they would forgive me for not stopping to talk.

When I reached the distant corner of the room, I steadied myself on the firm arm of the couch and knelt down next to the heavy Chippendale end table. Lifting up the front end of the table, I removed the hardcover book that had been wedged under the right front claw foot to keep the table from jiggling.

Still on my knees, I held the book up to the light and examined it. It was bound in brown leather with five raised bands on the spine, but it was so worn down and cracked that I couldn't make out the faded gilded title. I opened it to the title page and read *Pilgrim's Progress.* The printer was the legendary "Patriot printer," Isaiah Thomas. The book was dated 1790.

I let out a short, high-pitched shriek.

"Are you all right?"

I turned too fast to look up at Nathan an

44

strained my neck. "Ouch. No. Yes. I mean, I'm fine, but no, not really. Will you look at this?" Still on my knees, I shook the book at him, but didn't let go of it.

"It's a book," he said cautiously, as if he were trying to calm down a nut case. "Where'd you find it?"

"It's not just a *book*," I said through clenched teeth. "It's a priceless jewel of a book. It's the rarest of rare books. And it's being used to hold up a damn table!"

"Ah." He inched away. "That's not good at all."

"What was it doing there?" I demanded.

"I swear I didn't put it there," he said as he held up both hands in surrender.

"Of course you didn't." I wasn't sure if he was teasing me or not, but I didn't care. I was furious. Shaking. I wanted to beat somebody up. Or worse.

"Who would do something so stupid?" It was a rhetorical question. I didn't want to know. And I wasn't about to ask my hostess and thoroughly offend her. Instead, I glared at the offending table leg, then gasped. "There's another one!"

I dropped down to my hands and knees and scuttled around the side of the table. Just behind it, another book lay halfway under the couch. I grabbed it and stared at the dappled brown cloth cover, then turned and checked the black leather spine. *Gulliver's Travels.* Beneath that was the name of the author: SWIFT.

A wave of fatigue overwhelmed me and I leaned against the couch and closed my eyes. This book was at least one hundred years old, possibly older. It had probably dropped off the side of the couch when someone fell asleep reading. How long had it been hiding back here, lonely and forgotten? Hadn't anyone missed it? What was wrong with this world?

I knew my questions would sound ridiculous to anyone who didn't care about books as much as I did. For some reason, that thought depressed me even more than the missing books themselves did. I sighed, then opened my eyes and straightened up. Nathan Hayes stood nearby, watching me. Brave man. I almost felt sorry for him. It was obvious he thought I had gone off the deep end and now he was stuck with me for seven days.

But I was too livid to care about his feelings just then. I was more concerned about myself, frankly. I knew this anger had less to do with finding these books than with that blasted phone call earlier. But admitting it, knowing it, did nothing to calm the fury still burning in my chest.

The irony of the situation was almost funny. I had come to Grace's party to relax, have fun, and avoid dead bodies. But now the only thing I wanted to do was murder someone.

CHAPTER 3

"Let me help you up," Nathan insisted, grabbing my elbow and lifting me off my knees.

"Thanks," I muttered, steadying my legs as I stood. I had completely embarrassed myself again, but I didn't care. This was the kind of embarrassment I could handle. When it came to rescuing books, I was willing to do whatever it took. I pulled at my sparkly sweater to straighten it and brushed a few carpet fibers off my black slacks.

Nathan stopped a passing waiter and grabbed two fresh glasses of champagne from the tray. "Here. You might need this."

"You're right." I tucked the books under my arm and took the flute gratefully.

"Cheers," he said, clinking his glass to mine. "Here's to finding books where you least expect them."

"I'll drink to that." I took a sip of the expensive champagne, but I could barely taste it. And that was just sad. I'd lost the urge to indulge. I blamed it on the trauma of finding that poor book holding up the table.

"So what are these books?" Nathan asked, his tone tentative. He was probably scared to death of setting me off on another rant. And who could blame him?

"Oh, sorry." I hadn't even given him a chance to look at the books, so I handed him *Pilgrim's Progress*. I set down my champagne glass and looked at the other book more closely. Its cover was tan speckled calfskin and the title and author's name were gilded onto the black morocco spine. *Gulliver's Travels.* I opened it up and found the date on the title page was 1726.

Holy Mother.

I closed the book quickly. My head was in danger of exploding and I didn't want to damage the precious vellum.

"This dent in the front cover is unacceptable," Nathan said, scowling as he handed *Pilgrim's Progress* back to me. "But it's a stunning book. Do you want me to take it to the library with me?"

"Yes, if you wouldn't mind. But you ain't seen nothing yet," I muttered, opening *Gulliver's* to show him the print date.

"Whoa. Are you kidding?" he said, then

quickly lowered his voice as he took the book and examined it. "What was it doing behind the couch?"

"That was my question."

"Wait," he said, squinting at the book's spine. "This says it's volume two."

"Let me see." I took it back and stared at the spine. It wasn't gilded so I'd missed it the first time. But now I saw the faint indentation in the pale leather. VOL. II.

"So there's at least one more volume around here somewhere." I clenched my teeth together to keep from squealing again. "This one book has got to be worth thousands, so if there are two volumes, they belong in a museum."

"Yeah, I get that."

My exhaustion was growing, not only from the adrenaline rush of annoyance at finding the books, but also from my numerous attempts to keep from reacting to that silly phone call. My stomach hurt, too. "I'm hungry."

Nathan laughed. "Now, there's a non sequitur."

I shot him a quick look. "Did I say that out loud?"

"Yeah, but don't worry. Grace likes to eat early, so dinner should be announced any minute now."

"Good. I skipped lunch." And that was a sentence I'd rarely uttered in my whole life. How had that happened? I never missed meals. But now I remembered I'd been running around the house, packing and getting ready to leave for a week. I must have forgotten to eat.

"I could sneak you into the kitchen," he said with a grin. "I've gotten to know the chef pretty well."

I glanced around the room and saw Grace going from group to group, pointing toward the door. I hoped that meant she was giving directions to the dining room. "I guess I can wait a few minutes longer."

But after dinner, I was going to go straight to bed. I didn't want to inflict my bad mood on any other unsuspecting innocents tonight. I was too tired to tamp down my irritation at finding a rare book being used to hold up a table. Fine, I was willing to accept that in a house with twelve gazillion books, a few would get lost here and there. But stuck under a table? That was a new low.

I silently vowed to spend part of tomorrow morning searching the house for missing books, particularly that first volume of *Gulliver's Travels*. I figured I could go through a few rooms every day this week, hunting down wayward books. That would keep me occupied when I wasn't working in the library with Nathan. More than anything else, I wanted to keep busy this week. I didn't want to think about Derek with that . . . person. I would work hard and stay active, and to do that I would need to keep up my strength by eating a lot. Starting as soon as possible.

"There you are, Brooklyn," Vinnie said as she came up behind me.

Suzie was with her. "Time for dinner, kiddo. I'm starving."

"You and me both," I said.

Vinnie looked Nathan up and down. "Hello."

"Hello," he said somberly.

I quickly introduced my friends to Nathan and explained that he and I would be working together on book stuff this week. Vinnie continued to stare at him with such barely concealed curiosity that I had to wonder what she was thinking.

I twitched a little. She couldn't possibly think I was considering cheating on Derek with Nathan. Could she? Just because of a stupid phone call that I'd probably misinterpreted, anyway? Since the entire group was already walking toward the door to dinner, I would pull her aside later and explain that

Nathan and I would be working together this week. And nothing more.

As the four of us followed the rest of the guests down the grand stairway to the formal dining room, I took the opportunity to introduce myself to a few of the people around me. Grace's ex-partner from her computer game company, Peter Brinker, a tall, gray-haired man with what my dad would call a million-dollar smile, was friendly and outgoing and talked about the fun of creating games for a living. I liked him immediately.

"I'm his wife," said the woman on Peter's other side. She leaned forward and gave me one of those wiggly finger waves.

Peter laughed. "Sybil sells herself short. She's our CFO and we'd be lost without her."

Sybil shook her head. "I wouldn't go that far."

I never would have guessed that this was a woman who held such an important position. She seemed nice enough, but a bit bland. But then maybe that was the perfect personality type for a CFO. She wore her hair in a short black bob, similar to Grace's hairstyle. And her flowing fuchsia dress was identical to Grace's. It made me wonder if the two women were such good friends that they shopped and had their hair done together.

"Did you two meet on the job?" I asked.

"Yes," Peter said, taking Sybil's hand. "Sybil came to work for us and I was hooked from day one."

"Oh, stop," she said, brushing his arm.

Peter asked what I did for a living and I gave him the short version.

"That's fascinating," he said. "I love old books." He asked a few more questions as we walked downstairs. He was attractive and inquisitive and laughed a lot, and was in the middle of a story when Sybil nudged him. He turned away to listen to whatever she was saying and I thought for a moment that she'd meant to include me in her conversation. But then she flashed me a glance through half-closed lids and lowered her voice enough that I couldn't hear her. I took the hint and turned away.

Next to me, Suzie was conversing with a tall, wiry man with spiky white-blond hair. "And this is my friend, Brooklyn," Suzie said, and stuck her thumb toward me. "She's a master at restoring books and she solves murders in her spare time."

Stunned, I frowned as Peter and Sybil and several others turned around and stared at me with blatant curiosity.

"Excellent," the spiky-haired guy said, and stretched his arm out to shake my hand. "You must be really smart. I'm Marko Huntley. This is Bella Santangelo." He pointed toward the svelte, red-haired woman dressed entirely in black who followed behind him.

"Hi," I said cheerfully, trying to shake off Suzie's odd comment about me and murder.

"So you're, like, a true-crime nut?" Marko asked.

"What? No."

"Because I'm looking for beta testers to work on my zombie cops-and-robbers game. The working title is *Slaughter Beyond the Grave*. It's like, *CSI* meets *Body Snatchers*."

"Catchy, but I —"

"Hello," Bella said, her voice sultry and dramatic.

I turned to see that she had shifted positions and was now walking next to me. She carried an oversized martini glass and must have gotten a refill before she left the party, because it was filled to the brim with pink liquid.

"I was talking to her, Bella," Marko said, his tone a little whiny.

She reached across me and squeezed his hand. "I know, love, but I'm rescuing her.

55

Some of us just don't go in for zombies."

His lower lip stuck out. "Zombies need love, too."

"Go," she said, laughing.

He toddled off like a scolded puppy and I watched him strike up a conversation with Sybil. *Good luck with that one,* I thought.

Bella was watching him, too. "Don't mind Marko. He's like a twelve-year-old boy when it comes to zombies." She laughed. "And when it comes to everything else, too, now that I think about it."

"I don't mind him." I tried not to stare at her, but seeing her this close up made me realize how gorgeous she was. Her startling green eyes were fringed with long, thick black eyelashes. Her complexion was flawless and her lips were full and red. I was almost certain that was without any help from lipstick or makeup.

"Did I hear Suzie right?" Bella said softly. "Did she say you solved murders?"

I almost moaned. "She was joking," I said, brushing it off with a weak laugh.

"Really? Why would she joke about that?"

"Well, not joking, really. I guess it's true that I've been involved in a few cases, but —"

"That's perfect. I've been looking for an expert."

"I'm hardly an —"

"I'm working on an update to our company's *House Party Mystery* game. It's more on the traditional mystery side, unlike Marko's brain-sucking crime version. Maybe I can interview you later? I would love an insider's view of what it's like to be a witness to murder up close."

I could feel my heart pounding harder, and not only because these game people were so pushy. "Uh, sure, but I really don't think I'm very —"

"How'd you meet Grace?" she said, ignoring my stammering as she took a careful sip from her drink.

I was relieved to change the subject and launched into the story of how Grace and I met through Suzie. I mentioned my work with Grace's extensive book collection and remarked on the amount of bookshelves throughout the house.

"Books. I could work that into the game," Bella mused. "I'll bet you could kill someone with a heavy book."

I gulped at the thought, then noticed that Marko had given up on Sybil and was back to listening in on our conversation. "I suppose you could, but I hate to think of books being used to kill people."

She waved away my concern. "We'll talk.

I'll track you down tomorrow."

"You'll probably find me in the library."

Marko smirked. "And you can find Bella in the bar."

"You should talk, Marko," Bella said, then paused to sip her drink. "Mm, but Grace's bartender does pour the best cosmo I've ever had."

"Better suck it up," Marko murmured. "Dinner's about to be served."

She pouted. "And Grace always serves the best wine." She held up her glass. "Ah, cosmo, my love, I must bid you adieu." Then she drained the entire drink down her throat.

"Such a lush," Marko said with a snicker before turning to say something to Suzie.

As we reached the ground floor and walked down the wide front hall toward the dining room, Bella continued chatting with me. "We all used to work for Grace until she retired. Now Marko and I are the chief designers. Peter's still our boss."

"What types of games do you design?" I asked.

"Well, I did the original design for House Party Mystery, and I'm always updating it. And Girl Power was my design. But I'm most psyched about my latest creation. It's a post–World War Three, dystopian jungle-warrior tar-pit game. We're still working on a title, but it's totally sick. You'd love it."

"I'm sure I would," I said, even though I had no clue what she'd just described.

"Grace has the prototype up in the game room," Bella said, then snapped her fingers in time to her words. "Check. It. Out."

"I will."

"Coolio." Without another word, she set her empty glass on a small console table in the hall, then slunk around me until she once again walked close to Marko. The man didn't acknowledge her outwardly since he was deep in conversation with Suzie, but I saw him stealthily reach back and grab Bella's thigh. She slapped his hand away, but she was smiling. And his action signified his complete awareness of her nearness.

Body language didn't lie. There was more between those two than a mere office friendship. And even though I couldn't imagine what Bella saw in Marko, I was perfectly happy with yet another distraction this week. *Are they in love?* I wondered, though I doubted it.

In both appearance and attitude, they weren't exactly a match made in heaven. Both were tall. Marko looked to be in his early fifties, with pale skin and half-spiky, half-balding silver-blond hair. I estimated that Bella was in her late thirties.

Maybe it was uncharitable of me to think it, but she was simply too beautiful for Marko. Not that he was ugly, exactly; he was handsome enough in a quirky sort of way. I'd only just met him, but I'd already been treated to his devious smile and his proclivity for waggling his eyebrows suggestively. And his snickering. I suppose there were plenty of women who were attracted to the type of man who would never grow up. Bella had said it best: Marko was twelve years old in almost every way.

He continued to bounce around among the different groups, giggling for a few seconds and then turning to someone else. He appeared to have the attention span of a squirrel that had just spied a nut falling from a tree and was gone in a flash.

Was Bella really involved with Marko? My first impression of her was of someone who sauntered into a room like an exquisite gazelle and expected to be adored by all of humanity. But early in our conversation, I picked up on her quick intelligence and droll sense of humor, along with an underlying nervous energy that would probably be useful in the frenetic, competitive world of computer games and videos.

How Marko survived in that same world,

I had no idea. Maybe he had hidden depths. Or maybe his twelve-year-old mentality was perfect for that world. Whatever his secret was, it worked for him.

As we reached the ground floor and moved en masse toward the dining room, Suzie sidled up next to me and whispered, "I'm officially pissed off."

"Why?" I asked, concerned for her.

"See that guy in the boring gray suit?" She pointed out a man fast-walking ahead of us halfway down the hall. Hunched shoulders, small balding head. Then he turned and I saw the scowl on his pinched face.

"Whoa," I whispered. "Who is that?" He looked like a cartoon character, the smarmy kind of guy who would steal milk bottles from babies. Even from behind he looked disagreeable.

"Yeah," Suzie said with a knowing nod. "That's Grace's lawyer. I didn't know he'd be here. He's the biggest jerk. The fact that he's here tells me Grace must be planning to make some changes to her estate."

"Are you worried?"

"Of course she's not worried," Vinnie said. She had somehow materialized on my other side. "Suzie is Grace's favorite niece. She would never cut her out of the will."

"Don't let Kiki hear you say that," Suzie muttered. "She thinks she's the favorite."

"Kiki is a nice girl, but Grace loves you best."

Kiki was Suzie's younger cousin. I'd met her earlier and liked her immediately. She was a few years younger than Suzie and shared her semi-warped sense of humor. She seemed sweet and was frankly beautiful in a clean, wholesome way, with long dark hair and big blue eyes.

It had been a shock to find out during the cocktail party that Kiki's mother was Madge Crawford, the ill-tempered woman I'd met in the hall earlier. *Poor Kiki,* I thought, *having to grow up with a mother like that.* But, thank goodness, she seemed to have inherited her father's genial attitude.

Kiki's father, Harrison Crawford, was Grace's older brother. There was another sister, Jeannie, who was my friend Suzie's mom. But Jeannie had passed away five years ago.

Vinnie leaned closer and lowered her voice. "That Fowler man is not a nice person. I ran into him earlier this afternoon and he accused me of stealing his newspaper. Can you imagine? He cursed at me like a Bangalore cabbie."

"Damn," Suzie said. "I was watching him

at the party and he glowered at anyone who tried to greet him. I actually saw him push one of the other men out of the way when he went to the bar. I wouldn't be surprised to hear that he's the one trying to convince Grace to make changes to her estate, just to be spiteful."

He looked creepy, all right, but I would reserve my final opinion until I actually met the man. "His name is Fowler?"

"Stephen Fowler," Suzie grumbled. "Kiki thinks Grace will kick us all out of the will and leave all her money to some cat sanctuary."

"Grace has a cat?" I asked, perking up. "I haven't seen a cat around here."

"She's got a great cat," Suzie said, grinning. "Leroy. He's pitch-black and very cool."

I smiled at the image of a cool black cat and also at my unintentional changing of the subject. I was ready to talk about happier things. I was sick of being cranky and silently declared myself to be a negative-free zone for the rest of the evening. I would be upbeat, positive, and hopeful. And the subject of cats was a cheery alternative to lawyers anytime.

"Leroy is a joy," Vinnie said with more enthusiasm. "An excellent cat. Very friendly.

The best thing about being here."

"Okay, Vinnie," Suzie said softly, and Vinnie frowned, then nodded in what seemed to be a silent apology. Maybe they were tired of the negativity, too. It was a state I'd rarely seen the two of them enter.

"I can't wait to meet Leroy," I said, excited at the prospect of meeting a cat I could snuggle up with for a few days. Cats were a calming influence and lately I'd been thinking of getting one of my very own.

And while I didn't want to bring it up at that moment (because I was now an instrument of positivity in the universe), I couldn't wait to find out more about Vinnie's antagonistic feelings toward Aunt Grace, who, by the way, seemed to take Vinnie's snarky attitude in stride.

I recalled our conversation earlier that day, during our two-hour drive to Tahoe. Vinnie and Suzie had gone back and forth, filling in the gaps of my understanding of Aunt Grace. Vinnie didn't approve of Grace's lackadaisical attitude toward everything, including people. But Suzie described her aunt as whimsical and good-natured.

"She is most definitely whimsical," Vinnie had agreed, but added, "along with being fickle and unreliable."

"She's the youngest person I know," Suzie

had said by way of explanation, and it was obvious from her tone how fond she was of her aunt. Even though Grace was turning fifty and was retired from Gamester, the corporation she'd founded and helped grow, she was just a big kid at heart, Suzie insisted.

Grace had started out in the business by designing board games, but she made her millions creating pinball and video games. In the past ten years, she had moved her company into designing 3-D computer games. She was still crazy about every kind of game, puzzle, and magic trick. Even retired, she fancied herself a master gamester, and her huge home reflected her brilliant, idiosyncratic nature.

Vinnie's opinion of Grace was much less love-blinded. She felt that Grace played at being a kid because she didn't want to accept adult responsibility for her actions or decisions.

"Come on, Vinnie. She's not a mean person," Suzie insisted.

"No, no. She is simply a bit oblivious of others." Vinnie shifted in the car seat to look at me. "I suppose that's why she can come across as inconsiderate. But I don't wish to imply that she's mean."

"That's good to know," I said.

"However," Vinnie hastened to add, "I still

don't approve of her eccentric décor. I warn you, Brooklyn. Don't walk too close to the walls, because they've been known to move."

"You're kidding."

"No, I am not. Her house is a giant game board and subject to her ever-changing moods and whims. Please, please, don't walk under the giant mousetrap cage in the game room."

"Mousetrap cage?" I frowned. "Like the game?"

"Yeah," Suzie said, pleased that I got the reference. "Grace invented a game that had some of the same elements as Mousetrap, only there was more of a strategic game involved. Hers was called Cat and Mouse. I think it might've been the first game she ever came up with. She still has some life-sized props around the house from those early days."

"Yes, she does." Vinnie shot Suzie an ominous look. "She has that hideous mouse cage hanging from the ceiling, waiting to trap innocent bystanders."

"Almost sounds like you got caught in it," I said.

Suzie snorted and Vinnie batted her arm. "Yes, I was caught, and it was not funny. Yet Suzie and her aunt howled with laughter when it happened."

"Suzie, that was mean," I said, but I had to bite back a smile.

"Thank you, Brooklyn," Vinnie said. "They laughed, then walked out of the room, leaving me to rot in that cage."

"We came right back," Suzie insisted as she winked at me in the rearview mirror.

Vinnie scowled. "It was forty-five minutes later."

"It was ten minutes."

"I thought I would die in that stupid cage!"

"Hey, I've been caught in her traps before, too," Suzie said, then explained that she'd actually fallen through a trapdoor in one of the hallways. She'd landed on a huge pillow in the basement, but still. "Scared the crap out of me."

"Yes, that was too bad." Vinnie had tried to remain impassive, but finally choked out a laugh.

I was horrified but also curious. Who was this eccentric woman who liked to play games with her guests?

Giant mousetraps? Moving walls? Trapdoors? Maybe Madge was right to freak out in the hall earlier.

As we walked into the dining room, I was reminded of Grace's advice: "Take care,

watch your step, and nobody will get hurt."
I would have to remember that.

In the grandly formal dining room, we found that the seating arrangements for all fifteen of us had already been designated. I left my friends at one end of the table and tracked down my place card at the opposite end. I was seated between Nathan Hayes, Grace's new librarian archivist, and Peter Brinker, Grace's ex-partner. I could live with the arrangement, although I hated to miss out on the conversation at the other end of the table. Vinnie was seated between Suzie and Marko and the three of them were already laughing about something.

"Are you just going to stand there?"

I turned and stared into the face of Stephen Fowler. He looked even unhappier now than he had in the hall. I wasn't sure I'd heard him correctly. "What did you say?"

He scowled, grabbed my arm, and shoved me into the back of my chair. "I said, move it."

Instantly livid, I yanked my arm away, then took a quick look behind me. There was plenty of room for him to pass by me, so what was his point? I shook my finger at him. "Don't ever touch me again."

"Or what?" he taunted. What was wrong with him? Was he deranged?

"Or you'll regret it," I said evenly.

"Ooh, you scare me."

I was about to sputter incoherently, so I turned away, cutting him off. I gripped my chair and stared blindly at the place setting, hoping he would just walk away. Far away. I was shaking with anger. I wished I had a gun so I could pistol-whip him with it. That's how irrationally angry Fowler had made me. He had baited me deliberately and I couldn't understand why. I struggled to calm down, then carefully looked around again. No one seemed to have noticed our brief encounter.

Out of the corner of my eye, I noticed that Fowler had taken his place a few seats down on the same side of the table as me, thank goodness. I wouldn't have to look at his Grinch-like face.

I no longer had any interest in changing my seat to be closer to Vinnie and Suzie. It would only bring me closer to Stephen Fowler, and that would be intolerable.

What a horrible man!

"Hello again," Peter said genially, and pulled my chair out for me.

"Thank you," I said, and sat down cautiously. After the run-in with Stephen Fowler, it took a few seconds to remember that most people here were friendly and capable of acting politely.

Sybil was already seated on Peter's other side. It might've been my unsteady imagination, but I thought I saw her scowl as I took my seat. As soon as I looked back at her, though, she favored me with another one of her weak smiles.

I wasn't ready for another verbal confrontation, so I ignored my neighbors and spent a few minutes studying the pretty formality of the large room. The crystal chandelier in the center of the ceiling glittered in the candlelight. The table settings were gold-banded ivory set on hammered silver chargers. The delicate glassware appeared to be Baccarat. It was an educated guess; I'd seen similar pieces at Guru Bob's house. In front of every other place setting were pink cabbage roses and pale green hydrangeas compressed together in squat, square, etched-glass vases. The vintage arrangements lent an Old World charm to the table.

I settled back in my chair and let out a breath. I had tangled with obnoxious people before, but Stephen Fowler had spooked me badly. Maybe because his animosity came out of nowhere, completely unprovoked. He seemed to think I had done something unforgivable, but I hadn't, of course. It was possible that he was simply unhinged.

I scanned the room again and realized that Fowler was seated next to Sybil. Now, there was a happy duet.

Bella sat on the other side of Fowler, and Grace's brother, Harrison, held court at the far end of the table. Despite being married to the hateful Madge, Harrison seemed like a cheery sort and was presently chuckling at something Bella had said. He was of medium height and portly, and tonight he wore an expensive cashmere V-neck sweater in a bright green shade with a faded purple, tattered polo shirt underneath. I was willing to bet money that his wife hated that garish, motley outfit. But maybe that was precisely why Harrison dressed that way.

Whether by chance or on purpose, Madge was not seated next to her husband, but halfway down the table opposite Peter and right next to Vinnie. She was a little too close for my comfort. But Madge ignored everyone at the table by busying herself with folding and unfolding her white linen napkin. That was fine with me. I hoped her frosty, unspoken contempt for all of us would continue, because I really didn't care to be forced into another conversation with the woman.

By my count, there were three truly unlikable people at the party: Sybil, Madge, and Fowler. An odd party statistic, but it was true. Poor Grace, forced to invite them all — although, to be fair, while she couldn't have avoided inviting Madge or Sybil, I had no idea why she had invited that schnook Fowler.

A waiter filled my glass with wine and my mood lightened considerably. I decided it was time to ignore the three party poopers and get to know my immediate companions better. I liked Peter Brinker, found him easy to talk to and generous. And I wanted to find out more about Nathan. He was seated next to Grace, who sat at the head of the table.

Our dinner conversation was a bit forced at first, but the incredible food and excellent wines quickly loosened our tongues and inhibitions. Who could remain silent after tasting such incredible fare? The first course was a roasted beet salad with tangy goat cheese and caramelized fennel. This was followed by a pasta course of homemade linguini with wild mushrooms in a creamy, buttery, brandy-infused sauce that made me want to cry out in pleasure.

"I haven't had one bad meal since I moved here," Nathan said as he poured a touch more wine into my glass. "Grace's chef is worth his weight in gold."

"This pasta is sensational," I said as my taste buds moaned and begged for one more bite.

Grace overheard me. "Chef Tang is a gift from heaven. He's originally from Thailand but he studied at Cordon Bleu in Paris and worked in France for years before I was able to lure him here."

While I stuffed my face — er, enjoyed the fabulous dining experience — I glanced over at Vinnie and Suzie and wondered if I should've wangled a seat closer to them. They sat near Marko and Bella, who kept everyone in a good mood with their own banter and their kibitzing with other guests. Every few minutes, I would hear Marko's high-pitched, boyish giggle and it almost made me laugh.

Since I was seated with virtual strangers, our conversation was more sedate. I had time to observe at least five interesting things about my companions. First, as he'd mentioned earlier, Nathan had moved into the house two weeks ago and would continue living here while he worked on cataloging Grace's library. *Not a bad gig,* I thought, *especially if meals are included.*

Second, Grace preferred that her housekeeper, Merrilee Sweet, a pretty blonde in her late twenties, dined with the guests. I didn't have the slightest problem with that, but I noticed that Madge sniffed derisively when the lovely housekeeper sat down next to her.

Third, I learned that Grace's good friend, Ruth Kinsley, who sat on Grace's right, across the table from Nathan, was actually Grace's artist in residence and lived nearby on the property. She was given a monthly stipend, and her home was a cozy cottage surrounded by trees and woodland. Fascinating. I was about to ask her what type of art she practiced when Peter Brinker posed an unrelated question about her living conditions, and Ruth, a lively woman with long, graying hair and an infectious smile, went off on the wonderfulness of the heating and air-conditioning unit in the cottage.

Fourth, Harrison Crawford was truly a sweet, jovial man, but Madge continued to play the role of consummate shrew. Her attitude did not improve as the meal progressed, but Harrison let her foul humor roll off his back. Poor Kiki, though, having Madge for a mother. I learned that Kiki had an older brother and sister, Kieran and Celeste, but neither of them were able to make it to Grace's party. I wouldn't be surprised if they'd passed on the party because they couldn't take being cooped up in the same house as their mother for a week.

Kiki seemed to have inherited her father's geniality, luckily for all of us.

Fifth, Peter Brinker and his wife, Sybil, barely spoke to each other — unless Peter tried to converse with anyone else. Then Sybil would find any excuse to disrupt the conversation in order to tell Peter something that had just that moment occurred to her, apparently. She had interrupted me twice already, and while I understood it was probably because of her own lack of self-confidence, I was starting to dislike the woman almost as much as I disliked Madge. Sybil was so insipid that if it hadn't been for the fact that she was a high-powered CFO for a multinational corporation, I would've thought she was a rich, bored housewife whose only creative outlets were shopping and manicures.

But that wasn't nice of me. I hadn't gotten a chance to get to know Sybil yet, but I was willing to believe she would turn out to be very nice. Unlike Madge.

Wanting to stay with my new positive groove, I fought back my negative feelings toward Madge. How could I expect to be a font of optimism and hope if I abhorred someone? Hoping to readjust my downbeat attitude toward Madge — and Sybil, too, for that matter — I consumed liberal amounts of the smooth, full-bodied cabernet Grace was serving.

It worked. Halfway through the pasta course, I realized I loved everyone. Oh, boy. It was time to switch to water.

The main course consisted of a slab of rich polenta topped with ricotta cheese and drenched in a luscious, light, broth-based chunky tomato sauce with plump sausages and chicken that were both so moist and light they almost melted in my mouth.

The meal was essentially peasant fare, but in the hands of a talented chef, it had become haute cuisine. I wanted to lick my plate but figured that would be tacky.

"Was I right?" Nathan asked as he polished off his own meal.

"Incredible," I mumbled as I gulped down another bite of tender, fennel-infused sausage with a dollop of polenta smothered in red sauce. "I need this recipe." Tomorrow I would talk to Chef Tang and beg if I had to. This dish would be a perfect addition to my fledgling repertoire of things I could cook.

Dessert was a deep, rich chocolate soufflé with a generous side of whipped cream. There were no words to describe it, except

Oh, mercy.

"Attention! Attention!" Grace cried gaily as she tapped her fork against her crystal wineglass.

I caught Suzie's eye and she winked at me. I'd had enough wine that I winked back, and that's when I noticed that Stephen Fowler was glaring in my direction. I shivered as I looked away, then wondered if perhaps his eyes had been shooting daggers beyond me, toward Grace instead.

We all looked at her attentively. She appeared flushed and happy, no doubt from all the great food and wine, but also because she was surrounded by the people she loved. Well, except for Stephen Fowler and Madge. And Sybil, too, I supposed. I couldn't imagine Grace loving any one of those three.

I mentally smacked myself. *Be nice!*

"I'm so pleased to have you all here to celebrate my birthday. The Big Five-Oh! Heavens! I never thought I'd live this long."

I almost laughed. Grace was close to my mother's age but looked even younger, with her diminutive figure and cute hair, not to mention her youthful attitude. She waved her hands in the air theatrically. "Never mind. I refuse to get maudlin about my age, because I've never felt better."

We all hooted and applauded and Grace

laughed. "All right, enough about old age. Let's talk about some rumors that have been flying around. I'm about to quash one of them right now."

I turned in time to catch Sybil giving Peter a sharp look. Merrilee's face was serene, but Marko's frown lines practically obliterated his forehead. Stephen Fowler's face became even more pinched than usual. Bella slurped her wine, blissfully ignorant of the tension growing around the table. Suzie and Vinnie exchanged anxious but knowing glances, certain that Grace was about to announce that she was making changes to her will.

Instead Grace jumped up and grabbed what looked like a full ream of paper bound together by some sort of wide tape binding. "It's done!" she cried, waving the heavy document in the air. "Finished! My first novel! And you're all in it!"

CHAPTER 4

There was a moment of silence; then the entire group burst into noisy applause again.

"Congratulations!" Nathan said.

"Mazel tov!" Bella cried, and slugged down the rest of her wine.

"Wonderful, Auntie!" Kiki shouted.

Almost everyone at the table added their good wishes and cheery congratulations. I was glad the mood had lifted, because up until a few seconds ago I was afraid I would be dodging a number of steak knives aimed at Grace.

As the cheering died down, Grace placed the heavy manuscript on the table. She had tears in her eyes. "Thank you all so much. You make me feel like a superstar."

"That's exactly what you are," Ruth said, loyal as ever.

"Oh, Ruth. You're prejudiced," Grace said, patting her friend's hand. "But thank you. Now let me tell you all about this book. As you might imagine, the story is very near and dear to my heart. It's a roman à clef of sorts, about a smart, spunky woman who starts out with nothing and ends up creating a multimillion-dollar corporation that makes all kinds of games."

"Genius," Bella shouted.

For some reason her comment made me laugh, and a few others joined me. Next to me, Peter appeared contemplative. Sybil was practically scowling. Marko still didn't look too comfortable, but Bella was howling with laughter and pounding the table. She didn't seem at all concerned about the contents of the book, but maybe she was too tanked to care.

As Grace spoke, Sybil pretended to enjoy the repartee, but I could feel her vibe from two chairs away. She wasn't pleased. But then she hadn't looked very happy all evening. That went double for Madge. She looked positively furious. What was that all about? Had she already read the book? Did she know what was in it?

"Now, don't worry," Grace said. "The names have been changed to protect the guilty. You know who you are!"

More furtive glances were exchanged around the table. Some of the guests appeared intrigued, some looked suspicious, and some — Madge, of course, plus Stephen Fowler, and, surprisingly, Marko — looked downright annoyed. I leaned over, pretending to fiddle with a flower that had fallen from the vase, and caught a glimpse of Sybil. She looked like she'd been slapped hard. Interesting.

Personally, I couldn't wait to get my hands on a copy of Grace's book, but then I am a naturally curious person. Or just plain nosy.

"I've sent the manuscript off to a New York publisher," Grace continued, patting her chest as her emotions caught up with her. "But . . . I have copies! So everyone here will get a first look at it."

"Lucky us," Madge muttered.

Grace waved toward the antique sideboard along the wall. "The copies are stacked over there, so be sure to pick one up after dinner. And I mean this: I want you all to give me your honest opinions."

I wasn't an expert on these things, but I could pretty much guarantee she wouldn't want to hear too many honest opinions from this group.

"I've read it already and it's brilliant," Merrilee said, her tone earnest.

"Oh, there's an objective opinion," Peter muttered beside me.

Grace paid no attention to the grumbling.

"Now, enough about me. I want everyone to have fun this week! My niece Kiki is a certified masseuse and she's agreed to provide a selection of spa delights each and every day for anyone who's interested."

Kiki raised her hand, then stood so the guests would know who Grace was referring to.

"Catch me anytime," Kiki said, "and I'll schedule a massage for you. I do manicures and pedicures, too. I'll come to your room or we can meet in the pool house beyond the conservatory."

"How marvelous," Vinnie said.

A massage does sound wonderful, I thought. I would definitely be signing up for that.

Once Kiki sat down, Grace continued. "If you simply feel like curling up with a good book, my library has thousands on every subject imaginable." Grace favored me with a smile, then moved on, saying, "And of course there are walking paths along the lake and through the forest if you're looking for something more active to do."

"But I've heard there may be snow," Ruth said. "So bundle up if you go outside."

"Now for tonight's entertainment," Grace said, pressing her hands together in excitement. "Fritz, our piano player, has agreed to stay and play for two more hours in the music room, so if you want to dance or sing along, please do. You all know about the toys we have in the game room, and for anyone interested, I'll be reading tarot cards in the card room."

"I want to go first," Sybil said eagerly, surprising me. She had barely spoken all evening.

"And so you shall," Grace said, nodding regally.

"I've got dibs on the backgammon board," Harrison said. "Who's with me?"

"I'll play," Peter said.

Nathan raised his hand. "Me, too."

"I'll be at the bar," Marko said.

Bella raised her hand. "Me, too." For some reason, Marko found that hilarious.

"And tomorrow night," Grace continued, raising her voice to drown out Marko's snorting laugh, "as part of my homage to the great English house-party mysteries of yesteryear, we'll have a séance."

"Cool," Kiki said.

"Figures." Marko giggled as he nudged Bella. "House Party Mystery is still one of your best games."

"And best-*selling,*" she added with a wink.

"This should be interesting," Peter murmured.

Grace smiled and nodded in agreement.

I'd never been to a séance before, but it sounded like fun. It was too bad my mother couldn't be here. She would get a big kick out of communing with all her close personal friends in the spirit world.

Nathan sat back in his chair. "Knowing Grace, we should prepare ourselves for plenty of tricks and teasers during the séance."

"Well, of course," Grace said, causing a few of us to laugh some more. And a few of us weren't laughing at all. Interesting.

"I think there's a football game on tomorrow night," Marko said suddenly. "I was hoping to watch it."

"Yeah, it's a big one," Nathan said. "Bills versus Pats."

"We'll tape it and you'll watch it later," Grace said with a determined smile that quickly turned somber. "There's one more important announcement I'd like to make, but I've decided to save it until my birthday party on Friday night."

"How intriguing," Sybil said, though her tone implied the opposite.

"Another announcement?" Madge said under her breath. "Hasn't she made enough?"

Grace gazed around the table. "I'm afraid

some of you might find it shocking."

I took a quick peek at Suzie, whose lips were pressed together in a worried frown. Could Grace's coming announcement have something to do with changing her will?

"That's enough seriousness. I want to laugh." Grace raised her glass to toast her guests, then drained the contents in one gulp. "It's time for some fun and games."

Vinnie caught up with me in the hall, where I had stopped to admire a medieval shield of armor backed by two crossed swords. The swords were shiny, heavy, and sharp-looking. One of them would make a fearsome weapon if I were being chased through the halls by a madwoman.

And where had that thought come from?

Taking hold of my arm, Vinnie said in a confidential tone, "Suzie is now certain that Grace intends to rewrite her will."

"Does she still think Grace would cut her out?"

"It's of no importance to me, Brooklyn. You know we've done quite well with our art." Suzie and Vinnie were talented, well-known chainsaw artists who worked with large chunks of wood that came mainly from fallen trees rescued from the forest floor. Their award-winning designs had been displayed and sold in art galleries all over California.

"But I do worry that Grace will hurt Suzie's feelings," Vinnie said. "And some of the relatives aren't happy at all. Suzie tries to ignore their griping and sniping, but it's not easy. They're her family."

"But how do they even know it's true? They may be jumping to the wrong conclusion." I didn't want to mention that if Grace was serious about taunting her relatives with the possibility that she might change her will, she was taking this homage to the House Party Mystery game too far. Wasn't threatening to change one's will the ultimate cliché in terms of house-party machinations?

My gut reaction told me it wasn't true. Grace just didn't strike me as that mean-spirited. "Are all of Suzie's relatives here this week?"

"No, but the ones who didn't make it are being kept informed of all the developments, thanks to Madge."

Madge was really starting to fray my last nerve.

"I guess it's good for the family to stay informed," I said carefully.

"Madge is a grasping, bigmouthed money-grubber," Vinnie whispered, then added, "but otherwise, a lovely woman."

"Oh, Vinnie." I laughed and grabbed her in a hug. "I wish I'd been sitting closer to you guys during dinner."

"I wish you had been, too," she said, then frowned. "Brooklyn, I believe Grace may be trying to set you up with this Nathan fellow."

I grinned. "She can try all she wants, but it won't work. I'm completely nuts about Derek."

"Oh, good." She clutched my arm. "I was worried you might have taken a trip down to the deep end."

"You mean, *gone off* the deep end?"

"That's what I said."

I smiled. "I was upset earlier, but I'm not about to do anything stupid. I'll talk to Derek in a day or two and we'll smooth things out."

"Thank goodness. I don't want to see you unhappy."

"Neither do I," I admitted.

"Hey, what're you two plotting?" Suzie said as she walked up behind us.

"I was telling Brooklyn what your family thinks of Grace's big announcement."

Suzie waved her hand in a carefree gesture. "I'm not worried. Madge is a freak. Don't pay attention to her."

Vinnie and Suzie made a quick pact to ignore Madge's whining, and the three of us walked into the card room, ready to have some fun. Grace and Sybil were already seated at a small table in the corner, so we strolled over just as Grace finished shuffling a large deck of tarot cards.

Suzie got bored watching her aunt deal cards to Sybil and announced that she was heading to the game room to watch another *important* football game Nathan and Marko were already engrossed in. Vinnie and I remained to watch Grace read the tarot cards.

My mom had always been a big believer in tarot, so I'd grown up knowing what each of the cards signified. But it had been years since I'd seen anyone throwing the tarot, so I was looking forward to hearing Grace's interpretation of the cards.

Grace turned over the Six of Cups. "That means you radiate joy and affection."

Sybil nodded. "That's true."

What? I so disagreed, but I wasn't about to contradict Grace.

Grace threw down the next card and frowned. "Oh, the Page of Swords."

"What does it mean?" Sybil asked.

"It means your goals are in focus," Grace muttered.

"Good," Sybil said with a confident smile.

Vinnie flinched, then gawked at me. Her stunned expression was loud and clear: *Grace sucks at this!*

I completely agreed.

All of a sudden, Sybil screamed and jumped from her chair. "Get it away from me! Get it away!"

Was she hallucinating?

"For goodness's sake, Sybil," Grace said. "It's just a tarot card."

"Not the card, you moron!" She pointed a shaky finger toward the carpet and that's when I saw the tip of a black furry tail slink under the card table.

"It's just a cat." I frowned at Sybil. Not only was she being ridiculous over a small cat, but I couldn't believe she'd just called her hostess — and her husband's business partner — a *moron.*

"It's Leroy," Vinnie said soothingly. "Here, boy." She scooped the black cat into her arms. "Aren't you a pretty thing?"

Sybil shivered uncontrollably. "Keep that animal away from me. I'm deathly allergic. And I plain don't like them. They're vicious and . . . dirty."

Vinnie gave her a hard look and started to walk off, but one of the kitchen staff met her and carried the cat away. Vinnie and I exchanged another look. My friend was a staunch animal lover and owner of two cherished cats. Sybil was not making points with anyone tonight.

"Okay, the cat's gone, Sybil," Grace said, trying to regain some levity. "Let's continue with the cards."

"Fine." Sybil straightened her jacket and expelled a heavy breath. "Where were we?"

"I just threw down a card that means your goals are focused on something. I don't know." Grace waved her hand in the air. "Something good, like you should, uh, assert yourself. People like you. I think."

I shook my head. My mother would be chanting right now, trying to keep from correcting Grace's ludicrous interpretations. Beside me, Vinnie made a choking sound as Grace reached for the next card.

"Enough!" Vinnie exclaimed, unable to keep quiet a second longer. "That's not at all what that card signifies."

Grace's reading of the cards was so wrong, I had to wonder if she had ever done this before. Did she know anything about the tarot or was she making it up as she went along?

"The first card, the Six of Cups. It does have a connection to love and affection, joy, affairs of the heart, and even sex and fertility," Vinnie said. "But Grace's interpretation is too vague."

Vague? Her interpretation was laughable! Grace must be faking it. But the least she could do was fake it more realistically than she was doing. I barely knew Sybil, but even I could tell there wasn't an ounce of *affection* in her entire body. And *joy?* What a joke! Not that I was judging her. Well, I was, but that wasn't the point. It was Grace who should have interpreted the card differently. Why didn't she use a book? Tarot cards usually came with a book that interpreted them, even on a superficial level.

And if she had read the book, she would know that because the card was reversed and not facing Sybil, it could mean something altogether different.

Hmm. I guess I'd retained more of the tarot than I thought I had.

"There is more to see here, Sybil," Vinnie insisted before Grace could deal the next card. "The Six of Cups ties into your past more than any of the other cards. It suggests that it might be time to heal yourself from old wounds. And while the card does radiate an aura of affection, as Grace mentioned, that affection is often connected to related areas such as fertility, childhood, and family. It is simplicity. Forgiveness."

"Whatever," Sybil said.

But Vinnie was on a roll. "The card asks you to open your heart, appreciate simple gifts, observe the energy of children. A child is very much involved in the present. So the Six of Cups reminds us to remember the past, but live in the present."

Sybil had been staring at the ceiling, but now she glanced over at Grace. "Is she serious?"

Grace smiled at Vinnie. "I had no idea you were interested in the tarot."

Vinnie shrugged. "I'm interested in many things."

"Tell us what the Page of Swords means," Grace said.

"Really?" Sybil sighed heavily. "Can we just get on with it?"

"But, Sybil," I said, "don't you want to know more of the card's meaning? Isn't that the fun of it?" I tapped the card. "The Page of Swords doesn't just deal with goals. It has to do with one's intuition, one's insight. It's connected to your mental abilities and perceptions."

"My mental abilities are just fine, thank you."

"Of course they are." I smiled tightly.

"Brooklyn, you're an aficionado, too?" Grace clapped her hands. "How fun!"

"Isn't it?" Because Grace was trying to keep things light, I wasn't about to divulge the card's darker meanings. Each card within the suit of swords had a connection to intellectual pursuits and social interaction. But they could be aggressive, too, especially the Page of Swords. Some tarot experts even connected the card to acts of espionage and certain danger.

Like a sword, each card in the suit of swords could cut both ways. So when facing one way, the Page might represent a breakthrough in communication. If turned in the opposite direction, it could indicate confusion leading to a complete breakdown.

The Page of Swords indicated highly developed mental capabilities. It also suggested an ability to aggressively exploit or seize control of any situation.

But since Sybil didn't seem capable of seizing much of anything, including enthusiasm for the cards, I kept it short. "If there's a particular goal you had in mind, you might want to reconsider your means of accomplishing it."

Sybil's eyes narrowed. "Oh, really?"

"Yes. The Page of Swords sometimes indicates that your current course of action is faulty."

"Right," Sybil said, rolling her eyes. "And

I'll listen to you because a pack of playing cards is so meaningful to my life."

I'd forgotten who I was talking to. With a weak smile, I said, "Of course not. Sorry. It's just a game."

"That's right, Brooklyn dear," she said. "It's just a game."

"Then let's get on with the game," Grace said jovially, and threw down the next card.

Death.

Sybil squealed and jolted back in her chair. "Are you trying to kill me?"

Grace leaned forward. "Calm down, Sybil. It's just a game."

"You gave me the Death card, you twit!"

Twit? What was with the rude names?

My father had an old friend who, when he got overexcited, would begin swearing incessantly. It was almost like he'd contracted a type of Tourette's syndrome in those moments. But as soon as the excitement faded, he became a perfect gentleman again. Maybe Sybil had a similar problem. I hadn't heard her use such rude terms until now.

Vinnie flashed them both a disapproving look, but then she pressed a calming hand on Sybil's shoulder. "Don't be alarmed. The Death card can be a positive sign of change. It can indicate anything from tremendous spiritual transformation to the simplest modification in one's life. These are good things."

Grace smiled at Vinnie in admiration. "You're really great at this."

"I know a thing or two about a thing or two," Vinnie said cryptically. "Some take the tarot more seriously than others."

"Well, I'm just here to have fun," Sybil said pointedly.

Grace shrugged as she smiled at Vinnie and me. She dealt several more cards, then flipped over the Tower card.

Vinnie gasped and Sybil jerked around. "What's wrong? What does it mean?"

"Nothing. Nothing at all," Vinnie whispered, but her voice was as breathless as if she'd just run a hundred-yard dash. "I . . . I must go."

She backed away from the table and I pulled her the rest of the way across the room. "Are you all right?"

Still breathing heavily, Vinnie said, "That last combination of six cards, culminating with the Tower, indicates that chaos and peril are at hand."

"I know, I know," I said, and wondered what my mother would say about the Tower card appearing when it did. "But chaos can be a prelude to humility and, ultimately, wisdom."

"That is very pretty, Brooklyn, but coming on the heels of Death and a sword, the Tower card can only signify pain. Any other interpretation would be a sorry attempt to avoid the truth."

"But, Vinnie," I whispered, "this isn't a real reading. This is just Grace and Sybil fooling around with the cards. It doesn't mean anything."

She scowled. "Grace is playing a dangerous game she doesn't understand, and Sybil has had more than her share of cocktails tonight. It's a dodgy combination, Brooklyn, and in this house that can put a person in all sorts of peril. We must keep an eye on Sybil over the next few days. Anything could happen to her, and I don't mean that in a good way."

CHAPTER 5

Suzie came over to join us. "What's wrong with you two?"

Vinnie shook her finger at Suzie. "You must talk to your aunt about treating the tarot more responsibly. She doesn't know the kind of havoc she could be wringing from the universe."

Suzie glanced at me sideways, then patted Vinnie's cheek. "Somebody needs to get some sleep."

"I'm fine," Vinnie protested. At first I thought Suzie was patronizing her, but now I realized that Vinnie was exhausted. It had been a long day and the blowup over the Tower card seemed to have wiped her out.

"Of course you're fine, but I'm tired, too, so let's call it a night." Suzie spoke to her in the soft tones she'd use to calm a child. She wrapped her arm around Vinnie's shoulders, then looked at me. "I'm going to walk her back to the room. Will you be staying up for a while?"

"No, I'm ready to hit the hay, too," I said, and followed her as she guided Vinnie toward the hall. The two of them walked with me as far as the grand stairway. Then we all said good night and Vinnie and Suzie headed upstairs to their room on the third floor.

My Library Suite bedroom was on the ground floor, so I continued down the hall alone. I had a fleeting flashback of my earlier run-in with Madge, but the hall was empty and I made it to my room without encountering anyone.

I had left my bedside lamp on, so the room was cozy and warm enough. I got ready for bed, but something told me I wouldn't get much sleep tonight. Now that I was alone, I couldn't help but think about Derek.

I was over my angst about the phone call, but I still wondered why I hadn't heard from him yet. Did he even realize that I'd called? Did he know that the other woman had answered his phone? If he knew, did he wonder how I was reacting? Did he consider that I might be hurt or upset? Since I'd never known Derek to be unkind, I had to conclude that he didn't know about the phone call. I reminded myself again that I'd never known him to lie or cheat. He'd told me on more than one occasion that he loved me. And since he didn't lie, he had to have meant it.

So why was my stomach in knots?

"Why not?" I answered myself after I thought about the day I'd just lived through. This wasn't about Derek. It was about the scary run-ins I'd had with Madge Crawford, Sybil Brinker, and Stephen Fowler, three of the rudest people I'd ever met in one house. It was about bookshelves on the ceiling and a bizarre tarot card reading that still made my head spin. So my anxiety had nothing to do with Derek. How refreshing.

"So just go to sleep," I said aloud.

With determination, I lay down and pulled the covers up to my chin. The blanket and duvet were warm and toasty. The pillow was soft and fluffy. I would just close my eyes for a minute. . . .

I was startled awake by a heavy creaking sound, as if someone were sneaking into my room.

I lay very still, listening, wondering if I should roll off the bed and hide underneath it. At times like this, I missed having Derek around, but mostly I missed the very large semiautomatic weapon that he always carried with him.

Frozen in place, I scanned as much of the room as I could without lifting my head from the pillow. Light from the full moon streamed through the bay window, casting shadows on the walls and throwing parts of the room into complete darkness.

One thin shaft of light bounced off the glass-topped table by the love seat, illuminating the ceiling panels above.

One of them was swaying. *Oh, God.*

I rolled off the bed, certain that the ceiling was about to fall down on top of me. Slipping to the carpeted floor, I curled into a protective ball and waited. And listened. And shivered in dread.

When the noise wasn't repeated after several tense minutes, I decided I was being ridiculous and climbed back into bed. I tried to fall back asleep but couldn't. With my mind racing, I finally gave up trying. Instead, I sat up and turned on the light and glanced around. Sure enough, my room was not being invaded and the panel's swaying had stopped. I spotted Grace's manuscript on my nightstand and reached for it.

I was surprised by how quickly I got caught up in the story. Grace's main character, Greta, was a lonely child who spent most of her time inside her own imagination. She loved cards and magic, loved making up stories and games. She created her first original card game when she was seven years old.

Grace was obviously describing herself, except that Greta was an only child, while Grace had grown up with a brother and a sister. I figured she'd made Greta an only child to add more drama to the manuscript.

I was halfway through the fourth chapter when I finally drifted off to sleep, but it wasn't a relaxed sleep and the next morning I awoke feeling tired and a little groggy. I must have been too discombobulated by all the strange things that had happened yesterday, because I usually slept like the dead, even away from home.

I could blame my tossing and turning on that Euro wench Thomasina, of course. I was so ready to jump on a plane and fly six thousand miles just to experience the joy of smacking her upside the head. But in the light of a new day the effect of her behavior on me had faded, and I knew she had little to do with why I'd slept so fitfully.

I was literally surrounded by four walls and a ceiling filled with thousands of books. My mother had recently delved into feng shui and now insisted that if I slept near bookshelves, all those printed conversations in the books would keep me awake nights. How could you sleep with all those characters talking at once?

Yes, my mom could be a little wacko sometimes, but now I was beginning to wonder if some of her theories were true.

I climbed out of bed and stumbled to the bathroom to wash my face. That's when I remembered there were worse things than being tired and grumpy in the morning. There was the whole puffy-face thing, too. I splashed lots of cold water on my face but knew it was hopeless. The other house guests would take one look at me and think I'd either been crying in my sleep (not likely) or I was coming down with a cold (no way!). Whatever the reason, it wasn't pretty.

I threw on my sweats and made my way down the hall, where I ran into Merrilee plugging in the vacuum cleaner.

"Good morning," she said in the cheeriest voice I'd heard since Beaver Cleaver's mom greeted Eddie Haskell.

"Hi, Merrilee." My own voice sounded more like a bullfrog's. "I guess I overslept a little. Am I too late for breakfast?"

"Never," she said with a smile. She gave me directions to Grace's less formal family dining room located on the first floor off the back hall and outside the main kitchen.

I found the room easily, thank goodness. I didn't ever want to miss another meal again. A breakfast buffet had been set up and I approached it eagerly, then reconsidered when I saw Madge and Harrison Crawford sharing the table with Peter and Sybil Brinker.

I thought about grabbing a protein bar and hustling out of there to avoid conversation, but the aroma of fresh hot coffee and doughnuts grabbed me and I was stuck. I didn't know where this recent doughnut fetish had come from, but I wasn't about to question it as I headed straight for the stacks of buttermilk and jelly doughnuts and fluffy crullers that sat on a large warming tray. There were pastries, too. Bear claws, cheese Danish, apple fritters. I was in doughy, greasy, sugary doughnut heaven. I poured myself a cup of coffee, then grabbed a buttermilk doughnut and a chunky, sticky apple fritter.

"Oh, my God. They're actually warm," I said, my voice trembling in anticipation.

As an afterthought, I added a spoonful of scrambled eggs to my plate. A girl needed some protein every day.

I greeted everyone as I sat down, but didn't add much to the conversation. Instead, I listened as Madge complained about her lack of sleep.

"What was all that pounding?" Madge demanded. "It kept me awake all night. Did you hear it?"

Sybil frowned. "No, but we're up on the third floor. I slept like a baby."

"Oh, fine," Madge groused. "Figures Grace would stick us on the noisiest floor. You know she did it on purpose."

"Now, Madge, honey," Harrison began.

Madge smacked his arm and repeated through clenched teeth, "She did that on purpose, Harry. She's trying to get me to leave, and I'm warning you, it's working. If this keeps up, I'm driving straight to a hotel in Tahoe and staying there for the rest of the week. I don't care how much money she's promised you. It's not worth it."

Yikes. Cue the awkward silence. Peter and Sybil exchanged uneasy glances. I didn't dare make eye contact with any of them, for fear that my absolute disgust for the woman would be clear for all to see.

"Now, Madge," Harrison said calmly, "let's not get carried away. I'm sure the construction was a one-night thing. I'll speak to Grace."

"Construction, my ass," she muttered.

Was she really so thickheaded that she

didn't think her comments about money would annoy her husband? Maybe she was born with no filters between her brain and her mouth. Whatever her problem, I really disliked the woman. It didn't help that in the morning light her stretched neck and facial muscles and overly moisturized skin made her look like a shiny skeleton.

Note to self: rethink the whole face-lift issue. Of course, I had never considered getting one, but now I knew why.

"Grace still likes to experiment with new games," Peter explained. "She's always been an insomniac, so I guess she's been working at night lately. Can't wait to see what she comes up with."

Madge just rolled her eyes. "Yeah, yeah, I've heard all about her insomnia."

Then why couldn't she have more compassion for her sister-in-law if she knew she was an insomniac? Clearly they weren't close, but still. The woman was a real jerk.

Peter's explanation fit in with Vinnie's stories of how Grace was always looking for new ways to delight — or *deceive,* as Vinnie put it — her guests with new games and tricks. Suzie had told me that Grace often walked around the house, staring at the walls or gazing at the ceiling, and she was never without her tablet computer, on which she made notes about her latest ideas.

"Such an odd creature," Sybil murmured.

"Yes. Isn't she?" Harrison said, but his tone was cheerful. He caught me watching him and winked. I had to admit I liked him even more today.

Madge saw the wink and scowled. Pushing her chair back from the table, she stood. "I'm going for a walk in the woods."

Harrison stared at his half-eaten plate of food, then sighed and stood. "I'll go with you, my dear."

"Don't bother," Madge said sharply.

He laughed and turned to the rest of us. "She's kidding."

Madge grumbled something under her breath, then stomped out of the room, slamming the door behind her. Barely a second later, Merrilee opened the door and walked in, looking a little dazed. Clearly, Madge had shoved the door closed rather than keep it open for the housekeeper.

Madge was so offensive! In that moment, I wanted to track her down and slap her.

Despite the affront, Merrilee flashed me another bright smile. "I see you found our buffet."

"Yes, and your homemade doughnuts," I said. "Thank you."

Sybil stood, ignoring me as she walked

out of the room.

"We're off to explore the conservatory," Peter said, as he pushed away from the table.

"Enjoy," I said, but wondered how he could enjoy anything, being married to that woman. I felt the same way about Harrison. How odd to be in the company of two such genial, successful men who were both married to horrid wives. I suppose there was a lesson in there somewhere, but I couldn't begin to figure it out.

I was about to take the last bite of my buttermilk doughnut when I remembered last night's tarot card reading and Vinnie's dire warning that Sybil could be in danger and should be watched. Should I follow them? I stared at my doughnut and reasoned that since Sybil would be in the company of her husband, who appeared stalwart enough to protect his wife, I would leave them alone. So after gulping down the last of my coffee I escaped back to my own room.

Still feeling a little groggy from the lack of sleep, I took a long shower in the hope that it would revive me. It worked to some extent, and as I dried my hair and dressed for the day in black jeans, ankle boots, and a red turtleneck sweater, I considered my next move. I could always track down Vinnie and Suzie and see what they were up to. I also had big plans to get a massage, but that could wait until tomorrow. And I wanted to go to the library and see what progress Nathan was making on the book cataloging.

That reminded me of my promise to hunt down any wayward books and return them to the safety of the library.

I decided to start with my own room.

"A daunting task," I muttered as I glanced at all the books. But I could at least skim the shelves for anything of real value that might be better off and safer in the confines of the library. Plus I was anxious to check out those cool ceiling racks.

"Cool in the light of day, that is," I said aloud, reminding myself that I'd been scared boneless last night when I thought they were going to suffocate me.

Twenty minutes later I'd found six books on the shelves that I deemed too valuable to remain outside the library. I set them on the coffee table in front of the couch, then grabbed the remote control that operated the shelving up near the ceiling. I felt some trepidation after my first experience with the moving shelves and also because Vinnie had planted the seeds of suffocation in my susceptible little brain. But I forged ahead and pushed the power button, then pressed the button marked Number One on the panel.

I watched the shelf descend and marveled at this genius setup. I still wasn't sure why Grace had gone to all this trouble. Maybe she simply enjoyed a new challenge. Maybe one day she looked up and said, *Hmm, I'll build an elaborate yet nonsensical bookshelf on the ceiling. Why not?*

I could see her with her computer note-pad, sketching out a fancy design with her stylus. She liked pretty things, so the shape would have to be attractive and swirly. The wood itself looked expensive and intricately sculpted, and the pattern of fluttering petals sweeping across the ceiling like a surrealistic flower had probably appealed to her sense of whimsy. I would have to ask her where the idea had come from. In the meantime, it was a mystery, but a fun one.

As soon as the shelf was lowered to my waist level, I pressed Lock on the remote control. Venturing closer, I studied the books stored inside the sturdy boxlike shelf.

"Ah," I whispered, charmed by the set of twelve *Little House* books by Laura Ingalls Wilder. I pulled one out at random to examine its condition. *Little House in the Big Woods.* The dust jacket was still in good repair with no tearing, although there were some light stains. Stains weren't unusual when it came to the covers of children's books.

I opened the book to check the copyright page. It stated that the book was a first edition, followed by the letters *F — B.* I'd seen this type of code before in small-press books. The first letter, *F,* indicated the month the book was printed and the second letter, *B,* indicated the year. So if January was represented by *A,* a book with *F* would have been printed in June.

Figuring out the year was trickier, since it was anyone's guess what year represented the letter *A.* But judging by the book itself, the style of the drawings, and the font used for the titles, I would have guessed it was printed during the 1930s or '40s. And if that was accurate, then the book was in excellent condition. I checked the other titles and they all appeared to be in good to excellent condition, as well.

What a delightful little find. I wondered if the rest of the shelves hanging from the ceiling held complete collections. Only one way to find out. I pressed Ascend on the remote and sent the Laura Ingalls Wilder collection back up to its place just beneath the ceiling, then pressed Lock.

This was kind of fun. I found the button

for the second shelf and hit Descend, lowering the next shelf.

The books here were more of an eclectic blend, with a few old, well-read copies of *Tom Sawyer* and *Huckleberry Finn,* some mismatched Earnest Hemingways, and a number of philosophy tomes that had been nicely bound in matching black leather with red-and-gold gilding on the spines. The bindings had been commissioned by a book club, so while they were pretty, they weren't exceptionally rare or valuable.

I sent that shelf back up, then lowered the third shelf. It had reached eye level when a huge black creature flung itself at me.

"Eeeeek!" I screamed, and covered my face with my hands. "Oh, dear God."

What was that? I didn't want to know. I curled up and shuddered in fear that it would attack again.

"Mrreow."

I flinched at the sound, then had to rub away the second layer of goose bumps that had cropped up on my arms. It took a few long seconds to catch my breath, but I finally summoned the nerve to look down.

It was the black cat, looking very handsome as it sat on the carpet near my feet. "You're not exactly huge, but you scared the hell out of me. You know that?"

I could've sworn he looked up at me and grinned.

I was just thankful that my room was far enough away from the other guests' rooms so nobody heard my pitiful squealing.

"Hello, Leroy," I said, bending down to stroke his long, black coat. "You scared the bejeezus out of me. I don't think I've ever screamed quite that loud before."

"Meow," he purred, and rubbed his head against my ankles.

"I suppose you're proud about that."

He wasn't exactly the gigantic hobgoblin I'd envisioned, but given my reaction, he probably imagined himself a formidable fiend capable of bringing grown women to their knees.

I glanced at the ceiling. "How did you climb up there?"

"Meow."

"Hmm." I guess he wasn't ready to confess his secrets to me. But, obviously, cats knew how to get from here to there a lot easier than we humans did. "Were you the one making noise in here last night? I'll bet you were. Do you know that you woke me up?"

We stared at each other for another long moment. Leroy seemed amused by my one-sided conversation.

"I'm going to the library now," I announced. "Feel free to join me."

An hour later, Leroy and I were still in the library. I had given the books from my room to Nathan first thing, and told him about the other ones I'd found in the ceiling shelves. He assured me that he would check them out later. I warned him that the cat liked to hide up there, too.

"Leroy likes to hide in strange places," Nathan said, smiling as he bent down to scratch the cat's neck.

Nathan had set up shop at one of two antique rolltop desks placed at opposite ends of the spacious library. His laptop was set up in the center of the desk and notebooks and pencils were spread haphazardly across the surface.

"I'll start cataloging these right now," he said, and tapped a few keys on his laptop.

"I'd love to take a look at your catalog program when you can spare some time," I said. "I'm thinking about updating mine."

"No problem," he said absently, and kept working.

I took a leisurely stroll around the spacious room, giving thanks that there were no bookshelves hanging from the high ceiling. Instead, the ceiling was elegantly covered in dark wood with the ceiling surface painted a light cream color. Old-fashioned schoolhouse lights hung down from the center of each coffered panel to illuminate the room.

A sturdy wood library table and six comfortable chairs filled the center of the room and built-in bookshelves covered the four walls. There was a comfortable chair in each of two corners.

I cleared the second rolltop desk on the other side of the room of miscellaneous papers and still more books, then set up my own book-repair station. I ran back to my room to get my tools and supplies from my suitcase, then laid everything out neatly on the desk surface.

When I sat at the desk, I found that I could see out the window above it. There was a pretty view of the forest of pine trees that bordered the back side of the property.

"I'm impressed," Nathan said when I was finished setting things up. "You take your tools with you everywhere you go?"

I glanced up and was reminded again of how adorable and clean-cut he was. Smiling at my own thoughts, I said, "Not always. But Grace mentioned that she might have some repair work for me to do while I was here, so I came prepared."

"If what you found under that table last

night is any indication, this place could keep you busy for a long time."

"True," I said. "Too bad I don't travel with the kind of supplies it would take to repair that dented cover of the *Pilgrim's Progress*. If Grace wants it fixed, I'll have to take it home and work on it in my studio."

"She will," Nathan said. "It's too valuable not to restore it. And I hope we can find that second volume of *Gulliver's Travels* while you're here."

"Me, too. I would love to show the pair to my friend at the Covington Library."

Ian McCullough, head curator of the Covington, would be giddy over some of the books in Grace's collection.

Leroy settled down for a nap on the thick carpet under my desk. My rational mind tried to convince me that Leroy's napping at my feet had nothing to do with me; that the spot on the carpet was one of his regular haunts. But as I did on a regular basis, I ignored my rational mind and savored the personalized kitty-cat love instead.

I spent another hour doing minor repairs to several inexpensive hardcovers that had suffered from torn dust jackets, ripped pages, and flapping spines.

When I was finished with my repair work, I left the library and took a tour of Grace's house, just as she'd suggested the day before. I strolled through the public rooms, admiring Grace's magnificent furnishings as well as the quirky personal touches that seemed to pop up in the most unlikely places. On the third floor, halfway down the hall from the grand staircase, I was stopped in my tracks by the sight of an old-fashioned bright red English telephone booth. Curious, I checked the telephone inside. Sure enough, it was working. There was a little seat in there that swiveled out from the wall, too. How fun!

I continued my third-floor explorations, keeping a sharp lookout for missing books. Most of the doors were closed and I assumed they were guest rooms, but one door was ajar. Nailed to the door at eye level was a brass plaque that identified the small salon as the WONDERLAND ROOM. I walked inside and found it furnished with giant props from a recent remake of *Alice's Adventures in Wonderland.*

According to another plaque on one of the walls, Grace was an ardent fan of Lewis Carroll's creation and had come across the unusual pieces at an auction. The furniture was so massive that a ladder had been placed next to several pieces, including the eight-foot-high couch, in case any guests were interested in testing it for comfort.

I left the room humming an old Jefferson Airplane song about some pills making you larger or smaller.

A few yards down the hall was another cozy sitting room filled with normal, comfortable-looking furniture and a wide-screen television. I wasn't sure if anyone ever used the room, but I had the strongest urge to lie down on the couch and take a nap.

And yet there was no way I would sleep in this room, because in one of the corners a full suit of armor was staring at me. I stood next to it, amazed to discover that medieval warriors weren't very tall. At least the original owner of this fine suit wasn't, because I towered over it by a full three inches.

It was silly to feel chilled. There wasn't anyone hiding inside the armor, right? But then again, there could be spirits lingering. Maybe the suit's owner died while wearing the armor. Or maybe he killed a bunch of his enemies while he wore it. Those spirits could've followed the armor. But even if that was all baloney, I still wouldn't be able to relax with *him* staring at me.

I'd had a hard enough time using the powder room downstairs after discovering another suit of armor in there the first time I ever visited Grace.

"I didn't know anyone was using this room."

I jumped a foot before realizing it wasn't the suit of armor speaking to me. Spinning, I saw Harrison Crawford standing in the open doorway.

I patted my chest, catching my breath. "Hello, Mr. Crawford."

"Hello, Brooklyn," he said, sauntering into the room. "Please call me Harrison. I was just looking for a place to watch some TV and take a nap."

"I'm not staying, so you're welcome to use this room. I was just taking a tour and came upon this awesome suit of armor."

"There's a lot that's awesome around this house," he said. "It could keep you busy for a long time."

"I know. Grace is an amazing collector." I looked back at the shiny suit of armor. "Do you think you'll be able to sleep with that guy staring at you?"

"It shouldn't be a problem." He chuckled. "My wife accuses me of being able to fall asleep anywhere."

It figured that Madge would hold something as benign as that against him. "Is your wife going to join you in here?"

"Oh, hell, no," he said in a rush. "She's gone off for a walk in the woods. Said she wanted to do some bird watching. She's perfectly happy trudging about on her own."

Harrison was such a nice man. I was still trying to figure out what he saw in his unpleasant wife. I hated to be so negative — I was, after all, still trying to be a beacon of positivity — but I couldn't seem to help it when it came to Madge. "Well, Harrison, I'll leave you to your nap."

"Ah, I'll probably just watch the stock market returns." He plopped on the couch, grabbed the remote control, and spread the newspaper out before him on the coffee table.

As I headed for the door, I took one last look around the room. That's when I spied a messy pile of books on a console partially hidden by the open door.

"Wow," I whispered. The books were classic noir fiction. "Pulp fiction." I counted twenty-two of them. They were all paperbacks from the 1930s, '40s and '50s, by mystery authors like Agatha Christie, Mickey Spillane, Raymond Chandler, Erle Stanley Gardner, Dashiell Hammett, and others. They had the most fabulous, lurid covers imaginable, with scantily clad blondes and screaming redheads, bulging eyeballs, spilled cocktails, and black dial telephones.

The titles were wonderful, too, with some more suggestive than others. *Terror on the Train, Kiss Me at Midnight, Blondes Tell No Lies, Her Lips Were Blood Red, Call Me Wanton.*

One of the Agatha Christies, *4:50 from Paddington,* showed a woman's body flying from a train. It was so delightfully graphic, I almost giggled aloud. Most of the books were originally priced at twenty-five to thirty-five cents, but now they could be worth hundreds, maybe thousands of dollars. Especially as a collection.

"What's that you've got?" Harrison said.

"Some fantastic books." I carefully scooped up all twenty-two of the little jewels. "I'm taking them to the library for some special attention."

"That's nice," he said absently, and went back to his paper.

"See you later." I left the room and almost rammed into Kiki out in the hall.

"Have you seen my dad?" she asked.

"Yes, he's in there." I jerked my head toward the sitting room where I'd left Harrison.

"Oh." She glanced toward the door of the room. Then she frowned, but didn't make a move to go in and see her father. "Do you need help with that stack?"

"That's okay. I'm perfectly balanced right now."

She smiled. "Okay, catch you later."

I watched her walk into the room.

"Dad, we have to talk about Mom," she said.

"I wish you girls would try to get along."

"How can I when she's trying to kill —"

That's when Kiki closed the door.

What?

Damn! How was I supposed to eavesdrop on people if they closed the doors on me? I figured Kiki was just being an overly dramatic daughter talking about her mother, but my ears definitely perked up when I heard anyone mention the word *kill*. At this point, the ears-perking tendency had become part of my DNA.

I sighed, then fumbled with the books in my arms but managed to steady them. I walked carefully through the hall and watched every step I took as I descended the grand stairway.

I pushed the door to the library open and greeted Nathan. "Wait till you see what I found."

He instantly shut his laptop screen and followed me across the room to my desk. I lowered the stack of books carefully onto the surface and took a breath.

"Wow, these are fantastic," he said, picking up the book at the top of the pile.

"Aren't they? Be careful. Some of them are falling apart."

"I can see that." He turned the book over, then frowned as he opened the cover. "This one's in pretty bad shape. But still great. They don't make them like this anymore."

"I know. I can't do much except clean them up and check for any really bad tears. We should put them in archival plastic cases to protect them for the long haul."

"Good idea."

Finding the noir collection had made me wonder again if Grace might be interested in donating some of her books to the Covington. The paperbacks weren't really good for reading anymore; they were too brittle. But the covers were fabulous representations of the jazzy pulp art of a bygone era. They would make for a fun exhibit for the library.

Nathan grinned and held out the cover of the book he was holding. It was the terrorized redhead with her eyes bulging at the shadow of a knife above her. "Isn't she beautiful?"

"She really is." I reached for the Mickey

122

Spillane paperback. Its cover was fragile with age and barely hanging on to the yellowed text block. "I'll order a box of archival covers while I'm here."

"Good idea. They won't arrive until next week, so I'll take care of slipping the books into them."

"Thanks." I placed the Spillane back on the stack. "I'll bet there's more of these around the house. I thought I might put together a separate catalog for them. I think they would make a fascinating exhibit for the Covington Library, if Grace agrees to it."

"I don't see why she wouldn't." He walked back to his desk and pulled the rolltop down. I watched as he locked the desk and wondered if he wasn't going a little overboard with the security. But I couldn't really blame him. Like most people, he probably had his entire life on his computer.

He turned and said, "I'm heading out. Are you ready for the séance?"

I looked up. "What time is it?"

"Almost six."

"Are you kidding?" I frowned. "I must've lost track of time. I have to go get dressed."

He looked me up and down. "You're already dressed."

"I mean, for the evening. Don't want to

look like a slob."

He scratched his head, then shrugged, a typical guy wondering what this girl was talking about. "You look great."

"Well, thank you," I said, grateful for his words, yet still unwilling to wear dusty jeans to Grace's séance. "But I'm just going to stop by my room for a few minutes. I'll see you up there."

I was running late, but made it to the Gold Salon in time for the second round of cocktails. I ordered a vodka and tonic from the bartender and took a quick sip. Gazing around at the well-dressed guests, I was thankful I'd decided to change into chocolate silk pants, black heels, and a burgundy satin blouse.

"There you are," Suzie said. "I thought we were going to have to send out a search party."

"Sorry I'm late. I was working with old books all day and wanted to freshen up before the party."

"No problem, kiddo," Suzie said.

That's when I noticed what she was wearing. "Hey, you look really nice." I hoped I didn't sound too surprised. Suzie usually went for more of a butch look that often combined denim vests with motorcycle

124

boots and chains. But tonight she wore a pretty sleeveless black top in some kind of flowing chiffon material over slim black pants. Her normally spiky blond hair was now a sleek bob. And were those high heels she was wearing?

"Yeah, color me shocked, too," she muttered, and craned her neck to gaze over my shoulder. "But Vinnie's been on a kick lately."

I turned and my eyes almost bugged out of my head as I watched Vinnie approach wearing — oh, dear God — a little black cocktail dress. It was short and tight and clung to every curve she had, with capped sleeves and a sweetheart neckline that actually showed some cleavage. Her strappy black heels were seriously high and very sexy. She wobbled only once; otherwise, she looked like she'd been sporting stiletto heels her entire life.

Wait. Is she wearing makeup? Yes, I could see a glimmer of pale pink lipstick and soft gray eye shadow.

I leaned in close to Suzie and whispered, "Isn't this one of the seven signs of the coming Apocalypse?"

She snorted a laugh. "Doesn't my girl look hot?"

"Yeah," I said. "Vinnie, you look amazing."

"Thank you, Brooklyn." In a self-conscious gesture, she fluffed her hair, which, instead of hanging straight down her back in a demure braid, was curled around her shoulders in thick, lustrous waves. "I thought it would be fun for Suzie and me to play dress-up. Doesn't she look lovely?"

"You both do."

Suzie winked at Vinnie. "Never thought you'd catch me playing the lipstick lesbian, but it's kind of fun to see you all dolled up."

I took another sip of my drink. "Not that you guys don't always look perfect, but . . . wow."

"Thank you," Vinnie said, smiling her appreciation for my inability to speak coherently.

The men were gathered around the bar and I heard Nathan trying to convince the others to get a football pool going. Marko's silly giggle could be heard throughout the room and I wondered again what Bella found attractive about him.

Against one wall was a bountiful buffet table filled with hearty appetizers of every kind. Miniature quiches and taquitos, finger sandwiches filled with rare roast beef and horseradish sauce, Chinese dumplings with dipping sauce, chicken satay.

Once again, Chef Tang had outdone himself. And he would be serving dinner after the séance. I was so in love with him, and to prove it I was careful to eat as much as possible. I'd learned my lesson about skipping a meal.

"The séance is about to begin," Grace said in a clear, cheerful voice. "You'll want to take your drinks with you, but please place them on the floor by your feet. I can't have any beverages on the table interfering with the power of the crystal ball."

There were a few snickers at that. Bella and Ruth and some of the others hustled over to the bar and quickly ordered more cocktails. The rest of us followed gamely behind Grace, who led us into a slightly smaller sitting room next door to the Gold Salon. She called this room the Red Room. It was more than obvious why. Swaying streams of thick red velvet billowed out from the chandelier to the walls and cascaded down in a rich red waterfall. The material effectively covered any windows that might have allowed the moonlight inside. In the center of the room was a large round table cloaked in mirrored brocades and Indian print fabrics. Two rows of chairs circled the table.

Grace sat down at the table first and Ruth joined her.

"I brought you an iced tea," Ruth said, handing Grace a tall glass of dark red liquid.

"Mm, passion fruit, my favorite," Grace said, and leaned over to place the glass on the floor. "Thanks, sweetie. Sit here next to me."

Ruth took the chair to Grace's right and set her own glass on the floor. Then Bella grabbed the seat on Grace's other side and Marko sat down next to her.

"No glasses," Ruth murmured.

"Okay, just one more sip," Bella said, and took a serious gulp from her beverage before handing it to Marko, who placed both of their drinks on the floor.

Peter, Sybil, Harrison, and Madge rounded out the seating at the main table. Vinnie, Suzie, and I, along with Nathan and Kiki and Merrilee, took seats in the second row of chairs. Stephen Fowler straggled in last and sat down next to Kiki, grumbling as he did so.

As soon as everyone was seated, the lights dimmed and flickered as sounds of thunder were heard in the distance. It was obviously an old recording, complete with scratches and pops, but everyone laughed nervously.

Bella feigned girlish apprehension, inciting Marko to slip his arm around her. "Don't worry, Peaches. I'll protect you from the ghosts."

Peaches? I kind of liked that nickname, although I still wasn't sure I'd want Marko protecting me from anything.

Grace pulled the crystal ball closer. Looking around at all of us, she began to stroke and caress the large globe. Suddenly she cried out, "The spirits are restless! They know we seek answers."

Sure enough, that cued a series of scary sound effects, mainly lots of groans and moans from the spirit world. There were giggles and mock screams from the audience and everyone seemed to be having a jolly time. The lights continued to flicker.

"Grace Crawford," a baritone voice cried out from somewhere.

Grace gasped. "Uncle Cuthbert?"

Kiki, sitting next to Suzie, giggled, then whispered to the group, "We don't have an uncle Cuthbert."

"Silence!" Cuthbert shouted.

Kiki emitted a short shriek and hunched down in her chair. There were more giggles as Grace carried on a hilarious conversation with her dearly departed great-uncle Cuthbert. Apparently the story went that he had hidden his fortune in a tree trunk somewhere and Grace was trying to cajole the location out of him.

In the middle of Cuthbert's rant that all his relatives were drunken sots with no social skills and would never get a single rotten cent from him, there was a sudden raucous thumping of footsteps from somewhere in the house.

The noise startled me. One of the women seated at the table screamed.

"What is that?" Grace asked, glancing around. She sounded seriously concerned, but somebody chuckled and a few others joined in the nervous laughter.

Those footsteps sounded real to me, not part of the show. And they were growing louder.

I whipped around to stare at the closed door and caught Suzie's look of surprise mixed with alarm. We both frowned as the sound of boots continued to echo off the hard marble surface of the front hall downstairs. Seconds later they were stomping on the grand stairway, the heavy sound barely muted by the carpeting. Some man was coming upstairs in an awful hurry.

I rubbed at the sudden rash of goose bumps on my arms.

"Who the hell is that?" Peter asked.

A loud rumble of thunder roared outside,

for real this time. The lights dimmed and stayed that way. The pounding footsteps grew closer.

I recognized Kiki's nervous giggle. A glass shattered on the hardwood floor. Grace cried out. There was another giggle and someone else gasped, then made a choking sound. *Probably laughing too hard,* I thought.

There was some grappling and pushing of chairs, but I didn't pay any attention. My full concentration was riveted on the door.

"This is ridiculous," Peter said, pushing his chair back and standing.

But Nathan had already jumped up and beaten him across the room to the door. He yanked it open and yelled, "Who's out there?"

Is this part of the show? I wondered, as we all stood and stared in fear at the open doorway.

Two more women screamed as my dangerous friend Gabriel stalked into the room.

CHAPTER 6

Gabriel?

"Oh, my goodness," Kiki said on a sigh. "Am I dreaming?"

"Wow," Sybil whispered.

Madge pressed a hand to her heart. "You can say that again."

"Uncle Cuthbert, I presume?" Nathan said.

"I hope he plans to stay," Sybil whispered.

Kiki giggled again. "Yes, please."

"Oh, for God's sake," I muttered, letting go of the breath I'd been holding. Pushing a chair out of the way, I ran over and hugged him. "Gabriel, what in the world are you doing here?"

"Hey, babe," he said, and bent and planted a smacking kiss on my lips. He looked even taller and darker and more rebellious than usual in his weathered leather bomber jacket and dark-washed blue jeans. His black hair was windblown and his cheeks were ruddy from the cold. I guess I couldn't blame the other ladies for their swoony comments about him.

"Gabriel, you're late," Grace said next to him, her breath coming out in short huffs and puffs from all the excitement.

He gave her a cockeyed grin. "Hope it was worth the wait."

She slapped his arm. "Always, you scoundrel."

"Oh yeah," Madge murmured. "Definitely worth the wait."

Down, girl, I thought, but again, I couldn't blame her. The guy was eye candy personified. I watched as Kiki slid into one of the chairs as though she were boneless, then simply stared at him.

Gabriel scanned the room. "How's everybody doing tonight? Hey, looking good, Suzie."

"Back at you, pal," Suzie said, grinning. "Way to make an entrance."

"Whoa, Vinnie." Gabriel made a point of blinking, then narrowing his eyes to focus on her. "Nice shoes."

Vinnie beamed. "You are the sight for sore eyes, Gabriel."

"Not bad yourself," he said, then glanced down at his own attire. "Sorry. Must've missed the dress-code memo."

"There's broken glass on the floor," Merrilee said. "I'll ring for someone to clean it up."

"Thank you, dear," Grace murmured, as Merrilee dashed out the door.

"Something's wrong with Bella," Marko said sharply.

I whirled around and saw Bella slumped in her chair with her head thrown back, her gorgeous red hair backlit in the dim light. Her eyes were open but glazed over.

No. I tried to say it aloud, but the word stuck in my throat.

Marko gave her cheeks a few light taps, then shouted, "Something's really wrong here!"

My stomach lurched. This wasn't happening. Not again. It was impossible. Wasn't it? I stared at Gabriel, whose eyes narrowed in suspicion. Not at me, I assured myself, but even I was growing wary of people dying around me.

"What's wrong with her?" Sybil demanded. "Is she asleep?"

"She's drunk. What else?" Madge mumbled, and slurped her own drink.

"Shut up, you dumb bitch," Marko snapped.

Madge turned up her nose at him, but didn't speak again. No one did. Marko's threatening tone made everyone nervous.

He spun around and gave Bella's cheeks another smack or two. There was still no response, so he gripped her shoulders gently to help her sit up. "Come on, Bella. Wake up, baby." Marko's face was pale and his eyes were wide as he bent and pressed his ear against her chest. Lifting his head, he said, "She's passed out. I — I don't think she's breathing. Somebody help me."

Gabriel wound his way through the chairs and reached Marko just as the man was about to give Bella mouth-to-mouth resuscitation. Gabriel pulled him away brusquely. "Don't do that."

"I've got to! She's not breathing."

Gabriel moved closer and sniffed the air just above Bella's lips, then muttered, "Almonds."

"What're you talking about?" Marko grabbed the back of Gabriel's leather jacket and tried to push him out of the way. Gabriel didn't budge, but instead quietly nudged Marko back. Then Gabriel leaned in close to Bella and sniffed again.

Marko shook his hands and swallowed compulsively as Gabriel attended to Bella.

"She's been poisoned," Gabriel said, and pressed two fingers to Bella's neck. A few seconds later, he looked directly at me, his expression grim. Glancing at Grace, he said, "Someone needs to call the police."

Then he turned to Marko. "I'm sorry, man. She's dead."

No one protested when Gabriel took immediate charge of the situation. He suggested that we all gather in one room, and Grace led the way back to the Gold Salon — where the bar was, naturally. The buffet table had been restocked with hot chafing dishes while the séance was going on, and now the confused guests hovered nearby, unsure whether to eat anything.

Gabriel pulled Suzie and me aside and gave us our assignments. Suzie was to stay with the guests in the Gold Salon and make sure nobody left. She was to listen in on conversations, watch for nervous gestures, and keep mental notes for Gabriel.

"You got it," she said with barely concealed excitement.

"Merrilee has called the police," Grace said.

"Thanks," he said, and gave her a hug. "You stay here and take care of your guests. Brooklyn and I will see to Bella."

"Thank you, dear," she whispered. "I'm . . . oh, God. I can't believe it. Please, Gabriel. Find out what happened."

"I will."

Grace walked away just as Merrilee rushed up with a broom and dustpan. "I'll clean up the glass."

"No," Gabriel said, easing the broom from her hand. "It's too dangerous. I'll take care of it."

"Oh." She blinked, unsure of herself. "Is there anything else I can do?"

Gabriel asked for some plastic Ziploc bags and Merrilee raced off to get them. Then he turned and took my arm. "Do you have your phone with you?"

"Yes," I said, holding up the small shoulder bag I'd carried with me all evening.

"Good. Let's go."

We walked out of the room, but Nathan stopped us. "How can I help?"

Gabriel studied him for a split second. "Guard both doors. Nobody enters or leaves without me knowing about it."

"I'm on it."

Gabriel led me into the Red Room, closed the door, and locked it. Then he systematically studied the scene, barely touching or moving anything. He started with another quick examination of Bella and worked outward in a spiral, just as I'd seen the police do at other crime scenes.

He told me what pictures to take with my

smart phone and I complied, snapping shots of the room itself. Of Bella. Of the scattered chairs. Of the broken glass on the floor. I kidded myself that by keeping busy, I could avoid the fact that I was, once again, stuck in a room with a dead body.

At some point, Merrilee knocked on the door and handed the plastic bags to Gabriel.

"Good girl," he said, rewarding her with a dazzling smile. After she stumbled away (Gabriel had that effect on women), he used one bag to pick up the bits of broken glass and slip them into the other bag, never touching the glass with his bare hands.

"Nice glass," he said, holding the bag at eye level. "Used to be, anyway."

"Cut crystal," I said, taking a closer look at the chunks of heavy material. "The glass is etched. Might be an antique."

"Yeah," he muttered. "Won't find fingerprints on that etched surface."

We determined that the broken glass had been the one that held Grace's passion fruit iced tea. Had she been the real target?

Bella's cocktail glass remained intact on the floor by her chair, still half full. After I took a picture of the glass in its place, Gabriel carefully poured the liquid into one bag and slipped the glass into the other.

Once we were finished, Gabriel asked Nathan to help him lay Bella's body down on the floor instead of leaving her sprawled precariously on her chair. Then Gabriel told Nathan he could join the others in the Gold Salon.

Gabriel and I remained in the hall while I filled him in on all that had happened before and during the séance. I was in the middle of explaining how Bella had sucked down her cocktail when Gabriel gripped my forearm. "Wait a minute. Are you all right?"

I gazed up at him, bewildered. "Of course."

He stared at me with intent. "Brooklyn, don't bullshit me."

"What're you talking about? Okay, I'm upset. Someone just died in front of me. Again."

"No, it's something else." Frowning deeply, he searched my face and I could see sympathy in his eyes. "Something else is upsetting you."

"Are you kidding?" I swallowed nervously. Could he actually tell that I was worried about Derek? Wishing he were here with me at yet another crime scene? I knew Gabriel was perceptive, but this was ridiculous. I wasn't about to whine to him, so I stuck to the distress I was feeling about Bella. Which was the truth, after all. "I was getting to know her, Gabriel. She was amazing. Gorgeous but also smart and funny and . . . damn it! I'm completely flummoxed and pissed off and nervous. Here I am, once again in the middle of a damn murder scene. It's not fair. I was supposed to relax and enjoy . . ."

I shook my head. "Sorry for whining. I'm being a toad. This isn't about me. It's about Bella. We've got to find out who killed her. And why."

"Then let's do it." He walked with me down the hall to get away from any big ears that might be hovering in and around the Gold Salon. "Tell me everything that's happened since you got here."

I did so, starting with the run-in with Madge and sharing my thoughts about an apparent relationship between Marko and Bella. I listed all of Grace's announcements the night before, adding that Suzie was suspicious that Grace was planning to change her will.

I told him how much I disliked Grace's lawyer, Stephen Fowler, and made it clear that I wasn't the only one who felt that way. I went through the entire guest list, giving him my initial reactions to each person.

"Who all was drinking at the séance

table?" he asked.

"Good question." I recalled Bella and Marko bringing their cocktails with them. Ruth and Grace both had drinks, too. I wasn't sure about the Brinkers or the Crawfords. I mentioned that Ruth had handed Grace the glass of iced tea mere seconds before the séance began.

"While we were listening to you climbing the stairs, I heard someone gasping and choking. I thought it was laughter. There was the sound of chairs being pushed around. I wonder if Bella was trying to get up from her chair."

"Probably."

"I thought at the time that someone was just moving or standing up to get a good look at the doorway. I didn't realize they were the sounds of Bella fighting for her last breath."

Gabriel pulled me close and hugged me for a moment. Then he stepped back and folded his arms across his chest. "Since the iced tea had the poison in it, Bella must have drunk from that glass."

"Yes, but I think she would've noticed that it wasn't her glass immediately."

"You said she'd been drinking heavily," he said. "Maybe she realized it was tea and figured she could use a break from the booze."

"Maybe."

"So she went ahead and drank from the glass meant for Grace."

"Which means that Grace was the intended victim."

"Yes," he said. "So Grace may still be in danger."

"Exactly," I said, pleased that we were on the same wavelength.

He nodded firmly. "Grace has been a good friend to me and I don't have many. We'll have to make sure nothing happens to her."

"Cyanide?" Grace whispered as she paced the length of her private sitting room two hours later. "How could someone have poisoned one of my guests in my own home? And with cyanide, of all things. It's barbaric."

I had ended up in Grace's room with Suzie, who had insisted on keeping her aunt company. Vinnie, Gabriel, and Ruth were there, as well, and Merrilee kept popping in and out. She continued to keep us updated on whatever was going on with the other guests and also to let us know how soon the police would arrive.

The police had warned Merrilee that it

would take them a while to get to Grace's home. The drive from the town of South Lake Tahoe out to Grace's remote property was barely twenty miles, but it was starting to snow heavily on the winding mountain roads.

Earlier, Gabriel had taken each of the guests into another room, one at a time, to hear their versions of everything that had happened before, during, and after the séance. I was impressed by the way Gabriel had assumed control, rather like Derek would have done if he were here.

And for the umpteenth time that evening, I wished that Derek were here right now. I wondered what exactly he was doing at that moment. But then I quickly shoved all thoughts of Derek away. Thinking about him made me worry and miss him too much.

Our small group sat in numb silence in the sitting area of Grace's master bedroom suite. Grace and Ruth had both known Bella for years, so they grew teary-eyed as they shared their musings about their departed friend.

I stood next to Gabriel by the massive bay window that overlooked Lake Tahoe. Along the same wall was a set of French doors that led out to a private balcony.

Grace had explained that she rarely closed her drapes because the view was so glorious. She insisted that this little corner of the lake was so private that nobody ever came close enough to catch a glimpse inside. But I could feel the cold seeping in through the double-glass windowpanes, so I took it upon myself to pull the drapes shut and warm up the room.

"Why would anyone want to kill Bella?" Grace moaned to the group in general. She'd been pacing but had stopped to lean against the arms of the couch. She looked ready to drop.

Gabriel put both of his hands on Grace's shoulders as if to brace her. "Grace, the poison wasn't meant for Bella."

"I don't understand. Then who was it meant for?"

"You, Grace," he said, giving her shoulders a light squeeze. "The poison was meant to kill you."

Ten minutes later, after Grace had recovered from the shock, Gabriel asked everyone to leave the room for a little while. He and I needed to talk to Grace alone. But Ruth refused to leave her friend.

"I'm the one who gave her that glass," she wailed. "I could have killed her."

That was my thought exactly, but I kept my mouth shut.

Taking careful steps, Grace walked over and hugged Ruth. "Do as Gabriel says and leave us now. We'll just be a few minutes. I'll hear what he has to say and then I'll call you back in."

Ruth sniffled. "All right. But . . ."

Grace shook Ruth by the arms. "Now, don't be a silly goose. I know you weren't trying to kill me."

"Do you?" Ruth demanded. "Do you, Grace?"

Grace patted her friend's cheeks, then pulled her close for yet another hug. "Snap out of it, Ruthie. You're going to make yourself sick."

"I am sick. Sick at heart." She sniffled again. "You have to know I would never do anything to hurt you. Ever. You know that, don't you?"

I knew they were close, but was Ruth protesting too much?

"Oh, Ruth," Grace said. "Of course I know it."

Ruth nodded. "Good. That's good."

"Now, we've all had a horrible shock." Grace kept her arm around Ruth's shoulder and walked her to the door. "So I don't want you going back to your house. You'll sleep here tonight. We'll have a slumber party in my room."

"All right," Ruth whispered, and tried to smile.

Suzie opened the door and found Merrilee standing there. After a brief explanation, Merrilee took Ruth's arm. "I'll keep Ruth company until you're all finished." Then she led the older woman out of the room. Vinnie and Suzie followed them.

"We'll be right outside," Suzie said. Then Gabriel closed the door.

Grace looked from me to Gabriel. "I've never seen Ruth like that before. She's not a weak woman, but this has devastated her."

I wondered if Grace was being naive. Her friend could have killed Grace easily if she had taken one sip of that drink.

Grace and I sat down on the sofa and Gabriel took the chair. I touched Grace's knee gently. "Are you sure you're ready to talk about this?"

"Don't treat me with kid gloves, Brooklyn," Grace said. "I want to get to the bottom of it. I'm heartbroken that a dear friend had to die instead of me and I don't want it to happen again. I also don't want Ruth to suffer because of it. So let's put everything out on the table and talk some turkey."

"Okay, good," I said briskly. Grabbing a

146

notepad and pen from her bedside table, I sat in the chair closest to her. "I'm glad you feel that way. So let's start by making a list of the guests who have the most to gain from your death."

"Oh, dear," she murmured, and pressed her hands to her chest. So maybe she wasn't quite ready to talk turkey, but it had to be done.

"What about Suzie?" I continued breezily, as though I hadn't noticed her reaction. "She's got to be mentioned in your will, right?"

Her mouth dropped open. "Brooklyn, shame on you! You don't honestly think Suzie would do anything to hurt me. Do you?"

I gave her arm a comforting squeeze. "No, of course I don't. Not at all. We just need you to start talking that turkey talk."

"Well, I guess I asked for that." Her lips twisted to form a reluctant smile, but it faded quickly. "All right. Yes, it's true that Suzie would inherit money and property from me. And there's Harrison and Madge, of course, and Kiki, their daughter, along with a number of other relatives you haven't met yet."

"Kiki works as a masseuse," I said. "Is her business doing well?"

"Oh, you know how it is," Grace said lightly. "She's young and still trying to find out what she wants to do with her life. But she's an excellent masseuse nonetheless."

"I'm determined to get an appointment with her while I'm here," I said conversationally, hesitant to remind Grace that we were trying to pin down a killer, not chat about her family.

"You'll be glad you did," Grace said, nodding with enthusiasm. "She has wonderful hands."

Gabriel spelled it out for her. "Grace, does Kiki need money?"

"Oh." Grace blinked as reality sank in. "Oh, now, you can't possibly suspect Kiki. She's a vegetarian, for goodness sake. She's committed to universal peace and love."

"And poverty?" Gabriel asked.

"Don't be snide, dear," Grace chided quietly.

I was surprised to see Gabriel simply nod, accepting that he'd been chastised.

"Grace," I said, "please don't be upset. We're just trying to determine if Kiki might be desperate for money or not."

She sighed. "I'm trying to stay objective, but it's not easy when we're talking about my own flesh and blood. But I know you need answers, so I promise to try harder. As to your question, Kiki's not desperate at all. She makes a decent living, and she receives a generous allowance from her father. Which she often gives away to her special causes, I might add."

"All right, then," Gabriel said, joining her on the couch. "Now, what about your business associates?"

"Peter and I own equal halves of the business as well as most of the game patents and copyrights, except for the ones I invented myself."

"Has Peter ever invented anything?" Gabriel asked.

She turned and faced him. "No, Peter was always the organizational guy. He ran the business."

"So Peter and Sybil would profit from your death, too."

She waved the possibility away. "Yes, yes, but it's silly to think any of them would go to the trouble. They're all quite wealthy in their own right. Although . . ."

Gabriel's ears perked up. "Although what, Grace? What were you going to say? Something about Peter and Sybil?"

She sighed. "We had a little business meeting earlier today. It seems someone has been skimming money off one of the vendor accounts." Her eyes narrowed and she scowled, but she quickly brushed off whatever she was thinking. "It's an internal issue, nothing to do with what happened to Bella."

I glanced at Gabriel and knew he was thinking the same thing I was. Could Bella have been the actual victim of the murder after all? Had she been the one skimming funds from the company? Or maybe she had discovered who the embezzler was and that person had had no other choice but to kill her.

If any of those scenarios were true, then everyone who worked in the company could be suspect. Peter, Sybil, Marko, even Grace herself. Along with anyone whose money was invested in the company, for that matter. That list might possibly include everyone attending the party, except for me, of course.

"Why did they meet with you?" I asked. "Haven't you retired from the company?"

"I'm still the major shareholder," she explained.

"Do Peter and his wife stand to lose a lot of money from this theft?" Gabriel asked.

"No, no. None of us will lose money. Dear God, we all have more money than any of us will ever need. The company is extremely profitable. That account has already been closed and all of the passwords and routing numbers have been changed. And it's all covered by insurance, anyway, so it's not really an issue." She rubbed her forehead wearily. "I don't even know why I brought it up. I'm just flustered, I guess."

Gabriel leaned forward to rest his elbows on his knees. "Just a few more questions, love."

"Yes, yes," she said, her tone resolute as she straightened her shoulders and sat back on the couch. "I'm fine. Let's keep going. I want some answers."

"All right, then," I said. "What about Marko?" Feeling restless from sitting so long, I stood up to pace a little.

"Poor Marko." Grace dabbed the corners of her eyes with a tissue. "He's been with the company since we first started. Bella joined the team about ten years ago. I suspected that he was in love with her from the first day she arrived. He's so immature. I knew it would never work out. For someone as easygoing as he is, he can fly off the handle at the oddest moments."

"Could he be violent?" Gabriel asked.

"Oh no." She shook her head as she reminisced. "No, they were more like tantrums, really. Artistic temperament, I suppose, although none of the other designers ever behaved that way. Oh, and he used to be so cheap. It was almost laughable. He's gotten better, but Bella would never have tolerated that. Of course, we can't always choose who we'll fall in love with."

"No, we can't," Gabriel muttered.

Grace continued. "After seeing Marko's devastated reaction tonight, I'm sure he was in love with her. He couldn't possibly have killed her."

I let that comment go for now. "How about Merrilee?"

"Merrilee?" She was genuinely taken aback. Then suddenly she laughed. "Oh no, no, no. Merrilee isn't smart enough or mean enough to concoct such an evil scheme. She wouldn't hurt a fly, let alone another human being."

I sat down and took hold of her hand to soften the pain of the next question. "Grace, is Ruth in your will?"

"Well, of course," she said easily. "I'm her patron as well as her friend. I've set up a trust fund that will take care of her as she works toward her artistic goals."

"Does she know how much she would inherit?"

"We've talked about — Wait." She held up her hand like a traffic cop. "You can't possibly think Ruth had anything to do with this. We're very close friends. More like sisters, really."

Gabriel leaned farther forward to catch her gaze. "So you've told her how much she stands to inherit?"

She frowned at him. "Not exactly, but I suppose she might have an inkling. She's not a stupid woman."

"She handed you the poisoned drink," I said.

"That doesn't mean she was the one who added poison to the glass." Grace shook her head vigorously and refused to look at either of us. "No. It had to have been done by someone else."

"So someone else poisoned the drink and handed it to Ruth to give to you?"

"Yes. That must be what happened." She stared intently at her fingers as she fiddled with her rings. "Something like that, anyway."

"Grace, who do you think would do that?"

She looked up and her eyes were damp with tears. "I haven't got a clue."

Merrilee updated us with the latest information from the police dispatcher. There had been a major traffic accident on Highway 89, so the police wouldn't be able to make it to Grace's place before morning.

I stared at Gabriel, knowing what he was thinking. There was no way we could leave Bella's body unattended in that warm upstairs room all night.

I had taken at least a hundred pictures, so the police couldn't complain that we were mucking with the crime scene. Well, they could complain, but it was their own fault for not going to the trouble to get here faster.

I enlisted Suzie and Vinnie for help, and the three of us wrapped Bella's body securely in a clean white sheet. This time Gabriel snapped photographs, memorializing every step we took. Then Gabriel and Nathan carried Bella downstairs and outside. We all walked with them around the house to the root cellar located beneath the conservatory. It was below freezing and snow was still falling, so if my rudimentary knowledge of forensics was correct, Bella's body would decompose more slowly down here.

That thought gave me shivers. You'd think I would have become used to the realities of dealing with dead bodies by now, but no.

More pictures were taken inside the root cellar; then Gabriel locked the door with Grace's key and our small, intrepid group trundled back inside the house.

After Merrilee had arranged for a bedroom for Gabriel, she and Grace and the rest of the guests retired for the evening. I was wide awake, so I asked Gabriel if he would like to stay up and talk for a while.

He grabbed a bottle of wine and a couple of glasses while I snagged a plate of leftover appetizers and led the way to the cozy TV room I'd found earlier that day. It was a comfort to see that the short knight in shining armor still stood guard in the corner. He was a lot less scary now that I had company with me.

I sat on the couch and watched as Gabriel poured two glasses of wine. He first took a sip of the wine, then handed me the other glass and sat in the nearby chair.

"So what are you doing here, really?" I'd been wanting to ask him that question all evening and finally had the chance.

He stretched out his legs. "Grace invited me."

"But how? I can't believe you know her. Is this a small world or what?" I tucked my legs underneath me and nestled into the corner of the couch.

"She and I share a passion for books," he said, his smile enigmatic.

I narrowed in on him. "Did you steal one for her?"

"Brooklyn, Brooklyn." He shook his head and chuckled. "Let's just say we're old friends and leave it at that."

It was a reasonable question, given that shortly after the first time I ever met Gabriel he somehow managed to steal an extremely valuable book from my home. The book didn't belong to me, so the fact that I later discovered it in the home of the very person I had meant to give it to was somewhat mollifying. But still, I had little doubt that Gabriel was a thief for hire, among other occupations.

I sipped my wine for a moment, then decided to take his advice and change the subject. "So how did you figure out that Bella was poisoned? Can you smell cyanide? I don't think Marko smelled it. And how in the world did someone get cyanide into the house?"

He shrugged. "It's not that uncommon an ingredient. And I happen to have a good sense of smell. Only about forty percent of the population can detect the scent of cyanide."

"Really? I guess we're lucky you're one of them."

He said nothing, just took a sip of his wine.

"But seriously, Gabriel. Cyanide poisoning? Sounds like something out of the Cold War, don't you think?"

"It does. But it's still used all the time in herbicides and drain cleaners, usually under different chemical names. And it's found naturally in the nuts and seeds of some edible plants and some roots, too."

"Plants? Like garden plants?"

"That's right. Lima beans, bitter almonds, apricot seeds. But we're not supposed to worry because the government carefully regulates all that stuff."

"I wasn't worried until you said that."

And not everything was regulated, I realized, recalling the poisonous plants and trees that were clearly marked in Grace's conservatory.

I mentioned the plants to Gabriel and we discussed the remote possibility that someone had taken a cutting and somehow drawn the poison from it. I'd seen stranger things happen, so I wouldn't put it past a truly desperate person.

It was likely that the killer had simply used some kind of weed killer or cleaning agent. But before going off to bed, Gabriel and I made a date to search the conservatory tomorrow to see if any of the poisonous plants had been disturbed.

No, not *if*. Something had definitely been

disturbed; that much was clear. Now Gabriel and I were resolved to find out just how far someone in this house had gone in their attempt to kill our friend Grace.

CHAPTER 7

Bright and *way* too early the next morning, two police detectives and two EMTs finally showed up from the local police department. The detectives, whose names were Pentley and Graves, were a no-nonsense team. They told Merrilee to round up all the guests in the Gold Salon for interviewing, then asked to be taken to see the victim.

Gabriel and I led the way to the root cellar, where Pentley told the paramedics to unwrap the sheet to check that Bella was, in fact, there. She was, thank goodness. Then they wrapped her back up and Pentley gave the two EMTs permission to take charge of Bella's body.

I watched as the two burly men slipped her body, sheet and all, into a black zippered body bag. Then one of the EMTs ran back to their vehicle for a gurney to more easily transport Bella to the ambulance.

I breathed in the icy air. It was never a

fun thing to view death up close like that, but standing around with the cops and paramedics as they started down those cold concrete steps into the dark, dank root cellar? It really disturbed me. Especially since I knew that poor dead Bella had been lying there all night, waiting inside that earthen cavern on that icy slab for the police and EMTs to show up and declare her dead.

Bella hadn't deserved to die, but she also hadn't deserved to be wrapped in a plain white cotton bedsheet and stuck on the shelf of a funky old root cellar like a bushel of potatoes while she waited for justice to be served.

Rubbing my arms to fend off the chill, I added up the insults that Bella had endured. I put them all on a mental list of reasons why I wouldn't stop until I found her killer. I didn't care if that person turned out to be Grace's best friend, her worst enemy, or Grace herself. I was sick and tired and pissed off at people who killed other people, especially when I was around. It made me cranky and vindictive.

And yes, sometimes it was all about me, damn it.

Shoving my hands into the pockets of my thick fleece vest, I walked away from the activity. I didn't go far, just a few dozen feet, but it was far enough to take advantage of the sight of the early-morning fog hovering over the lake beyond the house. Snow had fallen during the night, so the mountains and trees surrounding the lake had received a light dusting of white. Everything looked clean and sparkly.

Staring up at Grace's home, I was overwhelmed by the grand eccentricity of the design. The outer walls were constructed from thick, heavy stone, but the style of the home itself was Queen Anne Victorian, complete with steep gables, a central tower, rounded turrets, and cone-shaped, or witch's cap, rooflines. Fanciful finials perched on top of the witch's caps completed the Victorian look. I was familiar enough with the design because Victorians of every style were ubiquitous in San Francisco.

Wrapped around the outside walls of the second and third floors was a labyrinthine maze of passages and walkways that led to balconies and porches and terraces outside the various bedrooms, parlors, and salons on the second and third floors. Some of the balconies were walled in by stone, while others were contained by pretty wooden spindle railings.

At the very top of the house was another

railing that surrounded a central section of the roof. A widow's walk, maybe? The view had to be incomparable from up there. I couldn't wait to explore it.

The overall feeling of the outside of the mansion was whimsically contradictory: heavily fortified yet charming. Almost otherworldly. An airy-fairy castle in the woods.

At last, the EMTs wheeled Bella's body over to the ambulance and loaded her inside. Then they took off, leaving the two detectives, Pentley and Graves, behind to conduct witness interviews and examine the crime scene.

"Sorry we couldn't get out here last night," Graves said.

"I guess the snow was falling pretty hard," I said.

"Yeah, the snow was bad, but we also got called to another murder in town."

I had to ask. "Do you normally get a lot of murders out here?"

"Not really," the taller cop, Detective Pentley, said. "Must be the full moon or some kind of weird planetary alignment or something."

"You think?" I asked, remembering there was a full moon the first night here. "Do the movements of the planets have an influence on the level of crime in this area?"

Graves snickered.

"Nope, it's mostly about drugs and alcohol," Pentley said with a straight face.

"Right." So I was being mocked. I exchanged looks with Gabriel. Fine. I could take it. And these cops would need their wacky senses of humor once they were dealing with the crowd staying at Grace's house.

By the time we got back inside, Merrilee had arranged for two sitting rooms to be used for the private interviews. She had stocked each room with a coffeepot, sodas, doughnuts, chips, and pretzels.

Merrilee was so competent and warm and intuitive when it came to providing guests with a welcoming space, I wondered why she was wringing her hands and fussing so much. It was almost as though she were the one about to be dragged off to the pokey. I knew in my gut that she couldn't be guilty of murder, so why was she acting like it?

I finally pulled her aside to try to calm her down. "Are you all right?"

Stressed out, she blew her bangs off her forehead. "I'm so worried we'll run out of potato chips. We're down to three bags."

"You're kidding, right?" I laughed, then scanned the sideboard with its abundant supply of snacks. "If we run out, it's not your problem. We'll just eat tortilla chips or pretzels. But it's not going to happen. You've arranged everything perfectly."

"Thank you, Brooklyn. I just worry."

"I know you do, but you shouldn't. We appreciate all that you do for us."

She still seemed to need reassurance so I stuck my tongue in my cheek and added, "In fact, I was wondering if there was any possible chance you'd consider coming to live at my house and doing this for me. I could use a running supply of snacks in my workshop."

"Oh, Brooklyn," she said, lightly swatting my shoulder as her chirpy laugh fluttered through the room. "You're so funny."

"I'll double your salary."

"Oh, stop."

I shrugged. "I'm just asking you to think about it."

She giggled and the hand-wringing ended. Seconds later, she was back to bustling about, making people happy.

The police interview process was long and slow and took most of the morning. It was a good thing there were plenty of books and games to keep us all occupied.

When it was my turn, I followed Detective Pentley into the small, blue-accented sitting room and sat on the least comfortable chair I could find. I wanted to appear serious, not overly relaxed, and a straight-back chair would help.

"Brooklyn Wainwright," he murmured as he wrote my name in a small spiral notebook. Then he looked up. "Tell me what you saw last night."

I pulled out my phone and clicked on the gallery of photos I'd taken the night before. He followed the pictures as I told him everything that had occurred. We went back and forth as I described the séance, before, during, and after. I told him how Ruth had handed Grace the glass of iced tea just as the séance was about to start. I told him that at least four people at the table had drinks, maybe more.

"So Bella had her own drink?"

"Yes."

"And Marko put both of their drinks on the floor by his chair."

"Yes."

"So why would Bella reach for the glass by Grace's chair?"

I thought about it. I'd seen Bella putting away the booze for two nights straight, so it was easy enough to surmise that she hadn't been thinking clearly when she reached for her cocktail.

I mentioned that to Detective Pentley,

who wrote everything down in minute detail.

I told him that Vinnie, Suzie, and I were the ones who had wrapped Bella in the sheet and he asked me why we'd decided to do that. I confessed that I'd been involved in a few crime scenes and I'd learned how important it was to preserve as much evidence as possible, including anything that might turn up on the body itself.

I gave him the names and phone numbers of detective inspectors Janice Lee and Nathan Jaglom, the San Francisco detectives I'd worked with on numerous occasions. He seemed impressed by my answers. I hoped he was, because I truly lived to impress the police with my knowledge of crime-scene procedure.

Then Pentley asked me how well I knew Gabriel.

"Very well."

"Are you lovers?"

"No."

"Why not? He's a good-looking guy."

"He's gorgeous," I said agreeably. "But he's not mine. I've got one of my own, thanks."

"And where is he?" Pentley asked as his eyes narrowed in on me. Was he trying to penetrate my soul? It bugged me, for some reason.

"Is that any of your business?"

"Depends."

"Right," I said. "Look, Gabriel is a good friend of mine. And it's a fact that he didn't even arrive until after Bella was dead."

Pentley scowled, knowing that was the bottom line.

I went on to vouch for Gabriel's integrity, compliment his supervision of the postmortem activities, and gush about his overall honesty. (That might have been a stretch, given the book-theft incident.)

I suggested that Pentley contact Derek Stone, former British naval commander and MI6 agent, if he wanted another, better reference for Gabriel's excellent and extensive experience in dealing with criminal behavior (on the good guys' side).

I didn't mention that Derek was my boyfriend, deciding that that was something else that was none of his business.

"I don't know what we would have done if Gabriel hadn't shown up when he did last night."

Pentley gave me a look so sharp, it made me wonder if I shouldn't be thinking about lining up my own good references. But he finally finished his questioning and told me

I was free to leave the room.

After two hours of interviews, the police spent another hour taking their own photographs and collecting as much evidence as they could find in the Red Room. As Pentley and Graves packed up their gear, Gabriel handed Pentley the plastic bags containing the cyanide-coated broken glass, the liquid from Bella's cocktail glass, and the cocktail glass itself.

"What the hell?" Pentley said, and shoved the bags into Graves's hands. Seniority had its benefits, apparently.

At the front door, Pentley issued one last warning: we were not allowed to enter the séance room or leave Grace's property until the police returned to clear them.

"It might be a few days," Graves added.

"We'll be in touch," Pentley said. "Thank you for your cooperation."

As they walked out, I looked around the room at the numb faces of the guests. The cops' warning had served to remind me — as if I needed reminding — that one of my fellow guests had been murdered last night. And, in turn, that meant that one of the people in this room was a murderer.

Cozy thought.

I scanned their faces again. I barely knew most of Grace's guests, so my sympathy fell on Grace and the people who had known Bella best. I could truly imagine the heartache and fear and guilt Grace was dealing with right now, after having a good friend die in her home. I had dealt with similar feelings of guilt before.

Absently, I checked my watch. It was a few minutes past noon. The police had been here for more than four hours.

"Well, that was unpleasant," Grace said soberly, standing up to address her friends and relatives. "I can apologize from now until kingdom come, but I'll never be able to make it up to all of you. I wouldn't blame you if you wanted to pack up and leave, but it seems you're all stuck here with me."

"None of this was your fault, Aunt Grace," Suzie said in protest. "We're all happy to stay and celebrate your birthday week."

"That's right," Kiki said.

I raised my hand. "I'm having a marvelous time."

"I wouldn't leave even if I could," Harrison said stoutly.

I caught Madge rolling her eyes in disgust. There were other positive comments, though I didn't hear any from Sybil Brinker or Madge, of course. But, then, I didn't really care if they were happy or not.

"Thank you, my loyal darlings." Grace

smiled bravely. "On the bright side, I can promise you great food and plenty of it all week long. We must keep up our strength, after all. So for anyone who's interested, Merrilee has set out a delectable buffet lunch in the informal dining room on the first floor, whenever you're ready to dine."

I was more than ready. I was half in love with Chef Tang already, based on the first night's meal. But then last night, when I dashed into the kitchen to return Gabriel's and my wineglasses, I'd had a chance to meet him. Chef Tang had generously shared his polenta and sausage recipe with me. I told him about my sister, Savannah, the chef and owner of Arugula, her new restaurant in Dharma, my hometown in the Sonoma wine country. Tang assured me that he would make it up to Dharma sometime soon to dine with Savannah. The chef and I were now the very best of friends.

"Come on, Auntie," Suzie said. "I'll walk with you to lunch." She threaded her arm through Grace's and strolled out of the room, followed by the others. I found Vinnie and we linked arms, too, and joined the crowd going downstairs to the dining room.

It was a quiet, reflective group today. Not that we all didn't have a lot to talk about. It just didn't feel like the right time yet.

Everyone was still rattled by Bella's death and the past four hours of grilling by the police.

The kitchen staff must have caught our pensive vibe, because they had outdone themselves trying to cheer us up.

Besides the main table overflowing with sandwich makings and breads and yummy salads of all kinds, two staff members stood at the ready to make omelets and dessert crepes for any who wanted them. There were at least twenty-five ingredients to choose from, all chopped, grated, and ready to go.

I decided on a Mexican omelet with onions, peppers, chorizo, avocado, sour cream, and salsa. And in case I was still hungry, I asked for a strawberry-and-banana-cream dessert crepe with hot fudge drizzled on top.

That would teach me to ever skip a meal again.

"I think we all need a treat to wash away the doldrums," Grace announced. "Tonight, after dinner, let's put on a show. This is a talented group, so I insist that you all perform something. Whatever you're good at. Or not. Pick something fun. Something entertaining. Make us laugh. We all need a good laugh."

"That's for sure," Harrison said.

"I'm not good at anything," Suzie muttered, then grinned at Vinnie. "Too bad we didn't bring our chainsaws."

"Ruth will read her poetry," Grace continued, "and I'll read a scene from my manuscript."

Merrilee clapped. "Won't that be fun?"

"Oh, please," Madge snarled under her breath.

I ignored the woman's mutterings and searched my mind for something I was good at, something that would provide some entertainment. I'd tried to learn piano when I was in grade school, but it had been disastrous. I liked to sing, but I wasn't very good. That didn't keep me from belting out show tunes when nobody was around to suffer through my caterwauling.

It was too bad I hadn't thought to bring along my mother's sacred-chanting love drum. I'd practiced on that thing and knew I could get a real groove going. But maybe Grace had something I could borrow. How much talent did it take to pound on a drum? I mean, besides the ability to keep time and the whole rhythm thing. I could do that.

"Oh, Vinnie, you must dance!" Grace said, her excitement rising. "Bollywood! Don't think you're getting away without performing tonight."

"Vishnu wept," Vinnie muttered.

I looked at Suzie. "Vinnie dances?"

"Like a freaking New Delhi Rockette," Suzie said, beaming with pride.

"Vinnie, I'm learning so much about you this week."

She grabbed my hand and squeezed it. "Brooklyn, I'll thank you to forget everything you've heard or seen by the time we get home."

I laughed. "Fine, but I still want to see you dance tonight."

"Yes, yes, I'll dance," she grumbled, and gave Grace a narrow look.

As the afternoon wore on, people began to get energized by the notion of performing in a talent show. Some of the guests traipsed up to the attic after Grace mentioned that there was a trunk filled with fancy outfits and costumes from a costume ball the company had thrown years ago. There were also plenty of outlandish props Grace had come across during her years as the queen of games.

I could hear musical instruments being played in the music room, mostly badly, but it was obvious that Grace didn't care about quality tonight. I knew that Vinnie had gone to her room to practice the dance she intended to perform. Had Suzie gone with her?

I hadn't seen Gabriel in a few hours, either, so I figured our inspection of the conservatory had been postponed. The snow was falling more thickly now, so I doubted he'd gone outside. Maybe he was in hiding, rehearsing the hula for the big talent show. But probably not. Gabriel wasn't big on public displays of, well, anything.

I missed my friends, but I had plenty to do on my own. I took off for the library to spend an hour or two fixing books. I was hoping Nathan would be there to keep me company, but the room was empty. Was he rehearsing for the talent show, too?

I sat at my desk and stared out the window at the gray sky. Snow continued to fall, and even though I was perfectly comfortable inside the house I shivered as I watched it coming down.

A sudden warm presence wrapped itself around my ankles. "Hello, Leroy."

He purred loudly as he searched for the perfect position, finally curling up on top of my shoes. I was pitifully grateful for his company as well as for the radiant heat he was providing to my feet.

I'd come across four more loose-hinged

books to repair, so I unwrapped my travel tool kit and popped open my little bottle of PVC glue. A bamboo skewer coated in PVC was my secret weapon when it came to loose hinges. I slid the thin stick in the gap between the boards and the endpapers, then twirled it until the glue was nicely distributed on both sides, while avoiding the spine.

It was a neat trick, one I enjoyed teaching librarians who were always dealing with books being damaged as they were checked in and out of the library.

Grace didn't have a book press, so I looked around for something else to use. I pushed my chair away from my desk and disturbed Leroy, who let out an aggrieved growl.

"Sorry, kitty," I said. "I know I'm a deep disappointment to you." I bent down to pet him and scratch behind his ears, silently begging his forgiveness. He must have granted me absolution because he purred and rubbed his head against my hand.

I stood and watched him slink off to find another comfy spot for his nap. Then I searched the room and found the perfect substitute for a book press. Each of the end tables next to the corner chairs had a heavy glass top. I could slip the books between the glass and the wood surface of the tables.

I arranged the two thickest books together on one table and set the weighty glass down on top of them. Then I did the same for the thinner books on the other table. Ten minutes later, they were all dried and fully repaired, so I returned them to their places on the bookshelves.

One job was done, so I faced another. The damaged *Pilgrim's Progress* sat on the corner of the center table. I'd been meaning to ask Grace if she would consider allowing the book to be showed at the Covington Library, but as with everything else I'd wanted to do today, there had been too many distractions.

I made a quick list of the other books I wanted to ask Grace about showing to Ian at the Covington. Then, grabbing the *Pilgrim's Progress,* I headed upstairs to find Grace. I would try her room first, and if she wasn't there I would hunt down Merrilee to ask where I could find her.

But she was in her room and answered her bedroom door after one knock. She looked tired and pale.

"Brooklyn," she said, swinging the door wide. "Come on in."

"I don't mean to bother you if you're trying to rest."

"Rest? After the past twenty-four hours

we've had?" Her laugh was devoid of real humor, but she managed a smile for me. "Not likely. Come on in."

Before I could enter, Stephen Fowler appeared from behind the door and blocked my way. The lawyer looked so aggravated, I took a step back.

"Stephen was just leaving. You *are* finished annoying me, aren't you, Stephen?" Grace gave him a pointed look.

"Don't be stupid," he grumbled, then glowered at me. "This house is full of pain-in-the-ass women."

"What is wrong with you?" I blurted.

"Shut up," he muttered, and stormed off down the hall.

I stared at his back, wondering what I had done to bug him this time. But I quickly brushed off the question. The man was pissed off at everyone. He was a born Grinch.

"Don't mind Stephen," Grace said. "He fancies himself a Doberman pinscher, but he's really just an old basset hound."

More like a slithery snake, I thought, but didn't say it out loud. Did she really not see how hateful he was?

"This is a treat," Grace said. "What did you want to see me about?"

Holding up the book, I said, "I wanted to

ask you about this book I found."

"Oh, book talk. What fun. Come sit down and we'll have a chat." She led the way to the sitting area by the curved bay window. "Shelly, do you mind if we sit here while you work?"

"Of course not." Shelly, a pretty, dark-haired young woman in her twenties, was dressed comfortably in jeans, a striped blouse, and tennis shoes. I was glad Grace wasn't the sort of person to insist on French maids' uniforms for her staff. I could picture someone like Madge enforcing that kind of dress code.

Shelly finished stuffing a pillow into a clean pillowcase, then looked at Grace. "Would you rather I come back and do this later?"

Grace turned to me. "Is it something personal or do you mind if Shelly stays and finishes up in here?"

"Oh, please stay," I said to the woman. "I'm just talking about books."

"That should perk her up," Shelly said with a fond smile for her employer. Then she went back to her work.

Grace's smile widened as she sat in the cushioned chair. "My people know me so well."

"That's so nice," I said, and took a seat

on the sofa. "You're surrounded by friends."

"I truly am," she said softly.

"How are you feeling?" I leaned over and touched her hand. "I know you and Bella were old friends."

"Thank you for that. I swear I've aged ten years in two days. I'm not even fifty yet, but . . . well, this isn't about me. It's about poor Bella. It's just horrible, isn't it? I can still see her in her chair, sitting right next to me at the séance. She was so full of life, and suddenly she was . . . lifeless, and . . ." Grace covered her eyes with her hand, then rubbed her forehead wearily. "And I'm so worried about Marko. They were very close. Marko has always been so flaky, but Bella seemed happy whenever she was with him."

"I'm so sorry." I'd already said it before, but couldn't think of anything better to say.

"Me, too." Grace shook her head and composed herself. "But that's enough wallowing for now. Let's talk about why you came to see me."

I stared at the book in my hand, but realized there was something else I was dying to know. "Why did you build bookshelves on the ceiling of my room?"

She laughed heartily. "Oh, aren't they wonderful? I saw something like them in a library on the outskirts of Cairo a few years ago. It was a small building, and in order to use the space wisely they had constructed those panels. They used ropes and pulleys to raise and lower the shelves. When I got home I was itching to design something similar. I think my petals are much prettier, and remote control makes it so easy. I hope you're enjoying them."

"I am. Thank you."

"I'm so glad. I had a friend visiting recently who never even noticed the petals on the ceiling. Can you imagine? I decided after she left that I would only allow that room to be used by someone with natural curiosity and a love of books. I think that describes you to a T."

"I'm honored." We smiled at each other in mutual admiration until I remembered what I was holding. "But that's not why I'm here. It's about this." I handed Grace the book. "Did you know you had this book in your collection?"

She looked at both sides of *Pilgrim's Progress,* then fanned the pages carefully. Thank goodness she was being careful, because I would've hated to rip the book out of her hands.

"I don't really remember. But it's nice, isn't it?" She rubbed at the indentation in the front cover. "Too bad about this dent, though. Do you think you could fix it?"

"Yes, I would love to fix it." I forged ahead with the truth. "Grace, I found this book in the Gold Salon. It was holding up one of the legs of a table. That's how the dent got there."

"Oh, dear." She sighed. "None of my staff is that silly. It must've been one of my nieces."

"Not Suzie," I said, horrified that Grace might think my friend would do it.

"Oh, good heavens, no," Grace said, laughing. "Suzie's not that dim."

I laughed with relief. "I'm glad to hear you say so."

Grace paused, thinking, then said, "It was probably Celeste."

I had to think for a second before recalling that Kiki had an older sister who couldn't make it to Grace's party this week.

"Next time she's here," Grace continued, "I'll tell her to be more careful with my nice things."

"On behalf of your books, I thank you."

She smiled. "You're welcome."

"There's one other thing I wanted to ask."

She sat back in her chair. "What is it?"

"I've told you before what I think of your collection, right? It needs a little organizing, but the books themselves are fabulous."

"That means so much to me, coming from you."

I held out *Pilgrim's Progress* again. "Grace, you might not realize, but this book is very rare and worth a lot of money. It's more than two hundred years old. The printer, Isaiah Thomas, is legendary in the history of bookmaking, too. And except for that stupid dent in the cover, the book is in excellent condition. It should be in a museum or a library collection."

"Well, that's wonderful." But she frowned and added, "Do you really think so?"

"I do, yes. If you were willing to part with it, I'm certain the Covington Library would pay a lot of money to have it. And then everyone who visits there could enjoy it."

As Grace pondered that possibility, I watched Shelly finish straightening up the bedroom area and then open the French doors to the terrace. She grabbed the broom leaning against the bedroom wall and began to sweep the ground, gathering up bits of dirt and grime with a dustbin.

"I'm sorry, Brooklyn," Grace said finally, "but I don't think I could ever sell my books. I love having them around me and I just don't need the money."

I leaned forward, undaunted. "Then you could make it a loan, or you could simply donate them. Your name would be whispered in reverent tones throughout the halls of the Covington Library forever."

She laughed. "I do like the sound of that. Let me think about it."

"I'm only talking about five or six books. Less than ten, anyway."

"I suppose I should be able to part with ten books. Shouldn't I?" She shuddered and rubbed her arms briskly. "It's getting chilly in here."

"The terrace doors are open," I said. "Do you want me to close them?" Without waiting for an answer, I stood and walked over to the doorway.

"Oh, I'll be fine," Grace said mildly. "Let Shelly finish out there. She'll only be another minute."

Shelly squatted down to sweep the last of the dust into the bin. Then she grabbed hold of the railing to pull herself up.

It was like watching a horror show in stop-action photography. The railing wobbled in Shelly's hand. Then one end snapped off the stone wall.

Shelly screeched in shock and fear as the entire railing swung out over the ledge with her hanging on precariously.

Grace screamed even louder.

"Hold on!" I cried. I raced out and lunged

for the railing itself, but it veered too far from the balcony. I had to scramble backward to keep from falling off the ledge myself.

The other end of the railing was still attached to the opposite wall, but the heavy metal hinge was being pulled away from the stone with every second that passed.

"Help me!" Shelly shrieked as she dangled in the air.

"Keep holding on," I shouted. "Grace! Call for help!"

Grace ran screaming into the hall.

I grasped the other end of the railing still attached to the wall. The screws were starting to give way from the extra weight of Shelly and the swinging motion of the rail itself. I wasn't sure I could hold it together.

Seconds later — although it felt like an hour — Gabriel rushed out to the terrace. "Don't let go," he told me.

"Hurry!" I said.

Shelly's screams made it impossible to hear anything, but who could blame her? She was swaying in midair almost three floors above the ground. If she fell, she would break every bone in her body. Or worse.

"Stop crying and listen to me," Gabriel said in a firm voice, and Shelly immediately quieted. As he flattened himself out on the terrace floor and stretched one arm over the edge, he continued to speak in a steady, serious tone. "Hold tight to the rail with both hands. I'm going to lift you up and onto the balcony and you'll be safe. Ready?"

"Yes," she said, gasping, her eyes wide with panic.

"Here we go."

He turned and looked at me. "Babe, do me a favor and hold on to my feet. Will you? I'd rather not go sailing off here, too."

"Okay." I knelt by his feet and grabbed his boots for dear life. "I've got you."

"That's my girl. Almost there," he said, cool and composed, calming Shelly down as he pulled the railing up. Spread out as he was, he had no leverage to work with, only his own upper-body strength.

A few more seconds of lifting and she was close enough for Gabriel to grab hold of her wrists. As he let go of the railing, Shelly squealed, but she was safer now than she'd been a minute ago. The railing tumbled down and clattered against the rocky ground below.

"Oh, my God," Grace moaned from the safety of the doorway. "Shelly dear, hold on."

"I've got her," Gabriel shouted. "You're

okay, Shelly. Wrap your hands around my wrists."

She did so, and he planted his elbows firmly on the stone terrace and used them as leverage to lift Shelly higher. The muscles of his lower arms shook with the strain, but he managed to get her close enough for her to latch onto the ledge.

"Let go of me, Brooklyn," he said.

I slowly, reluctantly released my grip on his boots, then watched him maneuver himself up onto his knees and pull Shelly all the way onto the floor of the terrace.

Spread-eagled on her stomach, Shelly began to weep and moan. Gabriel rubbed her back. Still on his knees, he reached down and managed to lift the young woman into his arms, then stand.

The man had some awesome calf and thigh muscles. I'm just saying.

"Get her inside," Grace said, stepping away from the open door so he could maneuver his way through with Shelly.

Gabriel carried her over to Grace's couch, where he laid her down. She curled into a ball and sobbed quietly.

"You saved her life," Grace said, and threw her arms around Gabriel. "That was heroic. She'd be dead if you hadn't been here and done what you did. I can't ever thank you."

"No thanks are necessary," he said, hugging her back. "I'm glad she's safe."

"I am, too," I said, staring at Shelly on the couch. "I hope she'll be okay."

Grace pulled a blanket off the back of the couch and laid it over Shelly. Grabbing some tissues, Grace then knelt on the floor and brushed Shelly's hair away from her face. "You're going to be fine, Shelly. I've called Ray and he's on his way back from town. He'll be here any minute."

"Who's Ray?" I asked.

Grace glanced up. "Shelly's husband. He's our handyman and takes care of everything around here."

Gabriel looked at me. "Do you know what happened?"

"Yeah." We stood on either side of the open doorway and stared at the dangerous spot where the railing had been only moments before. I told him exactly what I'd seen.

Gabriel ventured outside to examine the metal plate that had connected the wood railing to the wall. I inched closer and could see the marks and scrapings from some tool that might have been used to either weaken the screws or pry the plate loose.

"I'll go downstairs and find what's left of

the railing," he said grimly. "I'm willing to bet someone deliberately loosened the screws."

Grace came and stood in the doorway with her arms wrapped around her body for warmth. "I should've replaced that railing last summer."

I didn't think she'd heard us talking. "Was it coming loose?"

"No." Grace frowned and shook her head, looking more confused and older than I'd ever seen her before. "It seemed strong enough a few days ago. But I guess it wasn't. I feel just awful. She could've died. What in the world is happening around here?"

Gabriel gazed out at the view. "Do you go out on the balcony often, Grace?"

"Oh yes," she said. "I love it. I usually have a chaise longue out there, but it's been put away for the winter. But I can stay out there for hours, just staring at the lake and the mountains and the stars. Even on the coldest days of winter, it's beautiful."

"Then you'll want to get this fixed as soon as possible." Gabriel ushered us both inside and closed and locked the doors. Then he glanced at me. "Maybe you should stick around here while I go downstairs and check things out."

"Good idea. Let me know what you find."

"Oh, you must have better things to do," Grace said, squeezing my arm affectionately. "I'll be fine. I'm just going to read and watch over Shelly until she's feeling better."

But I wasn't so sure Grace would be fine. I was pretty sure someone wanted her dead.

CHAPTER 8

The good news was, Shelly felt a lot better and begged Grace to continue with her plans for the talent show.

The bad news was, Shelly felt a lot better and begged Grace to continue with her plans for the talent show.

It was bad news because I still didn't have any talent. But I was happy Shelly was feeling better after the horrible ordeal she'd been through.

We had all decided not to say anything to the other guests about Shelly and the railing incident. It would upset them and it would alert Grace's would-be killer that his or her scheme had been thwarted again.

Shelly's husband, Ray, had shown up finally, worried sick about her. Shelley had assured him that she was fine, but Ray insisted on carrying her back to their small suite of rooms on the third floor. Shelly flung her arms around his neck as they left

Grace's bedroom.

It was a sweet sight and, like I said, I was happy for her. But seeing the two of them together had brought the Derek issue back to the forefront. He wasn't here with me and, worse, he hadn't called. I could've gone a few more hours without being reminded of that hurtful little detail.

So maybe drowning my sorrows in the talent show was the best thing I could do right now. If only I had some talent.

It was getting late and I needed help. I went looking for Suzie and Vinnie and finally found Suzie in a corner of the game room, standing before a vintage pinball machine called Theatre of Magic. The game field featured an exotic-looking fortune-teller with a crystal ball, a Bengal tiger stalking the red-curtained stage, and lots of white rabbits that had escaped from a magical top hat.

"How's it going?" I asked.

"I'm winning," she said, and shoved her hip against the machine to force the silver ball to hit another rabbit. That won her another three thousand points. Must've been some rabbit.

While she played, I took a stroll around the game room for the first time and finally got a look at the dreaded mouse cage. It was bigger than I'd expected and hung from the ceiling, ready to fall and trap its next victim. Vinnie had not been exaggerating. The gold mesh cage was attached to a thick wire and was suspended above an empty corner of the room. It was maybe five feet across and tall enough for a six-foot man to stand inside it if it were on the ground.

The clinging and clanging of the pinball machine died down as the game ended. Suzie turned and noticed what I was staring at. "Yup, that's the offending cage. Don't let Vinnie catch you looking at it."

"Impressive," I said, staring up at the strange prop. "Does it really fall down and trap people?"

"Yeah. But it's never hurt anyone," she added in defense of her aunt.

I walked closer. "There must be some kind of electronic signal that activates it."

"I think so. Brooklyn, don't get too close."

"I'm okay." I got as close as I could without standing directly under the cage. Then I looked up. "There's got to be a path of light that triggers the cage to fall when it's interrupted."

"Like an automatic toilet?"

I gave her a wry look. "Something like that, although I was thinking more along the lines of an automatic soap dispenser."

She splayed her hands out. "But I'm a lot classier than you are."

I smiled. "True. And since you're so classy, I could really use your help."

"What? Is something wrong?"

"No, no. Well, sort of." Feeling a tiny bit embarrassed now, I fiddled with the knobs on the pinball game. "I've been searching my brain, trying to come up with something to do for the talent show. But I've got nothing."

She scrunched her face up, trying to think. "You could give bookbinding lessons."

I stopped and stared at her. "Really?"

She snorted with laughter.

"So I guess that's a no."

Rolling her eyes, she said, "Uh, yeah, Brooklyn, that would be a no."

"Fine." I thought for a minute. "I know. I can regale the crowd with my duct-tape horror stories."

She stared at me blankly.

I frowned. "So that's also a big fat no?"

"Good guess," she said.

"You're not helping."

"Sorry." She gave the pinball machine one more bump for good measure, then crossed the room. "Maybe we could do something together."

"Really?"

"Sure. I was going to pass on the whole thing, but we could figure something out."

I remembered my original idea from earlier that day. "Let's go to the music room. I want to see if Grace has any bongo drums."

"You play bongos?" Suzie said, as we walked out of the game room and down the hall to the music room.

"Well, sure," I said, staring at the huge metal cutouts of musical notes that decorated the walls. "Anyone can play bongos."

"Hey, I have a great idea." Suzie picked up a shiny silver flute from the bandstand in the center of the room. "You play bongos and I'll accompany you on the flute."

I blinked. "You play the flute?"

"Well, yeah," she said, frowning at me. "Anyone can play the flute."

"Shut up." But I was laughing now, too. Suzie's answer did not bode well for Grace's talent show that night, but maybe by performing together, the two of us would be able to provide some laughs. Laughs would be nice after everything that had happened around here in the past twenty-four hours.

I came across three old sets of bongos and tested them all briefly. I picked out the prettiest-looking one since they all sounded the same. And I sounded like a fool trying to imitate the beatniks I'd seen in those beach-blanket movies, but that was okay. I would just channel my dad, who easily could have been one of the original beat poets in a former life.

We ran downstairs to my bedroom to rehearse, but spent most of the time laughing so hard, our stomachs ached. After almost an hour of silliness, we had our act finalized. Suzie left to find Vinnie and get ready for the evening ahead.

I had more than an hour and a half to get ready, so I took a moment to jog down the hall to the library, just to check on things. Nathan's desk was closed and locked, so I assumed he was done for the day. I picked up a few of the books that were scattered on the reading table and began to shelve them.

"Oh, good. I was hoping I'd find you here."

I turned and saw Kiki standing in the doorway.

"Hi, Kiki. Come on in. Were you interested in finding a particular book?"

"No, just looking." She wandered around the room, studying the knickknacks and reading book covers, so I continued putting the books away. I had to stand on tiptoe to reach one of the higher shelves that Nathan had designated for nonfiction, and shoved a tattered copy of Benjamin Franklin's autobiography in its place between Michael J. Fox's latest memoir and Mahatma Gandhi's life story.

I heard Kiki suck in a big gulp of air before finally speaking. "I've been meaning to ask you something."

I stopped working and rested my hip against the table. "Okay. Go ahead."

"How do you know Gabriel?" She shook her head in frustration and started over. "What I mean is, what do you know about him? I mean, he's not your boyfriend, is he? Is he nice? He seems really nice. But sort of mysterious. Oh, God." She buried her face in her hands.

I swallowed a chuckle. So Kiki had a little crush on Gabriel. How fun for me. "He's not my boyfriend, Kiki."

She looked up right away. "He's not? Oh, thank God." She cringed. "I just mean . . ."

"It's okay, Kiki," I said. "Gabriel's a great guy."

"No. He's beyond great. He's awesome. He's so handsome. He's . . . I'm . . ."

I glanced at her sideways, afraid she might hyperventilate. "You like him."

She gaped at me as though I were some kind of a genius for figuring that out. "Oh, my God. I do. You can tell?"

Now I laughed. "Yes, I can tell."

She stopped in the middle of the room and let her head drop to her chest. "I feel like such a dolt."

"You're not." To distract her a little, I handed her a book and pointed at the wall. "Can you put that book back? It belongs on the third shelf up, right in the middle."

She took the book. Once it was shelved, she returned to the reading table. Her expression was deadly serious. "The thing is, Brooklyn, I'm pretty sure he doesn't know I'm alive. I've tried to talk to him, but he's always too busy and, well, I lose my courage. I was wondering . . . could you put in a good word for me?"

I gazed at her for a moment, but she took my silence the wrong way.

"You're right," she cried, throwing her hands up in the air. "I'm being an idiot. Never mind."

"No," I said quickly. "Just give me a minute to think."

She scowled at herself. "Okay."

I'd been enjoying her gushing, but now I was forced to take a mental step back and consider her request on its merit. Not that it was my decision to make, but I had to wonder if Kiki was the kind of woman that

Gabriel would ever be interested in. She was adorable and seemed very sweet and honest; hardly the sophisticated type of woman I pictured Gabriel dating. Of course, that might be a good thing. A while back, I'd come into contact with a woman who had been involved with Gabriel in the past. I was certain that he'd never loved her although they had lived together for a time. She was a tough cookie, as my mom would say. A little too tough, as far as I was concerned. Not a kind person at all, as it turned out. Because of her, I had since assumed that Gabriel preferred a more worldly type of woman.

Maybe Kiki would be a refreshing change for him. The thought made me smile. But then I took another minute to consider the man in question. Was there a woman in the world extraordinary enough to be capable of capturing his heart? I couldn't picture it.

Kiki was adorable, but she was an open book, so to speak. She had simple wants and needs and she carried her emotions on her sleeve for all the world to see.

Gabriel was dangerous, mysterious, elusive. Unattainable. I suppose every woman who'd ever met him fell in love with him, at least a little. Personally, I thought he was the second most compelling man I'd ever known — the first being Derek Stone, of course.

Since the two men were good friends, I'd had occasion to compare and contrast them. They were both tall, dark, handsome, protective, and hazardous to a woman's heart. But it seemed that Derek was happy to plant both his feet in my world and stay there. Who would have guessed? Certainly not me. But it had made me the happiest woman on the planet. Now, if he would just call, damn it . . . but never mind.

Gabriel, on the other hand, might never settle down. And why should he? He was the classic bad boy. No matter their age or demographic, women everywhere found him wildly attractive. And he loved them right back, in every shape and style.

For as long as he was in town, anyway.

Bottom line: he would break Kiki's heart. Could I do that to her? Was it my decision to make?

I whirled around — and knocked my head against Kiki's. She skittered backward.

"Sorry. Sorry!" she said, rubbing her forehead. "I was following you. I guess I'm a little anxious."

I blinked a few times and massaged my temple. "I guess so."

She reached out and touched my arm.

"I'm sorry I bothered you with this stupid request. I've never felt like such a fool. And over a man! It's so mortifying. Just forget I said anything."

"It wasn't stupid at all," I said, making my mind up in that moment. "I would be happy to put in a good word for you."

Her eyes widened and I thought she might be trembling. "Okay," she whispered, nodding as she stumbled toward the door. "Okay. Thanks."

"Kiki, wait," I said. "It doesn't mean anything. He's not the kind of man who will —"

She held up her hand. "I'm not looking for a wedding ring, Brooklyn."

Really? I thought. But I could only take her at her word. "Okay, then. I'll give him a heads-up."

"You rock." She grinned and walked out.

Nathan stood in the doorway and watched her leave, then looked at me. "What was that all about?"

"Oh, just a little favor between us girls."

"Then I'll just forget I asked."

"Probably wise."

I left him shaking his head and strolled back to my room. *Now what?* I wondered. It took me back to middle school, telling the boy that my girlfriend liked him. But I guess, emotionally speaking, some of us had never left middle school. Anyway, it wouldn't hurt to say something. And yet I worried. If I told Gabriel that Kiki was interested in talking to him, was I doing him a favor? She seemed so vulnerable. Would she faint if he smiled at her?

I put the problem aside for the moment while I showered and dressed for the evening's festivities. I chose black for the stage: black pants, black satin blouse, and pretty new black flats. To soften the look, I wound my hair into some kind of updo with loose strands falling and curling around my neck. It was an old-fashioned Edwardian style I'd seen in a magazine and I was only slightly shocked that I'd managed to pull it off.

Dangly crystal and silver earrings finished the look. I just hoped the things wouldn't fly off into the crowd when I got my wild and crazy bongo groove on.

While adding an extra touch of makeup — I was about to perform in a show, after all — I stopped to wonder if Gabriel had found the remnants of the railing from Grace's balcony. Had he discovered anything incriminating when he examined the loose screws? In all the excitement of rehearsals with Suzie, I had forgotten to track him down. I made a mental note to corner him during the cocktail hour to find out what he'd seen.

As I was about to leave my room and join the others for drinks and dinner, there was a knock on my bedroom door. Speak of the devil.

"Brooklyn," Gabriel said when I opened the door, "this is Ray, Shelly's husband and Grace's resident handyman."

"I know," I said, gazing curiously at the tall, sandy-haired man standing behind Gabriel.

The handyman, still dressed in jeans, a denim shirt with rolled-up sleeves, and a baseball cap, gave me a casual salute. "Hey."

"How's Shelly doing?"

"She's a lot better. Course, she won't shut up about this guy here." He grinned as he pointed his thumb at Gabriel. "So I've gotta put up with that. But I'd say it was worth it."

"That's good. Come in." I swung the door open wider to let them both into my room. "What's going on?"

Gabriel stopped and looked around. "Wow, babe. Have a few books, why don't you? This place was made for you."

"Glad you think so," I said. "Do you want to sit down?"

"Nope, just wanted to give you an update without any of the big ears listening in."

I smiled at Ray. I guess he didn't qualify as one of the big ears.

Gabriel caught my look and gave me a quick nod of assurance. "Yeah, Ray's cool. He tells me that Grace's balcony railing was in fine condition. He checks them all every month."

"That's right," Ray said, scratching his chin. "Grace is kind of a fanatic about sitting outside on her terrace, even when it's cold. So Shelly gets on my ass to keep everything out there in good condition. But I would've done it, anyway. That's my job."

"Did you see the damaged railing?" I asked.

"Yeah." He scowled. "The screws have been stripped. I don't get it. I just checked that railing maybe two weeks ago when I weatherized all the wood around the house. I always treat the railings and the eaves and the siding before the snows hit. I do that every fall."

"That's really smart," I said. "No wonder everything looks so nice."

"Yeah, until today," he muttered. "Damn it, Shelly could've died out there." Frustrated, he swiped his forehead with the back of his hand. "Anyway, I wanted to thank you both for saving her life."

"No problem, man." Gabriel slapped him gently on the back. "I was just glad I got there in time."

"You and me both." Ray nodded at me. "Well, you all should probably get going to dinner."

"Probably so," I said to Gabriel, then looked at Ray. "We're having a talent show tonight. Are you going?"

He stopped short of grimacing. "Shelly wouldn't miss it, so I guess I'll be there."

I laughed. "Sorry about that. But we'll try to give you some laughs."

"I can only hope." He walked to the door, then stopped. "I'll get that railing fixed tomorrow and it'll be good as new. And I plan on keeping a closer eye on things around here, too. Seems like someone might be up to no good."

"I know Grace would appreciate it," Gabriel said. "And we do, too."

"Yes. Thanks, Ray." Then something occurred to me. "Do you do a lot of work in the conservatory?"

"Nope. I'm not much of a plant man. I'm happy to dig holes and carry trees here and there, but as far as watering and pruning and such, that's not my thing. You might want to talk to Ruth. She's a whiz at all that."

I forced a smile. "Thanks. I will."

The door closed behind him and I turned to Gabriel. "Ruth again. She was the one who handed Grace the poisoned drink, and now she's a whiz with plants?"

He frowned. "We never did check out the conservatory."

"No. I guess we were a little too distracted this morning."

"Cops showing up at dawn tend to do that." Gabriel headed for the door. "Let's make sure we do it first thing tomorrow."

I grabbed my sweater, just in case it got chilly later. As we left my room, I looked up at Gabriel. "Are you ready for this talent show?"

"If you're wondering if I'm performing the hula or something, don't hold your breath."

I chuckled. "How did you know I was hoping for a hula?"

He grunted. "You got an act worked out?"

"You'll have to wait and see."

"I'm intrigued."

I put my hand on him arm. "Don't be. I beg of you."

We walked together in comfortable silence up the grand stairway and into the Gold

Salon. I was still stumped by Ruth's role in Bella's death. I was willing to give Grace the benefit of the doubt when she'd claimed that Ruth was blameless, but the question remained: Where had the woman obtained that poisoned glass? Had someone given it to her or had she picked it up at random off the bar?

I'd told my story to the police so I assumed they had questioned Ruth about it. Since she was still here and not behind bars in the county jail, I figured her answers must have satisfied them. Or maybe they were just biding their time. Did they want to sift through more evidence before making any arrests?

Maybe Ruth had completely denied handing Grace the glass. Maybe she'd told them a different story. Maybe the detectives had decided I was wrong or lying.

Maybe I should just ask the woman myself instead of driving myself crazy.

"Babe, you're mumbling to yourself," Gabriel whispered as we made our way to the bar.

"Am I?"

"Everything okay?"

"Yeah. Sorry." I frowned. "Just going over some things in my head."

"Memorizing lines for the big show?" he

said, smirking at me.

"Yeah, right," I said weakly.

"How about some champagne?" he said.

"Definitely," I said with a firm nod. Well, that was embarrassing. There was nothing wrong with talking to the voices in my head — unless everyone else was listening in. I sighed. It was just as well that Gabriel had interrupted me. My brain was starting to spin out of control with all the possibilities. I had to put the brakes on, so I changed the subject.

"Have you talked to Kiki since you've been here?"

"Grace's niece? No. Why?"

"She's pretty, isn't she?"

"Beautiful," he said carefully. "Why do you mention it?"

With a steady look, I said, "She would like you to talk to her."

He straightened up and his jaw moved back and forth as he took in my request. I guess I'd managed to surprise him. "What's this all about?"

"I'm merely passing on a message."

"Let me get this straight." He enunciated each word. "She asked you to ask me to talk to her."

"Not exactly," I hedged. "She just mentioned how much she admired you. A lot. I mean, really a lot. And she wished she could have a chance to spend time with you. Frankly, I'm not sure she'll survive if you actually speak to her."

"I've heard enough."

"Wait," I said. "I'm sorry. She's a nice girl and I like her. I don't mean to sound like I'm belittling her feelings."

He stared at me for another few seconds. "Thank you. I'll take care of it."

"But will you —"

"Brooklyn."

I smiled. "Got it."

"Good."

"Just . . . don't hurt her."

His eyes narrowed again. "I don't hurt women."

"You have no idea," I said, shaking my head.

The talent show was a huge success.

Peter Brinker began the show by performing magic tricks. I loved magic tricks! I was the perfect audience for magicians, because I was easily distracted. I knew that was how most magic tricks were pulled off, but I was always willing to play along. And Peter was actually pretty good at it. My hands hurt from all the applauding and Peter seemed to appreciate my standing ovation. It was never easy being the first to perform.

I thought Suzie and my flute and bongos act was stellar. Suzie's spontaneous tap-dance solo brought new meaning to the phrase *Get the hook!* I couldn't stop laughing and it seemed to be catching, because the crowd was cackling and hooting by the time we got to the big finish. Whether that was good or bad, I couldn't say. The happy news was, nobody booed us off the stage.

Ruth was next. We all straightened in our chairs and prepared for a decorous poetry reading. But who could've predicted that genteel Ruth's preferred style of poetry for the evening was limericks?

"There once was a gal from Nantucket," she began.

"Whoa," a man muttered from the row behind me. I turned and saw Gabriel wearing a sardonic grin.

Grace stood up immediately. "Now, Ruth."

"Let her finish," Marko said. He was chuckling for the first time since Bella's death.

The rest of the audience took up the chant. "Let her finish. Let her finish."

"I've got a bad feeling about this," Grace said, but she was smiling as she sat down and waved at Ruth to keep going.

Ruth didn't disappoint. The poem was as bawdy as everyone had expected, and as she took her final bow there were hoots and hollers and calls of "Encore."

"Maybe later," she said, patting her gray hair demurely, and sat down.

Heck, if I'd known I could've simply recited a bawdy limerick, I wouldn't have worried myself sick all day.

Grace stood and walked to the front of the room, carrying her heavy manuscript. She opened to the first page, coughed to clear her throat, and began to read. "I was a thin, lonely child. My father's business forced us to move every other year, and by the age of six the card game solitaire was my best friend."

I ignored the dangling modifier and smiled at Grace's portrayal of her central character. I had already read this part of the manuscript and was looking forward to reading more.

"Poor Grace," Suzie whispered. "So lonely."

That produced a scowl from Vinnie. "By the age of six I had eight noisy brothers and sisters. I yearned to be lonely."

"Shhh," I said, trying not to laugh. "She's reading about a fictional character."

"That's right," Suzie whispered. "Grace

grew up with siblings."

"A good thing, or you wouldn't be here," Vinnie muttered.

Grace read for another minute, then stopped and looked up. There was a beat of silence; then we all clapped and cheered loudly.

"Wonderful," I cried.

"More, more!" Suzie shouted.

I wasn't surprised to catch Madge rolling her eyes. She really seemed to hate her husband's sister. I didn't know why but I was starting to wonder how much and how deeply that hate was rooted. Deep enough to kill her? But why? Did her husband stand to gain such a great deal of money if Grace died?

Maybe Madge had been caught in the mouse cage like Vinnie. Maybe it had irritated her so much that she had come unhinged and was now ready to strike back at Grace.

That picture entertained me enough to get me through the next act, a painful rendition of the Up with People theme song sung by Sybil Brinker. What made it so awful wasn't just the fact that Sybil could barely carry a tune in a bucket. It was the song itself, a perky ditty that celebrated the idea that people were essentially good and that we were meant to get along with each other and be happy.

If Sybil Brinker believed one word of those cheery, upbeat lyrics, I would eat my wool scarf.

Halfway through Sybil's performance, I noticed that Vinnie was gone. I looked around but didn't see her in the room. Maybe she had slipped away to practice her dance steps.

The next to perform was Kiki. She jogged up to the front of the room, then did a cartwheel before beginning her performance, which was basically a yoga routine. She stood on one leg to start the Sun Salutation, then moved fluidly through each pose.

Two minutes later, she had mangled and twisted her body through five more impossible positions. By the time she reached Downward-Facing Dog, my neck hurt just watching her. Her nimble performance amazed me. I wondered fleetingly what Gabriel thought of it.

She ended the show by moving into Corpse Pose. I shivered as I watched her lying on the floor, not moving.

After a full minute, the audience grew restless. Kiki seemed to sense it because she finally jumped up and bowed deeply, mur-

muring, "Namaste. Namaste."

"Stirring performance," Grace murmured.

Suzie's snort was covered by our thunderous clapping. I applauded Kiki for having the guts to do that in front of all these virtual strangers.

And then it was time for Vinnie's performance. Suzie got up and started the CD player and an exotic drumbeat began to throb rhythmically. Then a penetrating, high-pitched female voice joined in, singing and repeating something that sounded like "Nananananananana." A male voice shouted "Hoy! Hoy! Hoy!" The plinking sound of a stringed instrument was added to the riveting drumbeat and a full chorus of voices joined and began a spellbinding musical number.

Suddenly, Vinnie jumped to the front of the room and began gyrating playfully to the music. It was meant to be sexy and flirty and fun, but it was more than that. It was riveting. Vinnie was a fantastic dancer.

She had changed her clothes and now wore a lavender chiffon sari with long matching scarves that floated up and down as she moved in time with the quirky music. She wore delicate sandals that seemed to curl with the shape of her small feet as she moved nimbly around the stage. She was mesmerizing.

Her fingers never stopped waving and snapping and convulsing as they performed their own fascinating dance. Her shoulders undulated and her feet moon-walked gracefully in a circle. Then she threw in a few disco steps and some King of Pop moves that brought her audience to its feet.

By the time the music ended, everyone in the room was waving their arms in the air and swaying and dancing with Vinnie. It was the perfect fairy tale via Bollywood ending to the talent show.

Vinnie took her bows to thunderous cheers and a true standing ovation.

"Thank you very much," she said. Suzie moved to her through the crowd and gave her a big kiss.

"Wasn't she great?" I said to Gabriel, who had been sitting behind me during the show.

"Blew me away," he said with a grin.

"Yeah. Me, too." I turned to look at him. "You didn't perform."

"No."

"I'm sure you're good at something. The hula, maybe?"

His mouth twisted wryly. "Not in this lifetime."

"Such a disappointment."

Then he leaned forward and whispered in

my ear, "What's going on over there?"

Frowning, I glanced up at him. Following the direction of his gaze, I found Sybil standing in front of a closet door I hadn't noticed before. I watched Sybil glance around as if to check that she wasn't being followed, then open the door just wide enough to skulk through and close it behind her. "Did she just walk into a closet? She's a strange woman."

"Grace went through the same door less than thirty seconds ago," Gabriel murmured.

I scanned the room again and did a quick count. Every one of our party was still in the room except Grace. And now Sybil. But the talent show was over and people would soon begin to wander off to the bar or the game room.

"This house has so many back hallways and odd passages. Sybil probably just found a shortcut back to her room. Maybe she was embarrassed. I would be. I would want to disappear if I'd been the one singing that stupid song."

Gabriel gazed at me. "Maybe."

"But you don't think so."

"She never ventures far from her husband. If she were going to her room, he would go with her."

It was interesting that Gabriel had noticed that. Also interesting was the fact that Peter was deep in conversation with Marko and didn't seem at all fazed by the absence of his wife. So maybe that meant he knew where she was. Maybe she was looking for a bathroom. Or maybe when we weren't looking, Sybil had whispered to Peter that she had a headache and was going off to bed.

But since it was Gabriel who had brought it up, I began to worry that something might very well be wrong. Gabriel tended to notice things that I wouldn't have given a second thought to. And once again Vinnie's words from the tarot card reading the other night hit me with a dull thud.

"We must keep an eye on Sybil over the next few days. Anything could happen to her, and I don't mean that in a good way."

But if Sybil was following Grace, why would anything be wrong?

Suddenly I wondered if the cards had meant that Sybil should be watched not because harm might come to her, but because she meant to do harm to Grace.

Could Sybil be trying to kill Grace?

Because of Bella's death the day before and Shelly's near-fatal fall off the balcony earlier, Gabriel's and my suspicion levels were off the chart. Still, it seemed so silly to worry just because both Grace and Sybil had used the same closet door to escape the rest of the guests.

"You're right," I said as I stood. "It might be nothing, but I'm going to worry until I see her again." I gave Gabriel a brief recap of what Vinnie had said after Sybil received the Tower card.

"Not that it means anything," I added. "Nobody believes in that tarot stuff, right?"

"If you say so."

"I do." I nodded absently. "So it's probably nothing. She's probably gone to bed."

"Yeah. So what's this?" Gabriel said, as he nudged his chin in the direction of the closet door.

I turned in time to see Madge sneaking through the same door that Grace and Sybil had taken moments ago. What was she up to?

"Now, that spells trouble," I muttered.

Gabriel took hold of my arm. "Are you staying here or coming with me?"

"I'm coming with you."

We tried to be casual as we slipped through what I had thought was a closet door. Instead we found a narrow hall that led from the Gold Salon, where the talent show had been held, to the game room. There we found Madge trapped under the mouse cage, shrieking.

So where was Sybil?

"Damn it," Madge yelled. "Get me the hell out of this freaking thing."

She continued shouting expletives and I wasn't sure what was scarier: seeing Madge trapped by that human-sized mouse cage or hearing her bellow and curse so much.

"Hold on," Gabriel said, and we both stared at the trap and its interior electronic mechanism, trying to figure out how to raise the cage.

"I won't hold on," she groused.

"You don't have much choice," I said. "We have to figure out how to raise the cage first."

"I'm sick to death of this freak house."

"You should be counting your lucky stars that we found you."

"Why'd you come looking for me?" she said, instantly guarded. "I didn't do anything."

I rolled my eyes. "We weren't looking for you." *We were looking for Sybil,* I reminded myself. Where had she disappeared to? As Madge continued to bitch and moan, I thought of my mother's favorite saying: no good deed goes unpunished.

"I have never been so disgusted or humiliated in my life." Her voice rose as she got going on a rant. "What kind of deviant moron devises cages for people to get trapped under? What is wrong with that stupid woman?"

I really didn't like Madge Crawford and that statement pushed me over the edge.

"That 'stupid' woman is a genius," I said. "She's made it possible for your husband to keep you in designer clothes and diamonds for the last twenty years, so I'd stuff a sock in it if I were you."

"How dare you speak to me that way?"

I laughed harshly. "I dare because you're a pain in the butt who whines and bitches about every little thing in the world and never shuts up. I'm surprised you were even invited to stay here at all."

"Babe," Gabriel said under his breath.

I glowered at him, but stopped talking. Guess I'd gotten carried away with my own rant.

Madge's nostrils flared as she hissed in a breath. She was furious, obviously, and astounded that anyone, especially a nobody like me, would dare speak to her like that.

I was surprised no one had done it before now.

Grace ran into the room. "Madge! Oh, dear. I'm so sorry you got caught. What were you doing in here?"

"None of your damn business. Just shut up and get me out of here before I press charges and have you all arrested for false imprisonment and mental anguish and assault and battery and —"

"Oh, shut up yourself," I said.

"Oh, dear," Grace murmured.

Gabriel searched the trompe l'oeil wall painting of a hillside in Burgundy and found a small electronic button disguised as part of a bunch of grapes growing in the sun. He pushed it and the cage rose smoothly, freeing the snarling, foulmouthed woman. She walked straight over to me and raised her hand to slap me across the face.

But I was ready for her. I had gone more than a few rounds with the notorious Minka LaBoeuf, world's worst bookbinder, and I knew a move or two myself. I grabbed Madge's arm and shoved her back, out of slapping distance.

She took another step toward me.

"Don't even think about it," I said, jabbing my finger at her.

Her face turned red and she gritted her teeth as she got madder and madder. But what could she do?

"I hate it here," she said loudly. "I hate all of you people."

"Right back atcha."

She stomped her foot, then stormed out of the room.

For several long seconds, the silence was deafening. Finally, I let go of the breath I'd been holding. "I'm sorry, Grace, but that woman is a mean, spiteful bully."

"No, I'm the one who's sorry, Brooklyn," Grace said. "She really is horrible. But Harrison is my brother and he's always been wonderful to me. I put up with her for his sake."

The question on my mind was, Why did Harrison put up with her?

Gabriel wrapped an arm around Grace's shoulder. "Harrison is lucky to have you for a sister."

She hugged him back and rested her head on his chest. "It's probably wrong of me to say it, but I'm glad the police won't let anyone leave. At this rate I would be all alone by the time my birthday came around."

"That would never happen," I said.

"Oh, that's sweet. I'm so pleased that I've gotten to know you, Brooklyn," she said, pulling me close to her other side. "Suzie's lucky to have you as a friend."

"I'm the lucky one," I insisted. Then, arm in arm, Gabriel and I walked Grace out to the wide main hall and headed back to the party.

I suddenly remembered we hadn't found Sybil. I opened my mouth to say something but was interrupted as a woman's scream shattered the air.

We all ran toward the sound that came from somewhere near the grand stairway. My throat went dry when I spotted Kiki lying motionless on the marble floor at the bottom of the stairs.

CHAPTER 9

Gabriel swore loudly and tore off down the stairs. I hurried to follow him, but had to be mindful of the slippery soles of my new shoes.

"Is she okay?" I asked when I reached the bottom.

"She's still breathing," he murmured, and slipped his hand beneath her neck. He gently lifted her head off the cold, hard marble floor to cushion her with his hands.

"Is she awake?"

"Not yet, but there's no blood."

"Thank God for that," I muttered.

"No, no," Grace moaned from a few feet above me on the stairs. "My little Kiki."

"She'll be okay," Gabriel said briefly, although he didn't sound all that confident yet. He ran his hands carefully along her shoulders and down her back, checking for broken bones, I assumed.

I heard the distant sound of tapping heels

on the marble hallway floor and looked up. It was Sybil, and she was running toward us.

"What is that?" she cried from twenty feet away, then gasped as she saw Kiki's inert body on the cold floor. "Oh, my God! What is happening to us?"

Gabriel looked up at her with annoyance shimmering in his eyes. "Quiet." Then he ignored her and tended to Kiki.

"Where were you?" I said to Sybil, then grimaced at my suspicious tone. This wasn't the time for an inquisition.

Sybil blinked at me. "I was using the powder room downstairs. I — I needed a few minutes to myself. To recover from that humiliating performance."

"It wasn't so bad," I mumbled. "All in good fun."

"It was horrific," she said flatly.

True, I thought to myself. I still didn't know if Sybil was telling the truth about sneaking off to the powder room downstairs, but I would wait to make sure Kiki was okay before jumping into a full-scale investigation of Sybil Brinker's whereabouts over the past few minutes.

More footsteps pattered down the stairs. I glanced up and saw Suzie and Vinnie, both wearing identical looks of horror.

"Kiki," Suzie said, her voice trembling as she wrapped her arm around Grace. "Is she . . . ?"

"Gabriel says she'll be okay," Grace whispered.

"Praise Lakshmi," Vinnie murmured, then began to chant softly in her native tongue.

I knelt down next to Gabriel. "Can I help?"

"I want to get her off the cold floor. Is there a room with a couch nearby?"

"The Blue Room," Grace said immediately, pointing down the hall. "First door on the right."

Gabriel laid Kiki down on the blue sofa, then knelt on the floor next to her, watching her slightest movements. I knew he was master of a hundred different obscure skills and had played at dozens of different roles throughout his colorful life. I just hoped that one of them was emergency medical technician, because I doubted even an ambulance would make it out here tonight.

Merrilee rushed in with blankets, a pitcher of water, and some hand towels. She spread a warm blanket over Kiki as Gabriel dipped and wrung out one of the towels and laid it on the unconscious woman's forehead. He slid another warm, damp towel behind her neck, then leaned back on his heels and waited and watched.

Ruth had joined Grace and the two women sat together on the nearby love seat, gripping each other's hands. Vinnie and Suzie paced the floor. I chose to sit on the sturdy coffee table close behind Gabriel, in case he needed anything. But essentially, we were all just waiting for Kiki to gain consciousness.

A few minutes had passed when I heard Kiki emit a soft moan. I felt Gabriel tense up as I watched her stir. He leaned close and brushed her hair back from her face.

"What happened?" she whispered, her voice groggy.

"You don't remember?" Gabriel asked.

"Somebody pushed me, hard. I fell."

Gabriel cast a quick look at me over his shoulder before turning back to Kiki. "Did you see who did it?"

Her eyes fluttered open. "No."

An hour later, Gabriel and I, with help from Grace and Suzie, had tucked Kiki into her bed. She was conscious and in pain, but essentially on her way to recovering completely.

Earlier, as Suzie had helped Kiki into her nightgown, I had attempted to ask her a question or two, trying to jog her memory. "Do you remember smelling anything unusual or hearing anything in the seconds before you were pushed?"

She tried to think, but her head hurt too much. I told her we could deal with it all in the morning. She assured us that she would try, because she was stumped as to who would want to hurt her so badly.

Wednesday morning I woke up early and dressed casually. Gabriel and I had planned to check out the conservatory this morning in hopes of finding some clue to Bella's poisoning. I wasn't sure he'd be up for exploring after what had happened to Kiki last night. But on the other hand, I should think he would want to find out who the culprit was, since it was probably the same person who had killed Bella.

I supposed I could go to the conservatory and search on my own, but I really wanted Gabriel there with me.

After the conservatory, I had been looking forward to spending some time with Nathan in the library, sorting through more books and making repairs. I wanted to check out his computer catalog program, too. I was thinking of investing in a new one for my home computer. But all that could wait.

As I slipped into a lightweight jacket, I

decided to first hunt down Gabriel and find out how Kiki was doing this morning. Then I would plan the rest of my day accordingly.

I walked out of my bedroom and stopped abruptly.

"That's weird," I muttered, staring at the wall opposite my bedroom door. The paneling looked completely different. My first thought was absurd: *I'm in the wrong hall.* But that was downright goofy, not to mention impossible. I had just walked out of the same bedroom I'd been sleeping in for the past three days.

I moved closer and realized the panels of the wall had been painted a new color. There was also an interesting art deco–style sconce in the middle of one of the sections. It was new. I was certain I would've noticed if it had been there before.

Glancing down, I saw that a new rug had been laid down over the old Berber carpeting. Or had I just not noticed these rich Oriental designs before? No, it had been wall-to-wall beige Berber yesterday, I was absolutely certain about it. What I didn't know was why Grace would have changed the carpets in the middle of the night.

I shook my head. I had to be wrong. Staring at the floor for another minute, I wondered if I'd been thinking of the carpeting in the upstairs hall instead of this one. That was one possibility. The other was that I'd been transported in the night to a parallel universe light-years away. It could happen.

On the way to breakfast, I noticed a few more odd things. I'd been using a shortcut through the library the past two times I'd gone to breakfast. But now when I opened the door that led to the passageway, there was only about ten feet of hall before it ended abruptly. There was a pretty window at the end, with a nice view of the forest. Still, where was the hallway I'd been using for two days?

I stared out the window in confusion. I didn't see the lake, only a forest of pine trees. So I wasn't facing north, as I thought I should be.

I suppose I could now relate to what Madge had been going through when I first ran into her. Because I could swear that two days ago, this hall had continued for another thirty feet, leading to another hall that led to the back entrance of the kitchen, where I'd found Merrilee. In fact, Merrilee was the one who had given me directions to come this way. Wasn't she?

Obviously I was mistaken. I mean, I'd clearly turned down the wrong hallway. There were lots of hallways in the house.

The front south hall, the back north hall, the east hall, the west hall. And that was just on the first floor.

"Yoo-hoo!"

I jolted at the sound, then stared down the hall. It was Grace! She was waving to me!

"Grace! Thank goodness," I cried. "I'm completely lost!" I walked toward her, laughing because she continued to wave at me. "I'm coming. I'm coming."

"Yoo-hoo!" she called again.

I stopped a few yards from where she stood and looked more intently at her.

"Yoo-hoo!" she said, and continued to wave in the same exact way she'd been doing for the past minute or so.

Quick shivers ran down my arms as I realized I could see right through her. It wasn't really Grace. It was a hologram.

Either that, or I had just crossed over into the Loony Zone.

"Oo-kay," I murmured, refusing to be sucked into madness. Grace was a great trickster and I tried to drum up some appreciation for her cleverness. But it didn't work. I just felt stupid. Were there hidden cameras recording my reactions? Maybe we'd show home movies later and everyone would have a good laugh.

"Fine." I turned and walked back to the other end of the hall, determined to start over. I'd lost my way somewhere along the line. If I could retrace my steps, I would figure it out. I was just a little stressed out, that's all. And who could blame me? We'd all had a few stressful days.

First, there was Bella's horrible murder by cyanide. Then there was the balcony railing that was tampered with to near-deadly results. Then Kiki's fall down the stairs that could've meant her death. And let's not forget the strange woman who had answered my boyfriend's phone. That could ruin a girl's day.

So, yes, I could admit I'd been going through more than my share of stress, which had clearly brought about a hysterical reaction. The result was that I no longer recognized the landmarks around me. And maybe I was having problems with concentration, too, because I must have made a directional error or two. No big deal. It happened all the time. *Recalculating,* as my car's GPS would say.

But as I stared from one unfamiliar wall to the other, I remembered Vinnie's complaints and Grace's warning to watch my step. Suzie and Vinnie had told me that when Grace bought this house, she had gutted it to create her greatest game board ever: her own home.

But moving entire hallways? Interchangeable wall panels? And carpets? A pretty window where a long hall had been? And there were paintings on these walls I'd never seen before. Was everything in the house moveable? Computerized?

There was nothing wrong with that, I supposed. A homeowner ought to be able to do whatever she wanted to do in her own home. Well, other than kill off her guests, of course.

And didn't that thought give me a warm, snuggly feeling inside?

I glanced at the formal lighting fixtures that hung from the ceiling, then noticed more attractive sconces mounted on the walls. Soft circles of light highlighted the expensive artwork. I moved closer to look at the paintings. I reached out to touch the frames.

There was nothing there!

"Oh God, I'm going bananas." But if I stepped back, the paintings reappeared. I waved my hand in the space where the painting was.

"More holograms," I muttered. Really good ones. I would have to compliment my hostess. If I ever saw her again.

I turned and started to retrace my steps, walking back the way I'd come. Then I stopped. If the hall had been changed to this extent, could there also be a new trapdoor in the floor? Or was I being ridiculous?

"I'm stressed out. Remember?" I reminded myself, and bit back an urgent need to scream. "Try to calm down."

And I was talking to myself again.

I stood where I was and looked both ways down the shortened hall. I was afraid to go either way, afraid to take a step in case I fell through a trapdoor. Vinnie would tell me that it was a reasonable fear to have in this place. That fear would keep you alive, she would say.

So here I was. Afraid to take another step in case of a trapdoor. Afraid of going crazy on the spot. Afraid if I didn't move I would faint from hunger.

Was there such a thing as hunger-induced psychosis?

Hunger pangs won the day. I needed nourishment, so I made my move. Carefully tiptoeing along either side of the carpet runner, I retraced my steps back to the door leading into the library. I felt safe for a moment. I continued down the newly decorated hallway, past my bedroom, where I'd started out in the first place, and followed the usual route to the sweeping grand stairway.

"I know where I am now." And from there, I started over, heading for the west hall this time. No new décor, no trapdoors or sliding paneled walls to trip me up. I was breathing easier by the time I entered the cheery informal dining room. And I was thrilled to see a familiar face at the table, gripping a coffee cup.

"Babe," Gabriel said without smiling.

I took in his stern expression, then noticed Madge sitting next to him. She kept scooting her chair closer and eyeing him with a look of hunger that had nothing to do with breakfast. Madge was hungry for Gabriel.

No wonder he stared at me with such complete focus. I knew I had to rescue him.

"I'll be ready to go in just a minute," I said.

"Good." He looked at Madge. "Excuse me." Then he shoved back his chair and stood. He looked at me and jerked his head toward the door, grabbed his coffee mug, and walked out of the room.

I got the message that I was to follow him. He probably had some vitally important news to tell me. Perhaps it had to do with Kiki. I really wanted to hear what he had to say, but I wasn't going to go anywhere until I got some food. I'd been wandering the halls for the past twenty minutes and I was peckish, to say the least.

If Madge's eyes had been laser beams, I would be dead by now. She was glaring at me as though I'd stolen her favorite teddy bear. But I managed to ignore her completely. She was pathetic if she thought that Gabriel would give her the time of day, but hope springs eternal, I suppose.

I grabbed one doughnut and a cup of coffee. Then I heard murmurings and knew that the big glazed monster on the end was calling my name. I couldn't ignore it. Nor could I ignore the chocolate-covered buttermilk beauty crooning at me.

And just in case, I went back and snagged an apple fritter. Because they contained apples, a good source of essential minerals. Yeah.

Dear Lord, I walked out of there with four doughnuts. It was too insane, so I ran back and returned the fritter to its platter. Taking a big bite of the glazed doughnut, I strolled out of the dining room and spied Gabriel standing halfway down the hall, staring out a window.

"What's up?" I asked as soon as I spotted him. "How's Kiki doing?"

He turned and his dark eyes studied me for a few long seconds. I stared back, momentarily captivated. I'm not sure how I could forget, but sometimes it slipped my mind that Gabriel was so gorgeous that some women would probably kill to get this close to him. His intensity seemed to grow as the silence lingered.

"Gabriel?" I said, mentally shaking myself. "What is it?"

The intensity passed and one side of his mouth quirked up. "You've got glazed sugar on your chin."

I raised my eyebrows. "That's it? That's what you wanted to tell me?"

"No, babe," he murmured, "but I can't talk to you without doing this first."

I held my breath as he took hold of my chin and brushed his paper napkin across that part of my face. Then he dabbed it on the corners of my mouth. "There. All gone."

"Um, thank you?" I touched my chin to make sure the crumbs were gone. There were possibly several hundred million women on this earth who would've been tingling with excitement if a man like Gabriel had touched them in that innocent, intimate way. I, on the other hand, was unfazed by his charms.

Oh, who was I kidding? I wasn't completely immune. You could count me in with those gazillion women, too. But while it was a total thrill to be standing up close and personal with Gabriel, Derek Stone was my guy. He was the one man who made me completely happy. So why wasn't he here right now? Why wasn't he investigating this gnarly murder case with me? Why wasn't he brushing crumbs off my chin? I missed my partner in crime.

Gabriel touched my arm. "Hey, are you crying?"

I jerked my arm away. "What? No. Of course not."

"Oh, hell. You are. Come here." He held both my elbows firmly while he stared at me. "What is it? What happened? Did somebody say something to you? Are you hurt? Damn it, Brooklyn, tell me what's wrong."

"Jeez, Gabriel. Chill out." I laughed but it sounded more like a wheeze. Something tickled my cheek and I took a swipe at it. My fingers came away damp. How annoying! I shook my head, sniffled, then smiled up at him. "I'm fine. I'm okay. Maybe I'm catching a cold. I just . . . oh, God."

He yanked me into his arms and hugged me tightly. After a minute, he whispered in my ear, "Where's the Brit?"

He meant Derek Stone, of course.

"On assignment in France," I said. "Or Belgium. Somewhere. He couldn't tell me exactly where he was going."

"So? What happened?"

I sighed. Gabriel wasn't going to let this go and I didn't feel like holding it in anymore. He was a good friend and he was a man, so I told him about the phone call in the hopes that he might give me some perspective.

"Babe, don't even go there," he said, his arm still wrapped around my shoulder. "Take it from me, that woman was pulling a number on you. She's obviously a drama queen and she means nothing to Stone. She's an assignment — that's it."

I hated to sound so insecure, but I had to ask. "How can you be sure?"

"Because I know the man." He shrugged, then held me at arm's length and admitted, "He's so crazy about you, it's an embarrassment to men everywhere."

I laughed, as he'd probably hoped I would. He eased his grip on me and I stepped back, relieved to have gotten it all out of my system. Gabriel seeing my tears was a little humiliating, but I'd get over it. Apparently the tears had been in there, just lurking behind my eyelashes, waiting for their chance to escape. Now that they had, I actually felt better. "Thank you. I know Derek wouldn't do what that woman was implying. It was stupid of me to give her any credibility at all."

"You got that right."

"I was doing fine for a while," I said, in my own shaky defense. "But I guess I'm overtired. And I just spent twenty minutes trying to find my way out of the maze of hallways, which nearly drove me nuts. But never mind that. It's just been so tense around here, what with Bella's murder and the thing that happened to Shelly yesterday and then Kiki's fall."

He took the hint and said, "Kiki's fine, just feeling a little achy. I checked with her first thing. She's resting in her room today."

"I'm so glad she's okay."

"Me, too." He gave my shoulder a light-hearted nudge to change the mood. "Look, Brooklyn. I'm no expert, but I think most of your stress came from worrying about your bongo act last night. I know you felt some performance anxiety over it."

"I did," I said, nodding. "There were a lot of high expectations."

He took my hand in his and we headed in the direction of the conservatory at the far end of the front hall. "That's understandable. The bongo is a dying art form."

"I'm keeping it alive."

"Just barely," he said with a toothsome smile.

I laughed. I was so grateful for his counsel and for the fact that we'd become such good friends that he was able to tease me out of my odd moods. "Thank you."

"For what?"

I shrugged. "Nothing."

He nodded sagely. "Snow's getting worse."

"I can see that."

We entered the glass-walled conservatory and he stopped to gaze out the window. "Power might go."

"Grace told us that there's a generator that'll keep the whole house up and running." I glanced at him. "Is that what you wanted to talk to me about?"

"What?"

"When I first saw you in the breakfast room, you indicated you wanted to talk to me about something."

"Nope." He looked around. "Just wanted to get a move on."

"Oh. Okay, we're moving." I got the point. Gabriel was usually a man of few words, so I didn't expect him to get all flowery. It was just nice to know he'd been concerned about me.

Outside, a thick blanket of white covered every surface. Snow was collecting on the branches of the trees, causing them to sag precariously. If it got much colder and the snow hardened to ice, the branches and the treetops might snap off.

I yawned.

"You sleeping okay?" he asked.

I started along the path and he joined me. "It was rough the first night, but I've been fine since then. Slept straight through last night. Why? Do I look sleepy to you?"

"Not playing that game, babe. You look beautiful as always."

I laughed. "I wasn't fishing for compliments."

He gave me a sideways glance. "You're a woman."

"Okay, fine," I said, rolling my eyes. "I appreciate the compliment. And I'm sleeping okay now. So let's get back to the topic."

His eyes narrowed. "Which was?"

"Power," I said, reminding him that if the electricity went out, Grace's generator would jump into action.

"Good," he said. "I plan on winning some money at that pinball game tonight, so I'll need the power working at full capacity."

"Really? Who are you playing against?"

He shoved his hands in his pockets.

"Suzie. And she cheats."

"Get out of here," I said, chuckling, and pushed him onward. "Let's go find us some poisonous plants."

It took almost two hours to examine every deadly tree and plant in the conservatory for telltale signs of scratched tree bark, torn limbs, or missing leaves. We almost overlooked it, but finally found what we were looking for in the most unlikely place. The dirt. Someone had dug up, then patted down, the dirt around the base of a cassava plant.

"Cassava roots are used to make tapioca," Gabriel said.

"How do you know that?"

"One of the many useless facts I've collected over the years."

I read the blue-tipped informational plaque that described the multileafed plant. "It says right here, 'The starchy tuber of the cassava plant is the basis for tapioca pudding and serves as an important staple crop throughout South America, Africa, and parts of Asia. The roots, leaves, and bark of the plant are used in herbal remedies to heal skin sores and snakebites.' "I looked at Gabriel. "Doesn't sound poisonous to me."

"Keep reading."

I skipped a few sentences, then continued. " 'If prepared improperly, the starch can produce cyanide, a deadly compound when consumed.' " I frowned. "But how?"

He shrugged. "When the root is chewed, it releases an enzyme. That's what turns into cyanide if it's not processed right."

I stared at him for a few long seconds. "You know way too much about this stuff."

"It's a gift."

I frowned. "My mom makes tapioca from a package."

"Pretty sure you're safe with that," he said.

I studied the cassava leaves that fanned out from the thin branches like green fingers. "There must be a few million people eating this stuff on an everyday basis. Are they all getting low doses of cyanide with every bite?"

"Some are," he said. "If it's consumed raw as part of a regular diet, it can cause poor vision, bad hearing, paralysis — all sorts of complications. In places where cassava is the main food source, malnutrition is rampant."

"I don't get that. Except for the whole cyanide issue, it sounds sort of nutritious."

"It's filling," he corrected. "But it's also very low in protein, so if that's all you're eating, you're going to be malnourished."

"Great," I muttered, frowning.

"Hey, guys."

We both turned and saw Ray walking toward us.

"Hi, Ray," I said. "How's Shelly doing?"

"Hundred percent," he said, thrusting his thumb up. "She's back to work and feeling good. Thanks for asking."

"Glad to hear it," Gabriel said, then waved him over. "Take a look at this."

We showed him where the cassava plant had been dug up and shared our suspicions with him.

"So you want me to dig it up again so you can check the roots?"

"If you have a few minutes and wouldn't mind," I said.

"I'm on it. We've got tools right over here." He jogged over to a small utility closet built out from the wall next to the house. Opening the door, he stepped inside and came out a few seconds later, holding a spade in one hand and a short heavy-duty shovel with a very sharp serrated blade in the other. "These should do the trick."

"I'll say," I murmured. That shovel would do some serious damage if it were used as a weapon.

Ray walked back to the cassava plant and began digging. Within a minute, the tops of the thick roots were exposed. A few minutes later, he was pulling out the three-foot-high plant and plopping it onto the dirt.

"Wow, those are big suckers," I said, staring at the chunky root ball. Extending out from the fibrous mass were eight or nine thick, gnarly tubers that were as big around as a healthy parsnip and as long as a good-sized carrot.

"These are actually kind of small," Gabriel said, tapping his knuckle on one of the roots. "They can grow as long and wide as my arm if given enough sun and good soil."

Ray touched his spade to the root ball. "Looks like a bunch of them were broken off here."

We both stared at the jagged stumps. Then I frowned at Gabriel. "So someone stole some tubers? Who in this house knows how to produce cyanide from cassava?"

He shook his head, equally mystified. "No botanists here that I know of."

"What's going on?" I muttered. It occurred to me that with the thousands of books in Grace's house, there might be one or two that described how to get cyanide out of a cassava plant. Or not. But you could certainly Google the information in seconds. Which meant anyone might have done this. But why?

Ray pointed toward the closet where the shovel was stored. "If someone wanted cyanide, they wouldn't have to dig up any roots and grind them into mash. They could find it easily enough in there."

"What have you got in there?" Gabriel asked.

"Drain cleaner." He shrugged. "Weed killer."

"Why do you need drain cleaner out here?" I asked.

"Once in a while the drains back up," he explained.

I looked around the room at all the drip lines and hoses and the rows of misters above our heads. "Of course. There would have to be drains."

He gestured down at the path we were standing on. "Underneath this layer of pebbles there's a whole system of drainage troughs that collect the excess water and send it down to a main pipe. That pipe leads to a filtration system. The water is recycled and pumped back inside to be reused by the plants."

"Very clever," I said, then thought of something. "But wouldn't the drain cleaner also be recycled back to the plants? That could kill them."

"No," Ray said. "When we're spraying for

bugs or washing the windows or unclogging drains, we use an alternate runoff pipe. That one leads to a lead drum that gets changed every month or so."

"Smart."

"Grace designed the whole thing," he said proudly.

"Figures," Gabriel said. "There's a complicated brain in that head of hers."

"I'll say." But I was thinking more about the hanging bookshelves in my bedroom and the holograms and all the switched carpets and hallways and panels inside the house, not some water-drainage design out here.

"Can I see what you've got in the closet?" Gabriel asked.

"Sure." Ray opened the door and reached inside to switch on a light. Gabriel walked in.

"Is this door kept locked?" I asked.

Ray shook his head. "Nope."

I nodded. Why would it be locked? Grace would never suspect anyone she knew of using the conservatory for such nefarious reasons as the ones we were considering.

"You might want to look at this," Gabriel called from inside the small room.

I walked into the closet and looked around. The space was well-lit and bigger than I thought it would be. It was wide enough to fit a narrow, waist-high workbench along one edge. Plant pots were stacked next to other pots that held small gardening tools, cloth gardening gloves, small stakes, spray bottles, and all sorts of other supplies, including bottles of plant food and weed killer. Leaning against the wall at the far end were shovels, rakes, and an extension ladder.

Under the workbench were two stools to sit on, plus a row of plastic clogs and some thick, colorful foam squares. I recognized them as kneeling cushions for working in the garden. My mother used them all the time and she swore they kept her poor old knee bones from crumbling to dust.

"This is the stuff," Gabriel said, holding out a red plastic container of weed killer.

"That's a brand-new one," Ray said from the doorway.

"It's half empty," Gabriel said, jiggling it lightly.

Ray frowned. "Just bought it a few days ago."

"But you said you didn't do much gardening," I said. "Did someone ask you to buy it?"

"Yeah, Ruth gave me a list of things to buy at the hardware store. She needed some weed killer, a bag of potting soil, and some small pots to start some seedlings. Guess it's coming on that time of year."

I exchanged looks with Gabriel. Ruth again. Her name kept popping up wherever there was a mention of poison. As Grace's close friend, Ruth also had easy access to Grace's balcony. Had she loosened the railing that almost killed Shelly? Had she put poison in the glass that killed Bella? Was she trying to kill her best friend?

Grace had allowed Ruth to live on her property for free. She considered Ruth her dearest friend. She had established a trust fund for Ruth's use in case Grace died. I had a feeling Grace would give the woman anything she wanted, so why would Ruth try to kill her own personal golden goose? Did she need the money that desperately?

It was premature of me to mentally arrest, try, and convict Ruth of murder, but that didn't mean I couldn't suspect her.

But could I really picture her digging up the cassava plant to concoct cyanide? So if it wasn't her, then who? And what about the bottle of weed killer that was already half gone? Was someone in the house in the planning stages of yet another murder?

CHAPTER 10

Nathan wasn't in the library, so Gabriel and I made ourselves comfortable at the center table with more cups of coffee and some freshly baked chocolate chip cookies I'd pilfered from the kitchen. We made lists of suspects and motives, then tried to draw lines between the two. I drew up a timeline and we attempted to fit the guests into it, trying to figure out who had been where, when they had been there, and what they had been doing. Then we tried to predict the killer's next move.

After an hour, I still had no clue. And even though Gabriel was an expert in this kind of stealthy home surveillance and was willing to search every guest's room for clues, he didn't know exactly what to look for, either.

I tried to help. "You should look for a bunch of gnarly old cassava roots. Check everyone's sock drawers."

He raised an eyebrow. I wasn't exactly being helpful. I tried again. "Could someone have set up a chemistry lab in their bathroom?"

"Think it would take a chemistry lab to process cassava?" he asked.

"That's the problem, isn't it? I don't have the first idea of what it would take to turn a cassava root into a deadly poison." Remembering what he'd mentioned earlier about chewing the root, I said, "Bella wasn't chewing anything; she was drinking. So the cyanide had to have been delivered in something closer to liquid form."

"True," he said. "But if they used weed killer, they would have to mix it with a strong-flavored drink to disguise the taste."

"The iced tea." I thought back to the séance. "When Ruth handed Grace the glass of iced tea, she told Ruth that passion fruit was her favorite flavor. Ruth said she knew that. Who else in the house would know that passion fruit iced tea was a drink that Grace wouldn't turn down?"

"Anyone who knows Grace knows that's her favorite drink." Gabriel shrugged. "Even I know it. Her staff makes it for her every day. It tastes awful, by the way."

"So why would Bella drink it?" I wondered. "She'd been drinking alcohol pretty heavily. Either cosmos or vodka tonics, I think. Why would she suddenly gulp down a glass of iced tea?"

"Maybe she figured she should sober up a little."

"Maybe." I had considered that very possibility earlier that week.

"Let's get back to the cassava conundrum," he said, then frowned. I had a feeling he was going through all the cassava facts he had on file in his brain. Finally he shrugged. "I guess you could put it in a blender. That might turn it to liquid."

"A little risky if you ever want to make margaritas again."

"But the cassava in liquid form would have a milder, more acceptable taste than weed killer."

"I'm glad you know that." I moved to my desk and powered up my laptop. "I'm going to do what I was taught to do years ago in library science class."

"What's that?"

"I'm going to look it up."

"Good plan," Gabriel said, stretching his legs out under the table. "I'll sit here and drink coffee."

"Excellent." I logged on to Google.

"These cookies are amazing."

"I know." I grabbed another one, tore it in

half, and took a bite. "God. I want to hire Chef Tang. And Merrilee. And Shelly and Ray. I'll take the whole staff."

"It's a good group," he said.

Forty-five minutes later, I glanced up from my computer screen and looked around. Gabriel was gone. Huh. Hadn't noticed him leaving. And Nathan still wasn't back. So maybe I'd gotten a little carried away with my research, but the good news was, I had answers.

I would track down Gabriel in a few minutes, but first I read over my notes. Cassava had turned out to be an interesting little food product. It was relied on as the main source of calories by some five hundred million people around the world. And yet I'd never even heard of it. But that said more about my provincial upbringing than about the plant itself or the people who consumed it.

Of course I'd heard of tapioca, one of cassava's main by-products. As I'd mentioned to Gabriel, my mom used to make it for our family on a regular basis. She would layer it with whipped cream and . . . well, thinking about Mom's fresh, fluffy tapioca and whipped cream just made me hungry. I had to get back to my notes.

While researching the subject, I'd found

out something awful that was totally unrelated to our murder investigation. Maybe I shouldn't have been so irritated, but the first article I read said that in many third-world countries, the women of the towns and villages were the ones who were in charge of processing the cassava plants. This left them all vulnerable to the cyanide gas that escaped in the process. A snarky voice inside me wondered why men couldn't get in on some of that action.

That was a little harsh of me, I guess. It's not that I wanted men to suffer, but why was it the women who were forced to endure the debilitating effects of cyanide poisoning? There had to be better, more modern ways to accomplish the job.

I dragged myself back to the exact question I'd been trying to research: How did someone process the cassava root so wrongly, so defectively that he produced cyanide? I tried to Google that phrase but got nothing, so I worked backward and searched for the *right* way to process the root.

The right way involved crushing the root with a mallet, then drying it on a wire sheet, then soaking it in vats of water, and finally rinsing it and baking it. And that's all it took, in theory, to effectively reduce the chemical substance in the root that induced the cyanide. It was incredibly time-consuming.

After reading over all my notes, I arrived at the bottom line: for a killer to produce cyanide from cassava root, all he had to do was chop up one or two tubers and add them to something that would disguise the flavor of the root itself. Say, a favorite meat loaf recipe. And voilà, death by meat loaf! Or whatever your food of choice might be.

So basically, after all of my cassava-plant reading and note taking, I concluded that Gabriel had been right in the first place. The most effective way to get to the cyanide was to chew the root raw. Who would do that?

But the real question was, Why would a killer go to all that mess and trouble when he could pop open a bottle of weed killer and accomplish the same thing?

And which one had been used to kill Bella? Had the cyanide come from the missing cassava root or from the bottle of weed killer?

If it was the cassava root, I had to wonder what kind of killer we were dealing with. A dumb one? A crazy one? Or maybe the guy was really smart and looking for a challenge. Maybe he'd heard about cassava and wanted to try a new twist on an old theme.

"I really hate this killer," I muttered. I threw down my pen, feeling frustrated. He — or she — was leaving me with more and more stupid questions and absolutely no answers.

I checked the time. Another hour to go before lunch-time. I had no idea where Gabriel had run off to, and I hadn't seen Nathan since last night. Was Nathan somewhere in the house, searching for missing books?

Or chopping up cassava root?

Now where had that thought come from?

"Nathan? A killer?" I said aloud, then shook my head. "I don't think so." He was too nice and he had a really good sense of humor. He was a librarian, for goodness's sake. But I had to admit, he more than met the smart criterion.

I shoved the idea of Nathan as a cold-blooded killer out of my head and considered my next move. I was a little antsy from my recent cup of coffee, so taking a nap wasn't in the cards. This would be a great time to get a massage, if only Kiki wasn't resting from her near-fatal fall.

"Hey, Brooklyn. How are you?"

I barely kept from jumping out of my chair. Nathan stood there smiling, unaware that he had scared the daylights out of me just as I'd been mentally measuring him for a lovely orange jumpsuit.

"Hi, Nathan," I said after recovering my wits. "I was hoping you'd show up."

"Yeah?" He emptied his arms of a pile of books he'd been carrying and stacked them on his desk. Then he sat and looked my way. "What's up?

"I wanted to take a look at your cataloging system. I was hoping you'd give me your opinion on the best one to buy for a small business."

"Oh. Sure. Let me . . ." He turned around and powered up his laptop. He fiddled with a few keys, then swore under his breath.

"What's wrong?" I asked.

"It's been freezing up lately." He closed the cover, then stood and slid the slim computer under his arm. "Listen, why don't I run to my room and get my bigger laptop and bring it down here?"

"I don't mean to put you through so much trouble."

"It's no trouble." He smiled as he shrugged. "I've got to get the other computer, anyway, since this one doesn't seem to be working."

"Well, if you don't mind."

"Don't mind a bit. Wait here and I'll be

back in a few minutes."

I watched him walk out. And that's when I noticed the papers Gabriel and I had left on the reading table.

"Oh, you knucklehead." They had the names of all the guests and the possible motives of each one. Nathan hadn't seen those, had he? I didn't think so. He would've looked at them more carefully.

I grabbed the papers, folded them up, and shoved them in my pocket.

"There you are."

I jolted, then leaned against the table. "Hi, Grace. You caught me by surprise."

"I'm so sorry. I should wear a bell."

I smiled at the picture of Grace with a cowbell around her neck. "Were you looking for me?"

"Yes. I've been thinking about your offer to take those books to the Covington. I think it's a good idea."

"Really? That's wonderful. I'll show them to Ian and keep you posted. Thank you, Grace."

"Well, I figured you're the expert. And I'm a fool if I don't pay attention to the experts I hire to give me advice."

"That makes sense," I said, smiling.

"Oh, you discovered my secret passion."

"I did?" I turned in time to see her pick

up one of the pulp-fiction paperbacks I'd found the other day. "Oh yes. They're wonderful, aren't they?"

"Yes," she said. "But they're just falling apart. What a tragedy."

"I'm going to order archival plastic covers for them, so at least they won't get any more damaged than they are."

"Thank you." She moved her fingers down the stack, reading titles. Then she carefully pulled out an Erle Stanley Gardner classic. "I remember loving every Perry Mason mystery I ever read. I had such a crush on that man."

"He won every case he tried."

"Yes, he was a real hero." She made a scoffing sound. "Unlike most lawyers these days. All crooks and thieves, one worse than the other."

I was taken aback by her unforgiving words and blurted, "But you invited a lawyer to your party."

She laughed. "Yes, I did, didn't I?"

"Sorry." I covered my mouth with my hand. "That is none of my business."

"Oh, I don't mind," she said, waving my worry away. "One of these days I should hire a more congenial attorney than Stephen, but I keep him on the payroll because he knows where all the bodies are buried."

Someone out in the hall gasped.

Grace and I turned and watched Nathan walk in with Merrilee. They both appeared to have overheard what Grace had said about her lawyer. It would've been humorous, except that with Bella murdered, the thought of bodies being buried could be considered a little creepy.

"Here's the laptop," Nathan said, overly cheerful as a way of avoiding all mention of what he and Merrilee had heard. "I'll get the program booted up in just a minute."

Merrilee wore a confused frown but didn't say anything.

Nathan touched her shoulder. "Thanks for walking me back to the library."

Merrilee's frown turned to a sunbeam of a smile. "You're welcome. Well, I'll be going now. Chef Tang is waiting for me to unpack two cases of olive oil."

"Can't someone in the kitchen do it?" Grace asked.

"They're busy with dinner prep," she said. "And I don't mind."

"It sounds heavy," Nathan said.

"The boxes are heavy but I can manage."

"I'll help you." He closed the laptop and slipped it under his arm. "Sorry, Brooklyn. I'll show you that program later." Then he grabbed Merrilee's hand and pulled her out the door.

But what's your hurry? I thought, as I watched them disappear. *Oh, but aren't they cute together?*

Yes, they were cute. But what about my catalog program? I was about to ask Grace what she thought of the twosome who'd just run out of the room, but she was frowning too hard.

"I'll let you get back to work, Brooklyn," she said distractedly. "I've taken enough of your time."

"Okay, Grace. See you later."

She scurried out the door. I had to wonder if she was going to chase after her errant staff members. Did she disapprove of canoodling among the hired help? I didn't think that would be a problem for Grace, but she didn't look happy, whatever the reason.

I glanced around and wondered what to do next. Since I was here, anyway, I could work on book-repair stuff. But I wanted to know where Gabriel had gone off to. Was he searching for tubers in sock drawers at this very minute?

"Brooklyn, there you are."

I flinched again. Good grief, this room was Grand Central Station today.

But when I saw Vinnie, I rejoiced. Finally

a normal person. "Hi, Vinnie. What's going on?"

She was back to wearing her usual jeans, sweater, and work boots, no longer high heels or a chiffon sari. Her black hair was pulled into a single braid down her back and she wore her signature row of five small hoops along the rim of her ear. Vinnie was a beautiful woman no matter what she wore, but I was glad to see she was back to her casual self.

She flung herself into one of the chairs at the table. "Don't tell Suzie, but I am going stir-crazy inside this house. I don't understand why, since I'm perfectly happy spending hours doing nothing in my own home. But here I'm pacing the floors and staring at walls." She waved her hand in the air. "Don't listen to me, Brooklyn. I'm cranky. How are you doing?"

"A lot better than you are, I guess." Gazing around the room, I realized I really was feeling good. "I've got plenty of books to work on and I love this library. There's a beautiful view of the snow falling on the trees. And I have my computer, so at least I'm connected to the world."

"Unless all that snow shuts everything down. We could freeze to death."

"Hey, you are in a cranky mood."

She grinned. "I'm positively foul, aren't I? Well, you're stuck with me."

"I'm okay with that. Where's Suzie?"

"She ran into Grace and decided to keep her company."

"That's nice."

"I guess so." Vinnie pulled her chair closer to my desk. "Since you have your computer here, can I log into my e-mail? I'd like to show you the video Jeremy and Sergio sent. It will cheer us both up."

"Okay." I switched chairs with her so she could navigate to her site. As we waited for the page to come up, I pulled the bottom drawer of the desk out and used it as a footrest. "Why did they send you a video?"

"They're taking care of Pookie and Splinters for us and they've been sending us updates via video. Isn't that clever?"

"Very."

Jeremy and Sergio were our neighbors in the San Francisco loft building where we all lived. Jeremy was a hairdresser and part-time performance artist, and Sergio was a talented pastry chef at one of the best restaurants in town. They had been living in the building for only a few months, but we had already become great friends. I couldn't have asked for better neighbors, especially since Sergio liked to bring home samples of the exquisite desserts he made.

"Here it is," Vinnie said.

The video came up on the two cats playing on a patch of carpet. Pookie's orange coat looked fluffy and full. Splinters was black and white and lean and strong. Pookie was frolicking with a string and Splinters was batting a catnip mouse across the floor. Both were having a wonderful time.

"Aw, they look happy," I said.

"I miss my babies," Vinnie said, but she was smiling.

I watched Jeremy teasing Pookie with the string and tried not to feel bitter. I loved Pookie and Splinters but they just didn't seem to love me back. I guess they still hadn't forgiven me for that one time when I forgot to feed them. I had left the house in a hurry and made it all the way down to the garage when I'd suddenly remembered. I rushed back upstairs to feed them and change the water in their bowls. I had been gone less than ten minutes but I knew they could read the guilt in my eyes.

"Who's the best little kitty-witty-booty-cutie kitty cat ever?" Jeremy cooed in that high-pitched voice we all reserved for communicating with tiny babies and adorable pets. "Pretty kitty-witty. Yes, you are."

"Oh, he's so good with them," Vinnie said

with a sigh. "They're having so much fun."

The camera panned up and Jeremy appeared on the screen. Waving, he said, "Hi, girls! Sergio says hi, too."

The camera bobbed up and down and Vinnie giggled. Apparently Sergio was operating the camera.

Jeremy continued. "Hope you're having the most faboo time with Auntie. Don't worry about your little darlings. We're all having the merriest time, too."

"Isn't he the best?" Vinnie said, looking at me.

I nodded. "He really is."

Jeremy said, "They love performing for the camera, so you'll probably get another couple of videos from us before the week is out. And yesterday Sergio found the most sensational place in the Mission District. The Pet Café. Have you heard of it? They make fresh cat food every day! The kitties adore it!"

Oh, great. Once again, I was being one-upped by people who were better at cat sitting than I could ever hope to be. Not only were they remembering to feed the cats, but they were also taking them out to dinner. It wasn't Pookie and Splinters's fault; it was mine. How could I blame them for loving everyone else in the world except me?

I had to stop right there and breathe. Given my emotional state the past few days, I knew it wouldn't take much for me to burst into tears again. So I gave myself a quick lecture. The fact that Pookie and Splinters might not love me had nothing to do with Derek not loving me. Good grief, Derek *did* love me. He had told me so repeatedly. And Derek didn't lie. Ever. So there.

And, damn it, Pookie and Splinters loved me, too. They were just a little reserved around me. Yeah, that was it.

And if I continued along this line of thinking I was sure to be carried off in a straitjacket before the week was through.

"Meow."

"Oh, it's Leroy," Vinnie said, patting her lap. "Come up here and watch Pookie and Splinters play, Leroy."

The black cat jumped up on my lap instead, placed his front paws on the desk, and focused on the computer screen. I stroked his back and scratched his ears, mentally thanking him for distracting me from another neurotic rant.

"Leroy loves you, Brooklyn," Vinnie said softly as she petted the cat.

I smiled. "I think he was more attracted

to the sound of Pookie and Splinters play-ing."

"Maybe so." The video ended and Vinnie sighed. "Want to watch it again?"

It was the last thing I wanted to do. "Um, I should probably get going on another book-repair job."

She gasped and jumped up. "I didn't mean to keep you from your work. I'll go now."

"Oh, God." My stomach twisted from the guilt and I grabbed Vinnie's wrist to stop her from bolting out of the room. "I don't know why I said that. You're not keeping me from any work, Vinnie. I'd much rather hang out with you than work."

"If you're sure."

"Absolutely." The gentle snowfall caught my attention and an idea popped into my head. "How about if we bundle up in our heaviest jackets and scarves and go for a walk in the woods?"

"That sounds wonderful. A change of environment is always a good thing and we'll work up an appetite for lunch."

I rubbed my stomach. "That shouldn't be too hard."

We both ran off to our rooms to grab our coats, then met five minutes later by the front door.

"Grace told me to take anything we wanted from the front closet," Vinnie said, opening the closet door. "She has everything in here. Down vests and hats and mittens and scarves and gloves."

"Good, because these gloves won't be warm enough." I pulled off my thin leather gloves, shoved them in my coat pocket, and found some arctic gloves on the closet shelf that fitted me perfectly. San Francisco could get pretty cold, but it was nothing compared to the frigid air up here in the mountains. Considering that, I took one of Grace's thick down vests off the hanger and slipped it on under my coat.

"I'm ready," I announced. I probably looked like the Abominable Snowman, but I would keep warm.

"Here we go," Vinnie said, and we traipsed outside.

The freezing air was a shock to my lungs, so I breathed in and out slowly until I was used to it. The snow crunched under our feet as we walked along the lake for a good distance. We turned and strolled back toward the house, then veered off into the woods. There was a nicely marked pathway through the trees so we wouldn't get lost.

"It's so beautiful here," Vinnie said.

"Do you and Suzie come up here often?"

"About once every month or so. Suzie and Grace are very close. Despite what I say about Grace, she's very good to Suzie and I love her for that. Suzie worries that the rest of the family isn't quite as nice to Grace as they should be."

"I don't know them all, but I would hate to be forced to spend time with Harrison's wife."

"Madge is appalling," Vinnie said, "but her kids are lovely. Kiki is very sweet. She inherited her easygoing attitude from Harrison."

"I'm glad," I said. "It would be awful to have more than one of Madge's kind around."

"It would be unbearable," she agreed.

At the sound of clomping footsteps we both turned. From deep within the trees Ruth stomped through the snow, carrying the same sharp-bladed shovel I'd seen Ray using yesterday in the conservatory. The edges were now coated with something dark. Dirt? Or was it blood? I swallowed convulsively.

"Hello, Ruth," Vinnie said cheerily.

"Oh!" Ruth gasped, then patted her chest. "Oh, Vinnie, you startled me. And Brooklyn. Hello, you two. My goodness, I never expect to see anyone out for a walk in the woods."

"Have you been digging?" Vinnie asked innocently.

"What?" Her face was blank for a moment; then she flinched as she realized what Vinnie was talking about. "Oh, the shovel. Yes. I had to bury something. I mean, nothing, really."

Was it something? Or nothing? What had Ruth been burying? A cassava root? A body? A shiver ran through me that had nothing to do with the cold.

Ruth seemed so preoccupied and worried that I finally asked, "Is everything all right?"

"Oh. Yes." Her hands flitted about. "I don't know what's wrong with me lately. I'm nervous as a bird. There are so many people up here this week. We usually live so quietly. But then again, maybe it's just the snow. I grew up in Florida so the cold weather catches me by surprise every year."

"It would stagger me every day," Vinnie said. "It rarely snows in my hometown in India."

I clapped my hands together to warm them up. "We've been known to get a little dusting in Sonoma, but it melts quickly."

We stared at each other in silence for a moment, watching our breaths turn to puffs

270

of fog in the subzero air.

"Would you two like to see where I live?" Ruth asked.

"I would love to," I said immediately, and Vinnie nodded in agreement.

"It's this way." She headed back the way she'd come. She dragged the shovel behind her, creating a shallow trough in the fresh snow.

It gave me the creeps until I realized we would be able to follow the trough back to the walking path. Had Ruth done it on purpose, then? Or was she using the snow to effectively wash blood off the shovel blade?

And there went my imagination again.

We tramped about a hundred yards through the trees until we reached a small clearing. Ruth's house was in the center. It was an adorable dollhouse version of Grace's Victorian castle.

"Come in," she said, holding the door open for us.

Vinnie hesitated. "You don't have any sliding panels or trapdoors in here, do you?"

Ruth laughed heartily. "No, thank goodness. Grace was good enough to limit her architectural peculiarities to her own house."

I walked inside Ruth's home and was

instantly charmed. The front room was cozy and inviting, with mahogany paneling and a round, used-brick fireplace in the corner. A small but efficient fire was going, filling the space with warmth.

The furnishings were simple but comfortable. A wide bar separated the front room from the narrow, Pullman-style kitchen. Cheery yellow curtains hung over the windows. An alcove across from the main sitting area held bookcases and a chintz-covered chair with a floor lamp for reading.

"It's lovely."

"Thank you," she said, looking around. "I love it here. There are two bedrooms down the hall and a good-sized bathroom. It's the best of all worlds. I have my privacy and plenty of room for my art. Plus I'm welcome to spend all the time I want in the main house."

"Especially around mealtime, right?"

"Absolutely," she said, laughing with me. "I never miss one of Chef Tang's meals if I can help it."

The snow was falling more rapidly now, so I said, "We should probably get back to the house before we're snowed in."

"You're right, Brooklyn," Vinnie said. "Suzie will be wondering where I've gone."

Ruth buttoned up her coat. "I'll walk with

you. I was on my way to the house when I ran into you."

She led the way outside and grabbed the shovel before taking us back to the pathway. I was having a hard time reconciling the possibility that Ruth, a seemingly delightful woman and good friend of Grace's, might be a cold-blooded murderer. But why had she handed Grace a drink laced with cyanide? And why had she ordered more weed killer? And what had she really been burying with that shovel?

Once again, I was stymied by too many questions but determined to find the answers before one more person in Grace's house was injured or killed.

CHAPTER 11

On the way back to my room, I had a sudden brainstorm and detoured up the stairs to Grace's room.

She was wearing her bathrobe when she opened the door. "Brooklyn, I was just resting up before getting dressed for the evening. Come in."

"Sorry to interrupt."

"Don't be silly." She pulled me into the room and closed the door behind me. "I welcome the interruption."

"Thank you." I strolled to the window and gazed at the calm surface of the lake. Then I turned and said, "It occurred to me while I was getting lost in one of your hallways this morning that you might be able to help solve our mystery."

She pressed her palm to her cheek, trying to look embarrassed. "Oh, I'm sorry you got lost."

"Oh, sure you are," I said, teasing her. "I

think you love doing that. But it was a little freaky. I didn't know which way to turn. You had new walls, new carpeting, new lighting fixtures, holograms." I glanced at her. "The holograms are really cool."

She smiled gleefully. "Aren't they?" Then she sobered. "Some people think I should go back to my real job instead of toodling around here, looking for new ways to torment my guests."

"You've worked your entire life," I said. "Now you're retired and entitled to do whatever you want."

"That's what Ruth says." Absently, she grabbed a lipstick off the bureau, stared into the full-length wall mirror, and applied a thin coating of a shiny, pink-tinged red color to her lips. "Now, what can I do to help?"

I paced the floor nearby. "It occurred to me that you might have cameras installed in some of the hallways so you can check to make sure your new designs and holograms are working."

Through the mirror, her gaze met mine. "I might."

"I'm not judging," I added quickly. "Just trying to see if your camera caught sight of a killer."

She flinched slightly at the word *killer,* then nodded. "Let's find out."

I followed her to the wall beyond her sitting room where a Monet painting hung, its muted pastel brushstrokes forming a pale lily afloat on a green pond. Grace pressed a corner of the heavily gilded frame and the entire wall panel slid sideways.

"In here," she said, and disappeared into the darkness.

My nerves screamed *Danger!* but I followed her, anyway, taking care with each step, praying I wouldn't step on the wrong patch of carpet and vanish through some trap in the floor.

Grace flicked a switch and the windowless room lit up to reveal her secret lair. Along the far wall was a massive architect's table with a high stool where Grace dreamed up her ideas. Charcoal renderings of various room designs were tacked to the wall above the desk. Supplies and tools were lined up neatly along the table's edges.

But the real action took place in the center of the room, where an ultramodern circular computerized control panel stood, as sophisticated and futuristic as anything NASA or Hollywood might dream up.

"Wow," I said, turning in a circle to take it all in.

"It's fun, isn't it?" Grace took her seat in the center module and began tapping keys on four different computers. "Sit here, Brooklyn," she said, patting the chair next to her. "Let's see what we can see."

An hour and a half later, I was back in my room, dressing for dinner. My vision was still a little fuzzy. Grace and I had fast-forwarded through four days of grainy videos, each of us keeping a sharp eye on two computer screens at a time. She had cameras trained on the four different hall-ways on three floors where her guests and staff passed freely all day long. Much of the action had streamed past me in a blur.

Several times, though, I'd slowed down the video to watch more carefully when a guest's movements caused me to suspect him or her of illicit behavior. But sadly, there was nothing sinister to be found on any of them.

As I finished buttoning my navy silk blouse, there was a knock on my bedroom door. I almost shouted out for the person to come in, but given the mischief that had been happening over the past few days, I decided not to take a chance on letting some killer into my room. Instead, I walked over to the closed door and said, "Who is it?"

"It's Merrilee. I have a package for you."

I opened the door. "A package? Who would send me anything here?"

"It doesn't say who it's from, but I found it inside the mailbox," she said. Then with excitement brimming in her voice, she asked, "Is it your birthday?

Frowning, I said, "Um, no. Thanks, Merrilee."

I took the box from her and she waved and strolled away. Closing the door, I stared at the box. It was similar in size and shape to a shoe box, and it was wrapped in brown postal paper. It was addressed to me, care of Grace Crawford, with her address printed in large block letters. But there were no stamps, no return address, and that was a big fat red flag waving in my face. I knew I should toss it out the window or call the bomb squad. And maybe I would later. But right now I was too curious to find out what was inside it.

Curiosity was quickly becoming my Achilles' heel. I knew it. Nevertheless, I shook the box. There was definitely something inside. It moved around slightly, but it sounded like it was well protected with paper or Styrofoam pellets. It was heavy enough that I thought it might be a book. Maybe one of the guests had hidden a valuable book in their room, thinking they would steal it, but their conscience had gotten the best of them and they'd sent it to me anonymously. It was possible.

I wouldn't know unless I opened it. I looked for an edge in order to begin ripping off the paper, then stopped and stared again at the empty space on the box where a return address should have been. And reconsidered.

I pulled out my cell phone and punched in Gabriel's number.

"Babe," he said on answering. "What's up? Where are you?"

"Do you have a minute?" I asked. "Could you come to my room?"

"Be there in sixty seconds."

He hung up and I resumed breathing. My insides glowed at the fact that he hadn't even asked why. He had just agreed to come when I called. He really was a true friend and I was so grateful that he was here this week with me. Maybe I was kidding myself, but his presence made me feel much safer.

Less than a minute later, there was a brief knock on the door; then Gabriel opened it and slipped inside. "What is it? What's wrong?"

"Thank you so much for coming." I held out the box. "Somebody just sent me a present."

"Give it to me."

I handed him the box and watched him search the paper for a hint of its contents. He shook it, turned it upside down, held it up to his ear and listened.

"It's probably nothing," I said.

"Who knows you're here?"

"Well, everyone staying in the house, of course. My mom and dad. Derek. Well, sort of. He knew I was coming here for the week with Suzie and Vinnie. He just doesn't know exactly where here is."

"Right." Gabriel nodded, then placed the box on the dresser surface. He pulled a small switchblade out of his pocket and sliced away the thick brown paper. Sure enough, it was a simple shoe box from a well-known company.

He looked up. "I doubt there are shoes inside."

"Me, too," I said.

I stood beside him as he pulled off the top, then slammed it closed.

I gasped and jolted back.

He whipped the box out of my sight, holding it behind his back. "You don't want to see what's in there."

"It's too late," I said, pressing my hands to my stomach as it roiled and burned with fear. "I saw it."

Inside the box a dead blackbird lay in stark repose, packed and held in place by lots of crumpled white paper.

"Oh, jeez." I slumped into a chair as Gabriel searched the box more thoroughly.

"Who brought this to you?" he asked.

"Merrilee found it inside the mailbox."

He rubbed his jaw with his knuckles. "Merrilee isn't capable of doing something like this."

"I don't think so, either."

"But almost anyone else in the house is."

"True. Except for Vinnie and Suzie. And Grace. And, well, I don't think Kiki is the type to kill a bird and stuff it in a box in the hope of scaring the life out of anyone."

"No, she isn't," he said gruffly. He knelt down on one knee in front of the small coffee table and pulled bits of paper out of the box, studying each piece, then lining them up on the table's surface.

"Someone is trying to frighten me into leaving," I said. "They think I'm getting too close to solving Bella's murder — which I'm not."

"Maybe not, but that's what it looks like."

"But who would do this? It's not like I've interrogated anyone lately. Well, I gave Sybil some grief last night. And there's always Madge."

His gaze met mine and he nodded. "She was pissed off enough to kill."

"Plus, apparently she goes bird watching." I shook my head. "That probably means nothing. But then there's Ruth. I think Vinnie and I interrupted her while she was doing something she didn't want anyone to see. She was carrying a shovel from the conservatory shed and I think there was blood on the tip of it." I gave him the details of our conversation with Ruth out in the woods.

"Maybe you should take the hint," he said. "Get out. Go home. You'll be safer. Hell, Stone would have my ass if you got hurt out here."

"Derek Stone isn't here and he hasn't called either." I sniffed once, then stiffened my resolve. I pushed myself out of the comfortable chair and began to pace around the room. "Let's agree not to worry about what Derek Stone will think."

"Babe." He stood and stopped me in my path, grabbing both my arms and pulling me into his embrace. It was strictly for comfort, and I was pitifully grateful.

"Besides, the police told us we had to stay."

"That means nothing if your life is in danger."

I nodded and rested my cheek against the soft fabric of his denim shirt. Once again, as he'd done on several occasions this week, he stroked my back slowly, rhythmically, as though he were trying to soothe a baby.

"What shall we do with the bird?" I asked finally.

"I'll take it out to the woods and dump it."

I eased myself back from him. "I'll admit I'm afraid. Anyone who would kill a bird to frighten me is a scary, screwed-up person. But I'm not leaving."

He took hold of my arm and led me back to the chair. I sat again, feeling more tired than ever.

"Look," he said, sitting on the table in front of my chair. "That bird was frozen and as stiff as a board. It's probably been dead for days. The killer must've found it in the snow and decided to have some fun with it."

"Some fun," I said, and shivered.

"All I'm saying is, whoever did this isn't as desperate or bloodthirsty a character as you think. Screwed up, yes. But this was just an accident of fate. Or convenience, more likely. He stumbled on the bird in the woods and saw it as an easy opportunity to frighten you. That's all. Whoever it is isn't a seasoned killer. He's not very smart, either. If and when we can get the police up here, they'll take the box and find it littered with fingerprints. Then we'll nail whoever did it."

"Well, that's something." I gazed up at him. "Thank you, Gabriel. I feel a lot safer having you around here."

Instead of smiling, he looked more concerned than ever.

"What is it?" I said. "Now what's wrong? You might as well tell me because I'll hound you if you don't."

"I know, and that's the only reason I'm showing you this." He took a breath, then opened the box again and pulled something out of it. "I found this underneath all that paper." He held up a Ziploc bag. Inside it was some kind of playing card. I looked closer. It was the Tower card from Grace's tarot deck.

"Chaos," I whispered.

By the time we sat down to another formal dinner that night, so much snow had fallen that the drifts had started to cover the downstairs windows. We hadn't lost power yet, but it could happen.

My thoughts were so scattered that I could barely focus on much of anything. But the thought of losing power was scaring me. I wasn't worried about the possibility of being trapped in the house with a killer, nor did I really care if we lost the electricity for a while. I didn't even care if we ran out of food. No, I was scared to death that if Derek tried to call me now, he wouldn't be able to get through.

Okay, running out of food was a close second.

But the very fact that food wasn't my prime concern only proved how twisted up I was inside. Maybe the dead bird had pushed me over the edge.

The only good news was that since my little emotional breakdown in front of Gabriel earlier that morning — gosh, it felt like that had happened days ago — I'd been much more successful at hiding my irrational feelings from others. I knew I'd been successful because Vinnie hadn't seemed concerned about me at all. And Vinnie, more than anyone I knew (except my mother), was highly sensitive to the moods of others. So that's why I figured I was putting up a good front.

And food was helping, as always. Dinner at Grace's house was a miracle cure for anyone who needed an emotional pick-me-up. Tonight, as they had done every other night, the kitchen staff served four courses, and one of those was homemade pasta. Color me happy.

I was nibbling at the corners of the delicate ravioli drenched in a delectable sage and butter sauce, listening to Nathan discuss the dire state of college baseball, of all things, when my ears perked up. Someone at the other end of the table was talking about me.

"At least five or six murders," Suzie was saying. "She's solved them all."

"It's true," Vinnie said. "We're all lucky that Brooklyn is here to share her expertise with us." Her hands were animated as she spoke between bites of pasta and sips of wine. "It's uncanny how she attracts death! But despite that grisly proclivity, Brooklyn is relentless in her quest for truth."

"It's a fact," Suzie said, waving her wineglass around to make the point.

"Absolutely," Vinnie said enthusiastically. Then she lowered her voice, as though she were sharing some gruesome secret with everyone. "Brooklyn deconstructs the mystery, studies the components, the clues, the telltale signs, then bravely confronts the murderer, and justice is served in the end."

There were actual cheers! Good grief. But among those who approved were several other guests who turned and glared at me.

Oh, dear. I thought we'd talked about dropping that subject after the first night when they'd mentioned it while walking down the stairs. Apparently not.

I grabbed my glass and took a deep slug of wine. This wasn't happening. Was it? The killer had already targeted me with a dead blackbird. Did he or she need any more motivation to try to get rid of me?

My good friends were *not* doing me a favor, bless their hearts.

"I had no idea you were practically a celebrity," Nathan said, his eyes warm with interest.

"I'm not," I said. "My friends are just being, um, kind."

And I desperately wished they would stop!

I looked across at Vinnie, and Suzie winked at me. I shook my head, hoping Suzie would get the message and change the subject. But instead, she jumped in with her own tale about the time I saved one of our neighbors from the clutches of a crazy killer.

This was not going to end well.

Gabriel was sitting on my side of the table directly across from Vinnie. I thought he might be able to change the subject, so I tilted my head forward to try to catch his eye. But he was smiling indulgently at Suzie's story and was no help at all.

And that's when it hit me that this might be a good thing. If we drew the murderer's attention to me, maybe we could catch him — or her — in the act. I took a bracing breath. This could work.

Nathan leaned closer, "So, you're saying you've never been involved in a murder investigation?"

I turned fast and almost speared him with my fork. Accidentally, that is. I was a little flustered, to say the least. "Um, yes. I've been involved in a number of murder cases and I've been face-to-face with more than a few desperate criminals. In fact, I have several San Francisco homicide detectives on speed dial." I almost groaned. Boasting about this stuff didn't sit well with me. I just hoped I wouldn't lose my appetite because the ravioli were still calling my name.

"So you were just being modest before?"

"Yes," I said, then lowered my voice. "I don't like to talk about it. It's not as if I go looking for murder. It just seems to happen wherever I go and I . . . hmm." I happened to glance up and saw that everyone was looking at me now.

Madge looked befuddled. "So let me get

this straight. Wherever you go, murder happens? Is that what you're saying?"

Sybil leaned forward, glaring at me. "Did you ever think it might be a good idea to warn the rest of us?"

"If she had warned you," Gabriel said loudly, shifting attention away from me, "would that have kept one of you from killing Bella?"

"One of *us*?" Kiki said, and her eyes widened as she gazed around the room. Had it just now occurred to her that we were spending every evening with a murderer? That we were all sleeping in the same house each night? Or that the person who had killed Bella was sitting here at the table with us right now?

"Yeah, one of us," Marko said, his tone belligerent as he scanned the faces of the guests. "Someone in this room killed Bella. And when I find out who did it . . ." He didn't finish the sentence, but the threat was clear.

"Oh, my goodness," Merrilee said, her voice shaky.

"But one of us is missing," Peter murmured.

I looked at him, then quickly checked around the room. Sure enough, one of the chairs was empty, but I couldn't remember who had been sitting there all week. How odd. "You're right."

"What? Who's missing?" Grace stood and looked down the table, then said, "Good heavens. Where's Stephen?"

I stood and stared at the empty chair, too. Stephen Fowler, Grace's loathsome lawyer, had many faults, but passing up a free meal was not one of them.

A quick search of his room confirmed that Stephen Fowler was missing.

Six of us volunteered to search the house. Peter took half of the first floor and Nathan took the other half. I went off with Gabriel. It was a sad statement, but I wasn't about to pair up with either Peter or Nathan. What if one of them was the killer?

Gabriel and I searched Stephen's third-floor bedroom more closely, then climbed the stairs to the attic. At any other time, I would've loved to stop and explore the dark, intriguing room with its old trunks and odd antique furniture, but I was on a mission. I traipsed behind Gabriel up the narrow stairs that led to the rooftop and followed the widow's walk briskly around the edge of the open space. Stephen Fowler was not in his room, not in the attic, and definitely not on the rooftop. If he had been outside, we would've found his body frozen solid.

Suzie and Vinnie searched the second floor, where the majority of bedrooms were located, but there was no Stephen to be found there, either.

Forty minutes later, Peter and Nathan left to join some of the men who were watching a football game in the Knight in Shining Armor Room. A few other guests were gathered at the bar in the game room. Some had gone off to bed. Gabriel, Vinnie, Suzie, and I found Grace commiserating with Ruth in the Gold Salon.

"You didn't find him?" Grace asked.

"Not yet. Sorry."

Ruth smiled at me. "The others were sure you'd be the one to find his dead, rotting body."

"Oh, great." I shot Vinnie a fulminating scowl. "This is your fault for talking about me like I'm some kind of Hercule Poirot."

She was undaunted. "I spoke the truth, Brooklyn. You are a marvelous detective. We are lucky to have you on the case."

Gabriel snorted as I threw my hands up in surrender. "Fine. I just hope the killer takes the bait you laid out."

"What are you talking about?" Gabriel said.

"If the killer thinks I'm on the case and is

afraid I'm about to nail him, he'll try to get to me first. And we can catch him in the act."

"Okay, it's official," he said. "I'm locking you in your room."

I smiled. "Very funny."

"I'm not laughing."

Grace sat at one end of the gold brocade couch and stared heavenward as though she were seeking forgiveness. "I'm a terrible person. I've known Stephen for years and I didn't even notice he wasn't in the room."

"Don't blame yourself, Aunt Grace," Suzie said, helping herself to a small glass of Baileys over ice. "None of us noticed, either."

"But I feel awful." She took a deep breath and let it go, then looked at us. Her face was a mask of shame. "Do you know, at one point during the first pasta course, I was thinking that dinner was so much more enjoyable tonight. I wasn't sure why."

"It did seem more convivial," Vinnie admitted.

"Yes." Grace pressed her hands to her cheeks, mortified by her uncharitable thoughts. "Because Stephen wasn't there."

Vinnie stood at the side of the couch and rubbed Grace's shoulder. "We have had many pleasant meals this week despite

Stephen's presence, so don't beat yourself up over that. But, Grace, why did you ever invite him here in the first place if you knew how unpleasant he could be?"

Grace stared at the carpet, once more unwilling to make eye contact with any of us.

Suzie squatted down and forced Grace to meet her gaze. "Aunt Grace, what aren't you telling us?"

Grace let out an exasperated groan, then sat up straight and faced us. "I invited Stephen only to annoy Madge."

Vinnie's eyes grew big and she quickly covered her mouth to hide the fact that she was laughing.

"Fine. I'm sorry," Grace grumbled. "But Madge is so negative. She says the most hideous things. Being around her is a constant chore."

Still anxious, she stood and began to pace. "I had no choice but to invite Madge, but I decided to keep her in line by bringing Stephen out here. I thought if Madge believed I was changing my will, she would be on her best behavior. In theory, anyway. She's still a royal pain in the ass."

Suzie nodded. "You got that right."

"I realize Stephen is simply atrocious, too," Grace said. "He's been so nasty to my guests. But how could I toss him out when that was the very reason I'd invited him? He kept threatening to leave and I kept telling him he couldn't."

"Maybe he did leave," Vinnie said.

I shook my head. "All his things are still in his room."

Grace's expression fell. "So he really is missing."

"I'm sorry."

But I was sorrier about something else. While I was glad to know that Grace wasn't really changing her will, I was now concerned that her attempt to thwart Madge might have had unintended consequences. What if Madge had arrived for the house party, seen the lawyer, jumped to the obvious conclusion, and decided to try to kill Grace before she had a chance to change her will?

I glanced at Gabriel. He must have been thinking the same thing, because he nodded briefly. But then he scowled. "Fowler couldn't have just disappeared into thin air. And he'd be a fool to wander outside in this weather."

"It wasn't too bad earlier," I said, then suddenly pictured Ruth and that bloody shovel. Had she lured Stephen Fowler into the woods, then smashed in his head and

buried him? Was that why she was so un-
nerved when Vinnie and I came across her
in the woods?

I shook my head, stunned by the direction
of my own thoughts. That theory was not
only absurd; it was impossible. The weight
differential alone would prohibit petite Ruth
from dragging Stephen's inert body through
the snow to a shallow grave and pushing
him into it.

Gabriel took charge again. "The four of
us will search the house one more time this
evening, only we'll each take different floors.
We can't go outside in this weather tonight,
so first thing in the morning I'll arrange for
a group to search the property."

"It might be time to call the police again,"
I said.

Gabriel nodded. "It would be nice to get
them involved in the search for Stephen,
but I doubt they'll be able to make it out
here with all the snow. Pretty sure we're on
our own for a few days."

"We're on our own," Grace whispered.
"All alone."

Her words were like icicles, drip-drip-
dripping down my spine.

That night in my room, I decided to call
my mother. After that dead-bird incident, I

needed some revitalizing energy, and my mom was the best one to go to for that.

She answered the phone and I said, "Hi, Mom. I hope I didn't wake you up."

"We just got into bed. What's wrong? Something's wrong."

"Can't I just call my parents to say hi?"

"Yes, you can, sweetie, and you do all the time. But I can hear a strain in your voice. Do you need an enema? I can recommend one that only takes two heaping scoops of espresso shaken with a pint of mineral oil."

I laughed to keep from gagging. "Thanks for that, Mom. But no." Seriously? An espresso enema? No wonder she had so much energy every day.

I reminded her of the house party and gave her a brief rundown of the week's events without going into too much detail. Such as various acts of mayhem and murder.

"You should get away from there," she said.

"We're snowed in for a few days."

"Oh, dear. I can hear in your voice how much negativity is bombarding you."

"Well, it's a beautiful place and most of the people are really wonderful, but . . . well, I just thought I'd call and say hi. I should let you get to sleep."

I heard her say something to my father, but her voice was muffled. Then she came back on. "Brooklyn, it's a wild coincidence, but I was just working on a new protective spell this afternoon. Put me on the speakerphone. You'll need both hands for this."

Oh, boy.

She had me sit in a comfortable chair with my hands resting on the arms and my eyes closed. I placed my phone on the coffee table before me.

Then she began to chant. "Oi! Ahh! Ron-jon-manna-roo-a-panja! Oi! Ahh! Ron-jon-manna-roo-a-panja!"

At least that's what it sounded like to me. She repeated the phrase a few hundred times more, her voice rising and falling, going deeper and then switching to a higher pitch. She would slow down, then speed up until she sounded like a record being played at the wrong speed.

My thoughts were centered on how utterly ridiculous it was to sit here and listen to my mother crooning and bellowing nonsense words over the phone.

And yet I could actually feel a comforting energy beginning to move through my body. It started in my hands and meandered up my arms to my shoulders. Then the energy split in two, half of it spreading up and warming my neck, then passing through my head, cleansing my thoughts and soothing my worries.

A different, more vibrant energy traveled down my spine, livening each vertebra as it passed through. When it reached my middle its pulsations softened and my stomach calmed down. The muscles and nerves around my hip bones relaxed and I felt myself dip deeper into the soft cushions of the chair. I uncrossed my feet and felt them tingle with vitality. Suddenly, I had happy feet, even though I had no interest in moving anywhere.

"Brooklyn?" Mom said. "Are you still there?"

"You probably knocked her out," my dad said in the background. "I'm feeling a little punchy myself."

"Wow," I whispered.

"It's a good one, huh?" I pictured Mom smiling at me through the phone.

"Oh yeah," I murmured, my eyes still closed. "It's a keeper. I feel great. Thanks, Mom. I really appreciate it."

"I love you, sweetie," she said. "Your dad sends his love, too. Take care of yourself and come visit us soon."

"I will. I love you both." I ended the phone call and got into bed. I felt warm and protected and happy for the first time in days. Whatever happened, I would handle it. I didn't know if my mother's crazy chant had given me the strength to take care of business or if I was just so happy to talk to someone from outside this house, but I had a new perspective.

Either way, I wasn't tired at all, so I picked up Grace's manuscript and ended up reading another fifty pages. It wasn't great literature. Then again, maybe that's why I was enjoying it so much. Her writing was vivid and accessible. There were racy sections, plenty of industrial intrigue, and enough good gossip to qualify the book as a good old-fashioned potboiler. My strictly amateur opinion was that Grace would make a killing on this book.

And by *make a killing,* I didn't mean she would get herself killed. (I reached over and knocked on the wood surface of the nightstand. You couldn't be too careful after even thinking something like that.) I meant only that she would make a boatload of cash. Not that Grace needed the money. Maybe she would donate her royalties to charity. But I was getting ahead of myself.

Even though the names in the book had been changed — Greta was the name of the main character — I could picture Grace doing everything the fictional Greta had done. There were a number of scenes in which she had reached a crossroads where choices needed to be made and questions had to be asked. She was a genius, but did that make her happy? Would she marry or stay single? Would she have children? Would she be happy at home with the kids? Running a successful, highly competitive business took so much of her time and energy. Was she one of those women who would be married to her job until she retired? Maybe she would live with girlfriends and travel. Would it be too late to live a full life then?

I put the book down and considered my hostess, Grace Crawford. Reading all of the life questions her character Greta was asking herself brought back a memory of the first time Suzie had driven me out here to meet her aunt. Ruth was there at the time, and while I didn't remember the specific conversation, I did remember wondering if Grace was gay.

Suzie had never indicated that her aunt leaned one way or the other, and Suzie was pretty open about things like that, considering her own situation.

It didn't matter to me. It was just interesting. Grace had introduced me to Ruth that day, and I had thought how remarkable it would be if they were lovers.

Now after I had been here for several days, it seemed odd that I had thought that back then. The two women were obviously close friends, but I'd spent so much time wondering whether Ruth might be trying to kill Grace that now I couldn't see them as lovers. How could someone's lover consider killing her? I suppose to some people the notions of love and murder weren't mutually exclusive, but it was still unacceptable to me.

I felt my cheeks warm up as another thought struck. I wondered if Gabriel and Grace had ever been lovers. Would I ever get the nerve to ask him?

Something else occurred to me and I stopped to consider the reasons why my mind was going down this particular path tonight. Maybe I missed Derek even more than I realized. But the fact was, there had been a moment earlier this week when I had seen Merrilee and Grace talking together. Merrilee's devotion to her boss was so deep-seated and real; I suddenly had wondered if maybe they were involved in a romantic relationship.

But that didn't sit right with me and it hadn't been long before I got to know Merrilee better and discounted that theory.

She was a sweet, simple woman who treated everyone, including her employer, Grace, with loving-kindness. I didn't think it went any further than that.

So all of my errant thoughts along these lines were idle speculation. And lest I ever forgot, I really didn't know what I was talking about. My gaydar has never been very sharp. In fact, it was nearly nonexistent. After all, I'd been engaged to my friend Ian for three months a few years ago, and had found out only recently that he was gay.

I shouldn't have been so surprised, though. He'd always had a highly developed feminine side and excellent taste in clothes.

I picked up Grace's book again and continued reading. Her heroine, Greta, had just filed papers to form her video game company. She and her best friend and business partner, Paul, were celebrating the milestone with a bottle of champagne. The next morning, Greta woke up in bed with Paul.

Uh-oh.

But I was smiling as I read how they both agreed that it would never happen again. I was surprised to find out that, despite their strong attraction to each other, it never did happen again. But something else did. Seven weeks later, Greta discovered that she was pregnant.

Unintended consequences struck again.

I woke up with a start. I thought I'd heard crying. Or a baby wailing? I must have been dreaming.

Blurry-eyed and sleepy, I glanced around. I thought for a second that it was morning, but then I realized I'd left the bedroom lights blazing. There was a heavy weight on top of my stomach and it took me a long moment to recall that I'd fallen asleep while reading a dramatic scene in Grace's thick manuscript.

In the book, Grace — or, rather, Greta — had just given birth to a baby girl. A beautiful little girl with a soft halo of pale blond hair, perfect tiny hands, dark blue eyes, flawless skin, and a sweet little pink mouth.

Greta had bitten back tears as she handed the baby to the waiting nurse. She never saw her little girl again.

Nowadays Greta would've kept the child and raised her alone, but thirty-some years ago, the stigma was too great. All the money in the world wouldn't have insulated her baby from the name-calling. She would be deemed illegitimate and worse. Greta couldn't live with that, didn't feel as though she had a choice, so she had given the baby up for adoption.

Soon after reading that part, I fell asleep.

"So it must have been a dream," I whispered to myself. But how much of that part of the book was true to life for Grace? She had referred to the book as a roman à clef of sorts. Was the baby real or fiction?

I shook my head at my thoughts. The fact was, there were no babies in the house. I had dreamed of babies crying simply because I'd been reading about a baby.

I checked my watch. It was 2:15 in the morning. Past time for me to sleep.

I switched off the lights and slid back under the covers. I lay still for a long time, listening to myself breathe, trying to empty my thoughts, trying to talk myself into falling asleep. But it wasn't working. I was wide awake now.

A baby whimpered.

"Oh, come on," I protested aloud. I was beyond tired and now I was hallucinating. I rolled my eyes at my own lunacy, then pounded the pillowcase and adjusted my head and neck into a more comfortable position.

"Now go to sleep." I released a heavy sigh, then forced myself to repeat my mother's chant as I tried to relax every bone and muscle in my body, starting with my feet and working my way up. It was working; I was dozing off.

And suddenly a baby's scream filled the air.

"No way!" That was a real baby! I jumped out of bed. Dashing to the door, I flung it open and looked both ways down the hall. The dim light revealed nothing. The hall was deserted. But now there was the steady sound of a baby crying somewhere in or near the house. Was it outside?

I raced back into my room, slid my feet into my slippers, and grabbed my down vest. I threw it on over my pajamas as I ran down the hall toward the front door. The closer I got, the louder the crying grew, and now I was certain the sound was coming from outside.

But it was freezing outside. What was a baby doing out in the snow?

Footsteps pounded on the stairway and I turned to see Gabriel racing downstairs right behind me in his black T-shirt and jeans.

"You heard it, too?"

"Yeah," he said grimly.

"Thought I was hallucinating."

"No, there's someone out there."

I was grateful for his presence. Even though I would've gone outside alone to investigate, I felt safer with Gabriel. Who wouldn't?

He nudged me away from the door and yanked it opened. Freezing air rushed into the house and I pulled my vest tighter around my pajama top.

Two women stood at the bottom of the stone stairs.

"Thank goodness," one of them said. "May we come in?"

The other one frowned. "We've been ringing the bell for a while."

"Must not be working," Gabriel said, and stepped outside to usher the two women up the slippery steps and into the foyer.

First to walk inside was a dark-skinned, middle-aged woman. She wore an expensive trench coat over nice slacks and carried a bundle of pink fleece in her arms. I assumed there was a baby in there somewhere, although I couldn't see one.

The second woman was a uniformed cop carrying a briefcase.

I moved to close the door but peeked outside first. The snow had stopped falling and someone, probably Ray, must have cleared off the circular drive. In front of the house an SUV was parked, exhaust fumes pouring out the tailpipe in a thick cloud.

"Your car's still running," I said.

"Just a precaution," the one holding the pink bundle in her arms said. "It's warm inside the car."

"I'll shut it off," Gabriel said.

"Thank you."

He dashed out into the cold and a moment later I heard the car door slam shut.

"How did you get through?" I asked. "According to the police, the roads are supposed to be closed."

The woman grinned. "My Land Rover drives through anything."

"Good to know."

Gabriel hurried back inside and shut the door. I led everyone down the hall and into the Blue Room, where we'd taken Kiki the night before.

"Some place you got here," the cop said, looking around at the impressive elegant blue-toned furnishings and up at the glittering chandelier.

"What's this all about?" Gabriel asked.

"Can I get you something to eat or drink?" I said at the same time.

"That would be wonderful," the older woman said in a grateful voice as she sat down on the settee. Leaning back, she rested the baby against her chest. "We've been traveling for hours. Thought we'd have to spend the night in Truckee, but the snowplows cleared the roads around ten o'clock and we took a chance."

"Why?" I asked, then added, "Sorry. But what are you doing here?"

Merrilee came into the room just then, still fumbling to tie her bathrobe around her waist. "I heard voices. Oh, is that a baby?"

"Merrilee, thank goodness," I said. "Could you arrange for a little food and something hot to drink for these ladies? They've been on the road for a while."

"Of course." She turned to the older woman. "Does the baby need anything?"

"I have a bottle if she gets fussy."

"Okay." She rushed out of the room on a mission to take care of her guests.

"Sit, please," I said.

The cop sat down next to the other woman and placed the briefcase on the floor between them. Gabriel and I took the two chairs opposite the settee.

Things still seemed a little surreal to me as I watched the older woman pass the pink baby bundle to the cop to hold. She grabbed the briefcase and opened it on the coffee table.

I had yet to actually see a baby inside all that fluffy fabric, but I knew there was one in there. I'd heard the crying. But what were these women doing here and why had they brought a baby with them?

"My name is Sandra Parish," the older woman said. "I work for Child Protective Services in San Francisco. Please call me Sandra."

"I'm Officer Angela Rodriguez," the policewoman said. "Just along for the ride."

"Oh no," Sandra said quickly. "That's not true at all. Officer Rodriguez is the reason I'm here, and I'm very grateful to her. She saved Lily's life."

The baby fussed and Rodriguez immediately handed the baby back to Sandra, who bounced the child lightly against her shoulder. The baby quieted instantly. It was warm enough that she removed the thick down blanket from around the baby, and I could see her pretty little face.

And I knew it was just a coincidence, but Lily looked just like the baby Grace had described in her book. The pale patch of blond hair; dark blue eyes; unblemished skin; tiny pink lips; and a button nose.

"I assume this is Lily?" Gabriel said as he stood and reached for the baby.

"Yes." Sandra smiled as she relinquished her precious pink cargo. Gabriel held the baby against his chest and the two visitors sighed audibly. Was there anything more moving to women than the sight of a strong man holding a tiny baby?

Merrilee walked into the room carrying a tray with crackers and cheese and a small pot of tea. She set everything on the coffee table and poured tea for the two women.

"This is wonderful. Thank you," Sandra said.

Merrilee looked at me. "Just call the kitchen when you're finished with everything."

"Thanks, Merrilee."

She left, and Sandra finished her small cup of tea. "Thank you again for the refreshment."

"There's plenty more," I said. "Please help yourselves."

Rodriguez put her empty cup on the tray. "Let's talk about Lily."

"Yes, let's," Gabriel said.

Sandra coughed lightly to clear her throat, then said, "Lily's parents, Theodore and Maris McClay, were both killed in a car accident earlier this week. Officer Rodriguez was first on the scene and acted quickly to save Lily, then called Child Protective Services to arrange for a caseworker to take charge of the child."

"Is that you?" I asked.

"Yes. I arrived at the police department

and took charge of Lily. The police and my own department both attempted to track down the next of kin, but found no one."

I glanced at Gabriel, who was walking back and forth across the room. He looked down and smiled at the baby, whose eyes were closed. Now, what female wouldn't want to be rocked to sleep that way?

The caseworker went on to tell us how they were able to track down the parents' lawyer. From him, they learned whom the couple had charged with guardianship of the baby in the event of their deaths. Sandra went to the new guardian's home, but was told that the person was out of town. Two very helpful neighbors informed her that the guardian was staying at the home of Grace Crawford near the town of South Lake Tahoe.

"And that's how we ended up here," Rodriguez said.

I frowned. "Who is Lily's guardian?" *And please, God,* I prayed silently, *don't let it be Madge.*

Sandra double checked her court forms. "Her name is Susannah Stein."

Gabriel whipped around and stared at me. My mouth fell open and I stared right back at him.

"Suzie?"

CHAPTER 12

Our Suzie?

I was pretty sure I would never forget the astonishment I felt at hearing Sandra's announcement, but I managed to snap into action. "Be right back."

Racing up the stairs to the third floor, I jogged down the hall to Vinnie and Suzie's room and knocked firmly on the door. After a few seconds I knocked again. And again.

Moments later a sleepy-eyed Vinnie opened the door. "Brooklyn? What time is it? Is everything okay?"

"No, Vinnie. It's not." I took hold of her arm and squeezed gently. "Can you please wake up Suzie and come downstairs with me?"

Her eyes widened in fear. "Is it Grace? Suzie, wake up! Something's wrong."

"It's not Grace," I said immediately. "I'm sorry I frightened you. Nobody's . . ." I was about to say that nobody was dead, but that wasn't true. Suzie's friends, Lily's parents, were gone. I couldn't be the one to break that news to them. "Grace is fine."

Vinnie clutched the lapels of my robe. "Then what is it?"

"It's . . . it's something else. Please, Vinnie, it's important. You and Suzie need to come quickly."

"Aunt Grace is okay?" Suzie asked, her voice groggy. She was out of bed and throwing on her bathrobe, but I could tell she was still half asleep.

"Yes, she's fine," I said, helping her with her robe. "But I really need you guys to wake up."

"All right, all right," Suzie muttered. "Long as nobody's dead."

Vinnie grabbed hold of Suzie's hand. "Okay, we're awake, Brooklyn. Sort of."

"Come on, then." I walked swiftly out the door and headed for the stairs.

"Can't you tell us what's going on?" Vinnie asked as they both jogged to keep up with me.

"You'll see soon enough," I said cryptically. I wasn't about to tell them about Lily all by myself. I wouldn't know where to start or how to say it. This was something they simply had to see for themselves.

Seconds later, we made it back to the Blue

Room and I introduced them to the two visitors. Gabriel stood in the far corner of the room, holding Lily. Vinnie and Suzie were still blinking and not entirely awake, so Sandra suggested they sit on the couch while she stood and patiently explained everything all over again.

Suzie got as far as hearing that her friends had been killed in a car accident. "No!" she cried, and jumped up. "No, that's impossible. I just saw them last week." She turned to Vinnie. "We had dinner with them. Right? We were celebrating. Maris landed a job at Apple and Teddy was going to start grad school. They just had Lily." She gasped. "What about Lily? Oh, my God, is she all right? Oh, my God. Oh, my God."

Suzie crumpled onto the couch. Vinnie wrapped her arms around her and Suzie sobbed into her shoulder. My own eyes were damp and so were Vinnie's. I felt so bad for my friends. I didn't even know Teddy and Maris, but my heart hurt for all that had been lost. This was such a tragedy, and there was more to come.

Vinnie finally looked up at Sandra. "What has happened to Lily?"

Sandra looked nonplussed, then realized that neither of the women had noticed Gabriel standing out of the way the whole time she'd been talking. Sandra motioned him forward and he strolled over to the couch.

"Lily's right here, safe and sound," he said quietly. "And beautiful."

Vinnie stared. Her mouth drifted open, then closed, and I watched her stiffen as realization dawned.

The movement caused Suzie to stir. "What? What is it?"

Vinnie shook her head slowly. "Oh, my . . ."

Suzie looked up then. "What's going on?"

Sandra put her hand on Lily's back in a protective gesture. "Teddy and Maris appointed you, Susannah, Lily's guardian if anything ever happened to them. They knew you would take good care of her. That's why we're here. We're turning the baby over to you."

"What?" Suzie shrieked.

Vinnie instantly grabbed her in a tight hug. "Shhhh."

"Vinnie, let me go," Suzie said, wide awake now and close to flipping out. Her eyes were red; tears streaked her cheeks. She wore an old bathrobe and her hair was sticking straight up, but she managed to look dignified as she faced the strangers across from her. "Now, look, lady. If this is some kind of a joke, it's not funny."

"Suzie, please," I said, and moved closer to stand by Gabriel and the baby. I took a peek, grateful that Lily was asleep and missing most of the drama. I knew how Suzie felt. This was a huge shock and she was so stunned she probably wasn't aware of what she was saying. So I kept my voice calm as I told her softly, "Of course it's not a joke. Lily needs you."

"But . . ." Dignity slipped and terror returned. "It's not possible."

"Suzie, come here," Gabriel said gently.

Suzie's eyes narrowed. "Why?"

"Suzie, don't be silly," Vinnie said. She stood and walked up to Gabriel, who turned the baby around so that Vinnie could take her. Vinnie rocked Lily in her arms, then pushed the thick blanket back so she could see her face better. "Poor little sweet thing, so tiny and all alone. But not anymore. Suzie, come say hello to our Lily."

Suzie shook her head, but it didn't mean anything and we all knew it. She was helpless against both the woman she loved and the baby who needed her. Finally, Suzie sighed in acquiescence. She stood and wrapped her arms around both Lily and Vinnie. They swayed together and I could hear Suzie's sniffles as she continued to mourn her friends. After several minutes,

Suzie finally opened her tear-filled eyes and whispered, "What are we going to do with her, Vinnie?"

"We will love her," Vinnie said, and passed the baby into Suzie's arms.

Early the next morning I dressed quickly and went to check on Suzie and Vinnie to see if they had gotten any sleep. I didn't want to knock and wake up the baby, so I quietly opened their door. They had fashioned a temporary bed for Lily by pulling out one of the wide dresser drawers from the bureau. It was padded with sheets and it sat on the floor by the side of their bed.

The baby was sound asleep and Vinnie and Suzie were both stretched out crosswise on the bed, watching every little breath she took. They were so caught up in their new daughter, they didn't even notice me.

Smiling, I closed the door, then went downstairs to find Sandra Parish and Officer Rodriguez finishing breakfast and about to take off for San Francisco.

Last night, Merrilee, the wonder woman, had fixed up a room for the two women to spend the night. They looked rested and ready for the long drive back to the city.

They both gave me their business cards to pass along to Suzie and Vinnie. Then I accompanied them out to their car.

As the women drove away, the front door opened and Gabriel and Kiki walked out.

"It's colder than I thought it would be," she said, wrapping her arms around herself.

"Go back inside," Gabriel said. "I don't want you catching a cold."

She smiled up at him and some kind of wordless communication passed between them. "Go on," he said. "We'll be back in a few minutes."

"Okay, but hurry." She scurried back inside and closed the door.

"I guess you two had that talk," I said.

"Yeah," he muttered, but refused to satisfy my curiosity further. Instead, he glanced around and said, "This is as good a time as any to look for signs of Fowler."

I knew it was useless to pry, but I took it as a personal victory that he looked so happy and relaxed this morning.

"Let's do it," I said.

The two of us walked around the yard, conducting what Gabriel called a perimeter search. We were looking for any signs that Stephen might have been dragged off or maybe just wandered away on his own.

I pointed toward the row of cars parked at the far edge of the back driveway. "Do we know what kind of car he drove?"

"I asked Grace. She said he drives an old silver Cadillac."

"For real? A silver Cadillac?" Of course he did.

"Yeah. Guess he's old-school when it comes to cars."

"He's old, anyway," I grumbled. That wasn't fair, though, since Fowler wasn't much older than my own parents. But I guess what my father was always saying was true. You really were as young as you felt. Stephen had to feel a thousand years old, he was such a crotchety geezer.

It was easy to pick out the classic Cadillac, with its garish fins and wide, shiny grill, from the line of cars.

"At least we know he hasn't driven off somewhere."

We approached the car cautiously. I didn't know what I was expecting to find. After what Suzie and Vinnie had said about me at dinner the night before, the expectation of the other guests was that I would be the one to find the dead body of Stephen Fowler. And then I would identify the killer, handcuff him, and toss him over my shoulder to carry him off to jail. Super Brooklyn.

But the car was empty.

I didn't know whether to be relieved or disappointed.

"Where is this guy?" I wondered, and turned in a circle to scan the larger area surrounding Grace's mansion. "Could he still be somewhere inside the house?"

"That's my guess." Gabriel cupped his hands over his eyes to block the sun's glare as he bent over and stared through the windows of the car. Finally he straightened up. "Nothing helpful in there."

"Where to next?"

His eyes narrowed as he looked around, then pointed toward the water. "Grace's property extends down to the shoreline and deep into the woods, and includes hundreds of yards of shorefront on both sides of the house. It's a few dozen acres at least."

"We can't possibly search it all," I said. "We'll have to call in the police."

"He hasn't been missing much longer than twelve hours," Gabriel said as we walked back to the house. "But you're right. That doesn't matter. We've already had one murder and one attempted murder. If we don't find him today, we'll need to call the police to come out to conduct a wider search."

"They should've come back here by now, anyway. We've kept the séance room locked all week in case they need to search it for more evidence. But how can they collect any viable evidence at this late date?"

And would you listen to me? I guess I'd learned something during all those brushes with crime scenes.

Gabriel shrugged. "That's their problem. Right now Fowler is ours. We'll search the house from basement to attic again." He turned and looked up at the house. "There are so many trapdoors and sliding panels and trick rooms, he could be anywhere. And we're going to check them all."

"Fine," I said. "As long as I don't fall through one of them."

"Why not?" He grinned. "It's kind of a fun ride."

I stopped and gaped at him. "You've fallen through a trapdoor?"

"On purpose," he specified.

"Ah. Right." I bit back a smile.

"It's true," he said. "When Grace was building the place I came out and played guinea pig for her."

"So what's with the changing walls and floors and stuff? Does she have attention deficit disorder or is she just bored with the same old thing?"

He thought about it for a moment. "I honestly think she set out to build a magical fun house. The thing is, when you fall through one of the trapdoors, you end up on a very safe slide that leads to a soft landing in the basement. It's a hoot."

It did sound like fun, now that he was describing it. Vinnie hadn't been quite so positive in her assessment, though. And I could see her point. Fun or not, it would be terrifying to suddenly drop through a trapdoor.

"Grace sponsors parties for foster kids and terminally ill kids out here and they have a blast," Gabriel said.

"I didn't know that," I said. "That's wonderful of her."

"She's just a big kid at heart."

Vinnie had said basically the same thing about Grace, but it hadn't been a compliment.

"How long have you known Grace?" I asked.

He thought about it. "When I first met her, she was still working in the city. So I guess it's been five or six years."

"Did you two meet because of books?"

"Books. Games." He shrugged, then added, "Tricks."

Tricks? But he didn't offer to explain that last item and I knew I wouldn't get any more information from him. Gabriel remained a mystery to me and I almost preferred it that way. I didn't know whether he was a thief or a hero, but I considered him one of my closest friends. I trusted him with my life, though not necessarily with my most valued books.

"Do you know why she moved out here?" I asked.

He took in the sweeping view of giant pines, rugged mountains, and a crystalline blue lake. "Seriously? You have to ask?"

I curled my hands inside my vest pockets as I followed his gaze. "I know it's beautiful, but it's so isolated."

"Grace is a very private person."

I blurted out my next question. "Were you two lovers?"

He laughed, then slanted a look at me. "You really think I would ever answer that?"

I smiled. "It was worth a try."

"Grace is a beautiful woman," he said thoughtfully. "But I don't think I'm her type."

I rolled my eyes. "You're every woman's type."

"Babe," he said, and smirked adorably.

"Well, you're not *my* type but . . ." I laughed, then shrieked like a little girl when he grabbed me and tossed me over his shoulder. "Put me down, you nut."

"Not until you —"

An ear-piercing scream from the house

stopped us both. Gabriel set me down and we raced as fast as we could to the nearest door. The screaming continued in short bursts as we stormed into the kitchen — and found Merrilee squealing in terror at the sight of Stephen Fowler. "They said he was dead! He's dead!"

I had to admit Fowler looked pretty bad. His hair was matted with blood and his face was streaked with dirt. His clothes were ripped and wrinkled and filthy. But he was very much alive and annoyed as hell.

"Where have you been?" I demanded, then almost gagged from the sight of dried blood that had dripped down his neck. I had a little problem with blood. I tended to faint at the mere sight of it. So I took deep breaths and looked away and thought of hot fudge sundaes.

"He's supposed to be dead," Merrilee whimpered.

"Oh, shut up, you idiotic twit," Stephen snapped.

"Don't talk to her that way," I said, just as Gabriel grabbed hold of Stephen's shirt and shook him once, hard.

"Hey! I'm the victim here," he whined loudly.

"That's no reason to take your crappy attitude out on Merrilee," Gabriel said, his tone deadly serious.

I laced my arm through Merrilee's and pulled her aside. "Who told you Stephen was dead?"

"Everyone was talking about him at breakfast," she explained. "They said he was as good as dead. Dead as a doornail."

At least she wasn't reporting that they blamed his death on me.

"So it scared you when you saw him," I prompted.

She nodded vigorously. "I thought he might be a zombie."

This was the first time I'd seen Merrilee act in such a naive and childlike manner. I had begun to think that Suzie was wrong about her, but now I could see that she was a bit challenged. She was beautiful as well as thoughtful and kind, and she ran Grace's house and staff professionally and competently. Seeing this sudden shift in her personality was a real eye-opener.

"You know there's no such thing as zombies, right?" I said gently.

"I guess so," she said, pouting. "But he's mean, too."

"I completely agree — he's a total jerk."

"Hey!" Stephen shouted.

"Zip it," Gabriel told him.

Merrilee's smile blossomed and grew.

"Thank you, Brooklyn."

I squeezed her arm in response, then let her go.

"Well." She rubbed her hands together. "The beds aren't going to make themselves, are they? I'd better find Shelly and get going with the chores." And just like that, she was back to her regular self. In a flash, she bustled off to take care of her people and her world.

Leaving Gabriel and me to deal with a wild-eyed, very cranky Stephen Fowler.

"He wouldn't tell you where it happened?"

"No," Gabriel said, glowering at the walls of the third-floor hallway. "The jackass would only admit that he was pushed, but refused to tell me where."

"So we're on our own again," I said, disappointed that Fowler wouldn't just walk upstairs with us and point out the spot where he'd fallen through the wall. Merrilee was right: the guy was a zombie.

"Pretty much," Gabriel said, knocking on another wall.

"But I thought you'd been through the trapdoors before. Don't you know where they are?"

"She keeps moving them," he muttered.

I ran my hand across a seam in the wall

panel. "Fowler was probably too embarrassed to talk about it."

We worked in silence for a few minutes, studying the surfaces of the walls, looking for a secret panel or a hidden doorway.

Gabriel's theory was that the killer, thwarted by Bella's death and Shelly's near miss, might have changed tactics. If Fowler were disposed of, then Grace wouldn't be able to change her will right away. The killer would have a reprieve and be able to take the time to plan the perfect way to finally get rid of Grace.

This assumed that the killer was someone who was actually mentioned in Grace's will.

Maybe it was a long shot, but if we could find the spot in the house where Fowler had disappeared, we might find a clue as to who might have pushed him.

"Merrilee had it right when she called him a zombie," I said crossly. "Wouldn't it be fitting if he turned out to be our killer? I didn't mean that. Not really."

"Yeah, I know. But it would solve some problems."

"Everyone hates him, anyway."

Gabriel leaned his shoulder against the wall and stared at its surface from the side. "The good news is that Grace was too distracted last night to make any changes in the configuration of these walls."

"Small favors."

"Yeah."

I smiled at the way he understood my shorthand speak. My entire family had a tendency to talk this way. It was a legacy from growing up with our great-aunt Jessica. She spoke in clichés so much that eventually she stopped saying the whole phrase and only uttered a word or two. "Saves nine," she would say, or "Once bitten." And we would all nod in agreement.

Derek had always gotten a kick out of that, too. My heart did a little twist at the thought of Derek, and I wondered if he missed me as much as I missed him.

Absence makes? I could only hope.

"Check out this panel," Gabriel said.

"What do you see?" I asked, moving closer.

"This seam here." He ran his hand over the wall.

I pressed against the wall and stared at it the way he had, sideways, trying to see if I could discern a gap in the panels. But instead my eye caught a flicker of white halfway down the hall. I jogged off to see what it was.

"Where are you going?" he asked.

I stopped at a small antique console. A

bouquet of freshly cut flowers had been arranged on a pretty white doily. Turning to Gabriel, I pointed to the floor. "Right here."

I stooped beside the console and grabbed a torn piece of paper off the carpet. It was the top corner of some kind of court document. I knew because I could see two thin vertical lines running down the side of the page with numbers next to the lines.

Standing up, I waved it at Gabriel. "Look at this. It's a small piece of some legal document. Stephen Fowler is a lawyer. Maybe he was carrying this when he disappeared."

"It's part of a legal brief," Gabriel muttered, staring at the torn fragment. "Makes sense."

"It sure does," I said, excited now. "So let's look right around here." I started pushing on the wall, testing random sections and panels. With a soft click, one section abruptly gave way and I fell forward, tumbling down into blackness.

CHAPTER 13

It wasn't that much fun after all.

I landed on my back — thankfully on something soft and welcoming — with a loud plop. I lay still, stunned, for several seconds, first trying to catch my breath and decide if I'd broken anything in the fall, and then trying to figure out where I was. I didn't recognize the room, but as I shifted position, it felt like I was sprawled across a giant balloon. It squeaked with every movement I made and felt like one of those giant bounce castles people rent for kids' birthday parties.

The initial shock wore off gradually, and then I started to appreciate the ride itself. Maybe I was hysterical, going crazy, but I didn't think so. Now that I was safe, I could see that the ride down had been kind of fun. Scary and bizarre, but fun. I could understand how kids would get a huge kick out of it.

But I still would have preferred some advance warning.

Suddenly from somewhere up above, I heard Gabriel yell, "Move out of the way!"

I rolled quickly. Gabriel plummeted down the chute and flew out onto the balloon pillow mere seconds later. A minor tidal wave erupted and I was bounced forcefully toward the edge. Oh yeah, an adult-sized bouncy castle; that's what this was like. And I was about to fall off.

He reached out and grabbed my sweater. "Don't fall on your head, for God's sake."

"Thanks. I'm okay." I lay back on the pillow as it settled, and stared at the cavelike ceiling. "Where are we?"

"This is the basement."

That made sense. It was more dungeonlike than anywhere else in the house. "It looks like it was carved out of stone."

"It was."

I ran my hands over the surface of the pillow, then turned my head and looked at him. "This thing is like one of those bouncy castles they have at kids' parties."

"You visit bouncy castles often?"

"Who doesn't?"

He smiled. "Good point."

I maneuvered myself around until my feet were dangling off the side, then slid down onto the floor. Gabriel followed me and we stood side by side and looked around some more.

"That was completely weird," I said, still a little shaky.

"Are you hurt?"

"No," I said after mentally surveying myself again. "It's just a strange feeling, suddenly dropping through space and landing on a big balloon — that's all. A first, for sure."

"Not a bad thing."

Since I'd survived and I had company, I was willing to go along with that. "I guess not."

The pillow's surface was at least eight feet across and it was almost three feet high. Plenty of room to catch someone plunging down the chute. I made my way around it and found a hose nozzle sealed in the plastic shell. It snaked across the floor to a small box with a plunger. I recognized it as a pump. A cord from the pump led to an electrical outlet in the wall. A timer was plugged in to the adjacent outlet.

"So they keep the landing pillow pumped up on a regular basis. That's very good."

"And Ray comes down here and checks it every few days."

"I'm glad to hear it." God forbid if the

pillow sprang a leak and collapsed. I couldn't imagine the damage a person would suffer when she came hurtling out of the chute with nowhere to land but the cold stone floor.

"Here's the rest of Fowler's legal document," Gabriel said, holding up the folded, wrinkled pages.

"I'm sure he'll be happy you found it."

"He's never been happy in his life."

"True." I took one last look around and that's when I noticed a dark smear on the blue surface of the pillow.

"Is that blood?" I shivered and sucked in big gobs of air as I took many baby steps backward. As I'd mentioned before, visible blood marks and I didn't mix well.

"Easy, babe." He examined the blood-stains up close. "Looks caked on. Must be Fowler's. He had a gash on the side of his head that probably bled here."

"Yeah, I saw it." My stomach rolled again and I fought the reaction. "Did he say how he hit his head? The fall onto the chute was painless. No sharp edges anywhere. And this balloon pillow couldn't have hurt him."

"He was whining that someone attacked him." Frowning, Gabriel added, "Someone could've hit him over the head upstairs, then pushed him down the chute."

And who could blame him? I thought, then chastised myself. Stephen Fowler, for all his foulness, didn't deserve any of this. "Maybe he was attacked once he got down here."

I worked out both scenarios in my head and neither made a lot of sense. "I don't suppose you noticed any blood on the chute."

"It was a pretty quick trip," he drawled, then turned serious. "My guess is that he was attacked in the upstairs hall, then pushed down the chute. When he woke up several hours later, it was dark. He was disoriented and couldn't find his way back upstairs until this morning."

"That makes the most sense, for what it's worth." And since Stephen wasn't talking, for whatever reason, all we had to go on was our guesswork. But it still didn't make me feel much better. "How do we get out of here?"

Gabriel turned and pointed. "That door over there leads to Grace's wine cellar."

"Really?" I raised my eyebrows. Coming from the Sonoma wine country, those were magic words. And in my own defense, let me just say that after falling through a trapdoor and sliding down into a dungeon, anyone would have wanted a glass of wine. "Let's check it out."

■ ■ ■ ■

I found a book in the wine cellar.

The underground room was even more cavelike than the bouncy-bounce room had been. The walls here were carved out of the bedrock stone beneath the house, too. But the ceiling was even lower, adding to the dark, cold feel of the long, narrow room. Gabriel found the light switch and turned it on, revealing a stone floor and row after row of wooden wine bins, all filled with dusty bottles of red wine.

Having grown up surrounded by vineyards, with parents who co-owned a winery and who had instilled in each of their children an appreciation of fine wines, I was always excited by the prospect of exploring a wine cellar. It felt like I was going on a treasure hunt. I never knew what gems I might unearth.

"Let's see what we have," I said, and pulled a bottle from one of the dusty slots. "Holy cow. I haven't seen a Kosta Browne pinot in over a year."

"Bring it upstairs," Gabriel advised as he scanned another row of bins. "We'll drink it at dinner."

"I will." I pushed back on the trickle of

guilt I felt over raiding Grace's wine cellar. After all, everyone at the party would be partaking of our bounty. Plus Grace had at least two cases of Kosta Browne down here. You couldn't find that wine anywhere. My father would be giggling and dancing in the street.

"I think we should drink one of these."

Gabriel looked up. "Take it with us."

"Okay." I pulled one bottle out and held it close. Then I scanned more bins and pulled out several more bottles, not to take but merely to identify the wineries. They were all excellent wines. "She's got great taste in wine."

"Yeah, she does."

I was almost finished with my hunt when something odd caught my attention. "No way." I reached inside one of the slots and pulled out a book. A *book?* Had someone actually stashed a book in a wine bin?

"This is getting ridiculous." I held up the book for Gabriel to see. "Who would be reading a book in a cold, dank wine cellar?"

"A book lover?"

"Very funny," I said, scowling as I studied the small book, a nicely bound volume of poetry called *The Open Road.* "If it had been a real book lover, he wouldn't have shoved it in a wine bin and left it to mold.

He's lucky it's not covered in parasites."

"Babe, you're giving me the creeps."

"Really? That may be another first." I stuck the book in my pocket to examine more closely in the brighter light of the library.

A minute later, Gabriel held up two more bottles of wine. "I just discovered two Jordan cabs I'm taking upstairs. Now let's get out of here."

"I'm with you."

An hour later, I sat at the library reading table, flipping through my portfolio of leather and cloth I'd brought with me for making or repairing book bindings. While searching the wine cellar earlier, I had come up with a brilliant idea for another birthday gift for Grace. I had brought her a set of bookends that I knew she would like. They were shaped like large brass pinecones, so apropos when you lived on the edge of a forest, I had thought. But the sad fact was, bookends would get lost in this giant house of books. So now I had an even better idea. I was going to construct a book box for her manuscript.

I cleared one end of the reading table and laid out my tools.

"What are you doing?"

I looked up and saw Nathan standing a foot behind me. I explained my plan and he decided to watch what I was doing.

"This'll take a while," I cautioned. "If you feel like dozing off, I won't be insulted if you leave."

"Fair enough, but I doubt I will." He pulled a chair closer. "It's always good to learn a new skill. Something to impress the girls back home."

I laughed. He was good-looking enough that all he had to do was walk into a room and he would impress plenty of girls. But I didn't say so, for fear he would think I was making a move on him.

I found a beautiful pale Japanese rice cloth with fragile cherry blossom limbs dotted with red flowers and buds. I measured it out and was happy I had enough material for what I had in mind.

"The steps for making this box are similar to making a book cover. Except that once you've covered the boards and spine as you would a book, you make two three-walled boxes and paste them onto each cover. One side is slightly smaller than the other, so they fit inside one another, forming the box. So when you close the book, the two boxes envelope the manuscript completely."

I simulated the box closing with my hands.

"Makes sense," he said. "I'm just missing the artistic ability to carry it off."

"Well, watch what I do and maybe you'll get the hang of it."

I showed him how to measure the size and shape of each piece, and then I cut them all from the heavy pieces of board I always brought with me. After everything was cut, I laid the pieces out in place on the table.

"The tricky part is in cutting the cloth to fit the walls. When you're making a flat book it's a lot more straightforward. But because we're constructing walls for this box there are lots of angles and edges. The cloth has to bend around the curves and the measurements have to be precise."

I continued to work, stopping occasionally to explain a particularly intricate step, such as creating the matching dust strip that was fitted over the spine. We used the same glass-topped table to press each side of the box, but we didn't have weights for the dust strip, so Nathan ran to the kitchen and brought back a heavy iron trivet to use. It worked just fine.

After two hours, the box was finished. I slipped the manuscript inside and folded the two sides together. And felt complete satisfaction at hearing the whisper of cloth against cloth.

"Fantastic," Nathan said.

"Thanks. I'm kind of thrilled that it worked out." Then I looked around at the mess I'd made and sighed. "And I just realized I'm exhausted."

"You probably have time to take a nap before dinner."

"I might do that," I admitted, and began the task of cleaning off the table and packing up my tools.

Dinner that night was a low-key affair. Stephen Fowler had insisted on dining alone in his room — until Gabriel suggested he would be safer if he was with the rest of us.

Even though it was probably true, I kind of wished Gabriel had let him go. Fowler's presence put even more of a damper on the evening than usual. Whatever frivolity we might have been tempted to enjoy on the occasion of Grace's birthday eve was effectively snuffed out by the obnoxious lawyer's gripes and groans.

They were accompanied by much eye rolling from the rest of us.

Fowler's snorts were bad enough, but we were also being treated to even more of Madge's unsubtle sniffs of disapproval this evening. I finally turned to Nathan for some work-related yet civilized dinner conversation. "If you're available, maybe you could show me that catalog program tomorrow."

He gritted his teeth in a grimace, but switched to a smile so fast, I thought I'd imagined it.

"Sure thing," he said, but that halfhearted attempt at a smile didn't fool me. He wasn't happy. Before I could ask him what was wrong, he turned his back on me to speak with Grace.

He wouldn't make eye contact with me after that. I tried not to take it personally as I twirled a few delicate strands of home-made fettuccine onto my fork and savored the mix of cream, butter, and pungent Parmesan cheese. Spectacular pasta, as usual, and the Kosta Browne pinot noir I'd found in the wine cellar was an exquisite pairing.

Fantastic food, wonderful wine. A darling new baby in our midst. Who could be unhappy when we had all that to celebrate and enjoy?

So why was Nathan so irritable? Was his computer still on the fritz? Maybe, but I was pretty sure his chilly response to me had nothing to do with his computer. He'd made it more than clear that he didn't want to talk to me. Was it something I'd said? Or was I just being overly sensitive?

Fowler's presence had cast a dark cloud over the table, but this change in Nathan wasn't related to Fowler.

And just like that, I was suspicious again. Was Nathan not speaking to me because of what Vinnie and Suzie had said about my detecting skills last night? Maybe that's why he'd decided to stay and watch me build that book box. Maybe he'd been keeping an eye on me. Was he worried? Or fearful of my tendency toward rooting out bad guys and bringing them to justice?

Even if Nathan was afraid or guilt ridden, I was tired of being suspicious of everyone. Tired and fed up. Why couldn't I just relax and enjoy life? Why was suspicion my semipermanent state these days?

Well, there *had* been a murder, I reminded myself, along with any number of suspicious acts since then. Who *wouldn't* be suspicious?

Fine. I couldn't snap my fingers and make my suspicions go away, so I decided to fiercely embrace them. All through the salad course, I pondered what might be wrong with Nathan. What had changed? Why was he avoiding me? Did he have something to hide? Like, say, a cassava root mixed in with his gym shorts?

For most of the meal, I watched him out of the corner of my eye. He was distracted tonight, overly friendly one minute, moody the next. When Marko asked him about a football game airing that weekend, Nathan scowled and told him football wasn't everything. Huh? The world's biggest football fan was turning down an invitation to watch the game? Was he angry at Marko, too?

Strangely enough, it comforted me to know that it wasn't just me he was angry with. The only person he was genuinely happy to talk to was Merrilee. But that didn't mean anything. Everyone was friendly with Merrilee. Except for Sybil. And Madge, of course. It went without saying that Madge didn't like anyone, but Merrilee seemed to garner a large portion of her wrath. Probably because she was so nice. Or maybe it was because she was "the help."

Now, Madge was a person who deserved my suspicion. She hated everyone and everything. She criticized the staff, whined about the weather, even complained about the pasta. The pasta! Oh, it didn't taste *bad*, she insisted. There was just too damn much of it.

The fact that she'd asked for second helpings two nights in a row wasn't a detail anyone was willing to mention.

She was bad tempered, condescending,

and not very bright. A deadly trifecta. Sadly, though, I couldn't see her experimenting with a cassava root. I wasn't even sure she'd know how to pronounce it.

It made me wonder all over again just what Harrison saw in her. But then, the reasons why couples got together and stayed together were a mystery for the ages.

That thought made me glance at Peter and Sybil Brinker. In a way, Sybil was almost worse than Madge. Her passive-aggressive reaction to events was creepy. She tried to come across as pleasant, but she was just plain icky. There was no other word I could come up with. At least not after drinking two glasses of wine.

Happily, though, suspicion didn't slow my appetite down any. As I finished the last bit of my tiramisu and drained my coffee cup, Grace took pity on all of us and stood, signaling the end of the dinner hour.

"I'll be in the card room doing tarot card readings," she announced, clutching the back of her chair. "And Harrison has promised a rousing game of backgammon with anyone willing to take a trouncing. We're also showing the new Scorsese film in the media room at the far end of the third-floor hall. Oh, and the music room is open, as well."

"Finally," Peter muttered, and shoved back his chair.

I turned. "You're happy the music room is open?"

"Very funny," he said, standing. "No, just happy this meal is over."

I pushed back my chair. "At least the food is always phenomenal."

"Sometimes that's just not enough."

I recoiled. "What planet are you from?"

He finally cracked a smile and I felt like I'd achieved something monumental.

The others seemed to feel the same way Peter did as we all rushed to leave.

I hurried to catch up with Vinnie and we walked down the hall together. "What a vibe, huh?"

"What a lovely dinner," she said simultaneously.

"What?" I said.

"I'm sorry, Brooklyn," she said at the same time.

We were both amused at how we kept talking over each other. "You go first," she said.

"The vibe at dinner," I explained in a low voice. "You could slash it with a butter knife."

"I don't understand. We had a lovely dinner."

"Well, sure, the food was great, but what

345

about . . . ?" Then it dawned on me why she was so happy. "You had Lily with you."

"Yes." Her smile was rapturous. "She is such an angel. Suzie has gone to the kitchen to get her a bottle. She'll be right back."

"I'm glad." I leaned against her in weary camaraderie. "My end of the table was dismal. Everyone's uptight or morose or just plain bitchy."

"I'm so sorry, Brooklyn," she said, patting my arm. "Come sit with us next time."

"I will."

"Grace only stuck you at that end of the table to pair you up with Nathan."

"I suppose so." I smiled. "You'll be glad to know it doesn't seem to be working out."

She laughed. "Thank goodness."

"And despite all the angst, my appetite is as healthy as ever."

"That's my Brooklyn."

We made it to the card room in time to see Fowler arguing with Gabriel. "I may be stuck in this godforsaken house, but that doesn't mean I have to socialize with you heathens any more than necessary."

"You're right," Gabriel said. "It's time for you to leave."

"Fine." Fowler sniffed. "Good night."

Gabriel grabbed his arm and squeezed. "I suggest you go straight to your room and lock your door."

Fowler's eyes grew wide and his lips trembled. Was he only now remembering how dangerous it was to be left alone on the third floor? He bolted from the dining room as if he were shot from a cannon.

I watched him leave, then gave Gabriel a nod. "Well done."

Gabriel smiled artfully at me, then shifted his glance to Vinnie. "Everything okay with the baby?" he asked her.

"Everything is wonderful." Her hands were pressed together in a little prayer of thanks. "Bless you both for your part in bringing us all together."

Gabriel lifted his shoulder in a casual gesture. "I was just holding the kid."

"An experience Lily will treasure forever," Vinnie assured him with a smile.

I laughed and gave her a quick hug. "I'm thrilled for you and Suzie. And I'm right down the hall, don't forget. If you ever need a babysitter . . ."

"Thank you, Brooklyn," she said. "We are so grateful to you. You are the very best neighbor in the world."

Since the rest of the guests were filtering into the card room, I figured all of us had concluded, at least subconsciously, that there was safety in numbers.

Peter, Marko, Harrison, and Nathan gathered around the bar with after-dinner drinks. The four men had developed a loose-knit friendship, but now I watched Marko and wondered. Here he was, stuck in this house with the person who had murdered his longtime friend and possible lover, Bella. Was he mourning her loss? Was he bent on revenge?

In the beginning, I had considered Marko a grown-up kid, a consummate slacker. He seemed like the kind of guy who could stretch out on any couch in the world and fall asleep in an instant. But now, without Bella around, he seemed antsy. Like he wouldn't know how to sit quietly if someone paid him to do it. My original impression still stood: he was an annoying twelve-year-old kid in a fifty-year-old body.

At that moment, nobody was paying much attention to him, so he was cantankerous and loud and getting worse by the minute. But I watched him study the others out of the corner of his eye and I saw him change tactics. He grew more somber and solicitous. One of the men said something to him, then the others joined in. And just like that, he was acceptable again.

So maybe Marko wasn't as drunk as they thought he was.

I couldn't figure him out. The slacker routine was real, but he could also be devious. He hadn't laughed as much since Bella died, but every so often, his irritating giggle filled the room. And he did snicker and snort once in a while when he and the other men gathered at the bar.

I hated to say it, but watching Marko made me recall an article I'd read recently that talked about sociopaths and how they were much more prevalent in our society than people thought. The article had a checklist of personality traits that seemed to coincide with some of Marko's. The fact that I couldn't pin him down on any particular topic, couldn't decipher any true emotions emanating from him, made me wonder if he had some of those sociopathic tendencies. For one thing, I didn't think he was mourning Bella at all. Had they truly been a couple? Or had Bella simply been an easy port in a storm, so to speak?

And the way he had maneuvered the conversation to include him again a minute ago was suspiciously manipulative.

And yet, I wondered if maybe I wasn't being fair to him. Maybe in the quiet of his lonely room, Marko suffered greatly from the loss of Bella. But out here with his three amigos at the bar, he had to put on a show, get all tanked up and party hearty. Show that he was ready to do whatever it took to be part of the gang.

The four men scoffed and guffawed as they tested each other's knowledge of trivial football statistics — Nathan excelled at the statistics game — and compared their favorite rock-concert performances. And now they were moving on to the subject of single-malt scotches.

I had brothers; I knew where this was going. Sure enough, the bartender brought out more glasses and lined them up on the bar. A single-malt taste test was about to be conducted, sure to be accompanied by plenty of laughing and drunken back slaps.

Nathan's gloomy mood seemed to have evaporated. So maybe it was just me, after all. It didn't matter. For the time being, I'd lost interest in trying to figure any of these people out.

At the other side of the room, Gabriel huddled with Grace at the tarot table. They were deep in conversation and she wasn't dealing the cards, so I wondered if he was regaling her with the story of our adventure through the trapdoor earlier.

"Oh, there's the baby," Merrilee cooed, drawn to Vinnie and Suzie, who sat with Lily in a quiet corner.

I pulled a side chair over and joined them.

"Wanna hold the kidlet, Brooklyn?" Suzie asked.

"Absolutely," I said, and took the little darling into my arms. I inhaled the sweet scent of baby powder and wondered if anything could be softer than her pale pink cheeks and tiny baby fingers. After a few minutes of hugging and rocking the baby, I looked at my friends. "This could get addictive."

They both smiled in agreement. Even though Suzie and Vinnie had suffered through grief and tears and sadness and doubt that day, their faces now showed nothing but joy. They were clearly enchanted by the baby.

Everyone was happy about Lily. Over the next hour, most of us, the women as well as the men, found ourselves taking turns paying visits to the baby and her new moms. There were comments and questions about everything from her tiny toes to her pretty face, her appetite and her attitude, her diaper preferences and her college prospects.

Some of us already had nicknames for her. She was barely six weeks old and already a beauty. I found it sweet and so amazing that my friends had fallen so deeply and eternally in love with the little bean.

"Grace took us up to the attic, where we found the most fabulous crib and bassinet," Vinnie said. "It's vintage, more than a hundred years old, but it's perfect for Lily."

"I'm having it sanded and refinished," Grace said. "It'll go in the new nursery." She went on to describe the construction plans for a full nursery in one of the third-floor suites. She reminded Merrilee that they had to schedule their contractor to come out next week. Then the two of them discussed the best ways to childproof the house. Grace couldn't wait for Lily's visits and suggested a two-weeks-a-month schedule from now on.

I shot Vinnie a look, thinking this wouldn't sit well with her, but she smiled serenely. The fact was, she couldn't seem to stop smiling. Her entire attitude toward Grace seemed to have changed over the past day or so. Was it all because of Lily? I wondered, but then realized Vinnie had begun to warm up to Grace when the older woman had confessed her true reason for inviting Fowler to the party.

The mellow sounds of jazz filtered through the room. Kiki begged for a tarot card reading. Peter played backgammon with Harrison. Madge flipped through a magazine and Sybil drank too much.

"Hey, pretty lady," Nathan said, and sat down next to me.

I laughed at that ridiculous line, but still flirted a bit with him. He was suddenly attentive to me again, probably due to the abundant shots of Scotch he'd just tossed down his throat. He was a nice guy, but my heart wasn't in it.

I stood and said good night to everyone and headed off to my room. But once I got into bed, sleep was out of the question. I picked up Grace's manuscript and continued reading where I'd left off the night before.

For three fascinating chapters, Greta was entangled in a scandalous industrial-theft problem. No one knew who was selling the company's top-secret ideas to the highest bidders, but suspicion was growing throughout the company and nobody trusted anyone.

Greta hired lawyers to file restraining orders against her rival companies, but there were ways around the orders.

She brought in a team of undercover detectives who set up a sting and several employees were caught in the web. She fired them all, including two of her favorite game designers, people she'd worked with for years.

After the firings, things calmed down for a while. Greta and her board of directors breathed easier. Then weeks before Greta was to bring out their biggest game ever, a multimillion-dollar 3-D video reenactment of Battle of the Alien Worlds, their biggest competitor announced their newest game coming on the market one week before Greta's.

It was the exact same product! Only the name had been changed slightly to War of the Galaxy Invaders. It was a blatant rip-off and Grace — er, *Greta,* was furious. The thief was still working for her!

Greta had always prided herself on her people skills. She was a genius with games, but she was also a decent person. Her employees had always loved her because she respected them and rewarded their efforts. But now she was stymied and hurt. Who among her workers had betrayed her?

The thief was never caught. There was never another incident of industrial espionage, but the damage had been done. Greta was never quite the same effervescent charmer after that.

I closed the book, shaken by the depth of emotions the story touched in me. I hated that Greta's experience had extinguished some of the lightness within her.

Troubled, I stared at the pages. Had an ongoing proximity to murder done that to me? Had it made me more harsh? More judgmental? More suspicious of human nature? I hadn't thought so before, but now I was afraid I might be wrong.

Hell, just that evening at dinner, I had looked around the table and mentally accused a good number of Grace's guests of murder. What did that say about me? Okay, yes, there actually *was* a murderer among us, but did that excuse my readiness to mentally accuse everyone in the room?

I put the manuscript on the nightstand and turned off the light. While wrestling with the pillow to find the perfect spot for my head, I questioned whether the part of the book I'd read tonight was factual or not. Earlier in the week, Grace had told us that the company had recently suffered a loss of some money. Someone had been skimming funds. But she didn't seem too concerned about it.

In her book, though, the crime had been industrial theft. Someone had stolen her idea. Her creation. For Grace, that would be like stealing her soul. That loss would plague her much more than the loss of money would.

But was it true? Had *Grace* been plagued by an industrial thief as *Greta* had been? Or were those chapters pure fiction? Before I dozed off to sleep, I made a mental note to ask Suzie about it in the morning.

Sometime in the middle of the night, I was awakened by another strange noise. Unlike the last time I heard noises in the night, I was certain there was someone inside my room. Was it Bella's murderer?

The moon was obscured by heavy clouds so my room was cloaked in darkness. The floor creaked with every other step the prowler took toward my bed. I was frozen in fear, but knew I had to do something to save myself, knew I had to make a move.

Did he have a gun? Maybe he was planning to slip a dose of poison into my glass of water. Either way, I couldn't stay in bed, waiting for something to happen.

Just as I was about to spring into action, a noisy "Meow!" erupted from one of the ceiling panels. Then Leroy pounced down and attacked.

A loud gasp erupted, followed by a grunt. My intruder raced to the door and escaped.

"Damn." I jumped out of bed and ran after him, but by the time I reached the hall, the person was gone.

Soft fur bumped against my ankles as Leroy wound himself through and around my legs, purring softly. I let go of the breath I'd been holding and bent down to pick him up.

"My hero," I muttered against his soft fur. "You saved my life."

He had also helped reveal who my intruder was. I'd heard that gasp and was fairly certain I knew. The question now was whether or not that person was also Bella's killer.

CHAPTER 14

For some reason, I woke up feeling lighter and happier than I had in days. We were close to finding Bella's killer, but that wasn't the only reason I felt good.

I was comfortable in my own skin again. I wasn't sure why, but I refused to question it. I was just relieved to be rid of the psycho girlfriend who had invaded my body and brain since that fateful phone call to Derek. The real Brooklyn was back.

Hallelujah.

As I brushed my teeth and fixed my hair, I thought about my mother, who was a big proponent of dream therapy. So maybe I had worked out all my doubts and fears in my dreams. Who knew? But once again, I wasn't going to ponder it too deeply, because, let's face it: my mother was also a big proponent of curried-ghee facials and astral trekking.

Today was Grace's birthday. The day

would be a long one and tonight would be jam-packed with drinking and partying — and, with any luck, unmasking a killer. I decided to track down Kiki and do something I'd been yearning to do all week. I was going to get a massage.

Two hours later, I was in my bedroom, lying prone on Kiki's portable massage table, completely wiped out and still groaning from the glorious pummeling I'd just received.

"You do great work, Kiki," I whispered.

"Thanks," she said. "But promise me you'll work on that tension in your shoulders. That stuff will make you old if it doesn't kill you first."

"Those are wise words," I muttered. "I promise. Thanks."

"You're welcome." She tucked the sheet around me, then said, "And thank you, Brooklyn."

"You're welcome." I opened one eye. "For what?"

She smiled softly. "For Gabriel."

"You mean . . ." I stopped. Why was she thanking me? What had he done? Oh, God, she'd already fallen in love and he was going to break her heart. "Look, Kiki, I never —"

She laughed. "It's okay, Brooklyn. We just talked. He's wonderful. I've never met anyone like him, and I have you to thank for making it happen."

"I just gave him the message, Kiki. So . . . what did he say to you?"

"He told me about his big move. He said he'd sworn you to secrecy, so I don't blame you for not telling me. It's so exciting, isn't it?"

"Uh, yeah. It sure is." I had no idea what she was talking about.

"Imagine moving to Antarctica for the next five years to study the flight patterns of polar birds. That takes dedication. I had no idea he was a scientist. But it makes sense, doesn't it? The way he took complete charge of the murder investigation until the police got here? He's so clever. A true Renaissance man."

A scientist? I choked on a laugh, then coughed to disguise it, happy I was lying facedown so Kiki couldn't see my expression. "He truly is."

"I was so inspired by his story," she continued, "that I've decided to go back to school and get my degree in physical education."

"That's wonderful, Kiki. Good for you."

"Thank you." She patted my shoulder.

"Wish me luck."

"I do," I said, relaxing again. "Good luck."

Then she walked silently out of the room.

Ten minutes later, I had gained back enough of my strength to slide off the table, pulling the sheet with me. After a leisurely shower, I dressed, then walked down the hall to the library to shelve the book of poetry I'd found in the wine cellar yesterday.

I opened the library door and saw Nathan and Merrilee talking quietly. They immediately hushed up as I walked in.

The old, suspicious Brooklyn might have felt a little paranoid. But the newly refreshed Brooklyn simply chalked it up to their personal business and not my problem.

"Good morning," I said cheerfully. "I was just returning another book found in a strange place." I briefly explained how I'd come across the book in the wine cellar.

Merrilee stuttered a good morning, then dashed out of the room.

I watched her go, then glanced at Nathan. "Was it something I said?"

"No," he said, scowling. "It's something I said."

His frown was so forbidding that I didn't even bother to ask. He turned and stared at his computer screen, and I ignored him, refusing to relinquish my good mood.

Instead I turned to work, always the best distraction for me. Laying a white cloth out on the reading table, I placed the poetry book I'd found yesterday in the middle of the cloth and stared at it for a minute.

It had been a pretty little thing once upon a time, providing companionship and inspiration to some poetry lover who had probably carried it in his jacket pocket when he went on walks through the woods.

At least that's what my imagination conjured up. I liked to picture it as a beloved book whose owner had taken good care of it always. Sadly, the owner had died and the book had fallen on hard times.

Now I examined the cover and, except for the heavy dust and grime and some age spots where the leather had faded, it appeared to be in good condition. I dusted and cleaned it thoroughly with another soft cloth. Then I went through the book page by page, using a thin, stiff brush to swipe away the bits of dirt and film that had collected over the years due to neglect and poor storage conditions.

The paper itself was in decent shape except for the ubiquitous foxing that occurred in old books. The small brown spots of mildew or dirt were difficult to avoid and hard to get rid of once they had appeared.

In my workshop at home, I had several methods of lightening spots like these. But I hadn't brought any of my bleaching supplies with me, so the spots would have to stay for now.

After placing the poetry book on Nathan's growing pile of books to catalog, I went back to my desk and pulled some pretty endpapers from my pack of supplies. I used them to wrap the book box I'd made for Grace, then took colored strands of raffia and made a rustic bow.

I noticed the piles of vintage noir paperbacks were still on my desk. They'd been stacked to the side, out of the way, to make more room for my computer and tools. But now I wondered again what the best thing to do with them might be. They would find a loving home at the Covington Library, if only Grace would allow me to take them. They could be displayed under protective glass to halt their aging process somewhat. Otherwise, if they were stuck on a shelf here, even if wrapped in archival plastic, I was concerned that they might eventually perish.

Absently I picked up the book on top of the stack. Agatha Christie's *And Then There Were None.* Sudden shivers tickled my spine as I recalled that the story revolved around a number of strangers who were invited to a party at an isolated mansion. The first murder victim in Christie's classic tale died of cyanide poisoning.

I set the book down quickly and rubbed my arms to calm the chills.

I promised myself I would deal with the paperbacks later and went to find Suzie and Vinnie. I tracked them down in the small dining room off the kitchen. Vinnie was drinking a cup of tea while Suzie was just starting to feed Lily a half bottle of formula.

"Hi, girls," I said. "How's our baby?"

"She is a darling ray of sunshine this morning," Vinnie said proudly, as she tucked a clean dish towel under Lily's chin.

Suzie grinned at me. "How you doin', kiddo?"

"I'm kind of a little ray of sunshine myself," I said, determined to keep the conversation light. "I feel good. Slept well, had a massage, wrapped a present for the birthday girl. Then I came looking for you guys and here you are."

"So, what's up?"

I helped myself to a cup of coffee from the sideboard and sat down next to Suzie. "I wanted to ask you about something I read in Grace's book."

"Oh, dang. I haven't even started reading

it," Suzie admitted guiltily.

"Well, you've had your hands full," I said.

"True," she said, smiling down at Lily. Then she looked up at me. "So what about it?"

"I'm just curious. Did Grace ever talk about having a corporate thief in her company?"

Suzie thought about it. "I've got a vague memory of that. It happened years ago when I was pretty young. I remember my mom and dad talking about it. They said Grace lost millions of dollars, but more importantly, she lost a video game to a competitor. I think that hurt her a lot more than the money."

"I'll bet."

"So you're enjoying Grace's book?" Vinnie said.

"I am," I said. "I didn't think it would be as good as it is, but it's fascinating. I'm just trying to figure out what's real and what's fiction."

"You should ask Grace," Suzie said. She pulled the bottle from Lily's mouth to check how much was left. "She loves talking about the book."

"I will. I guess she would love to hear that I'm enjoying it."

"Oh, you know she would." The baby

began to fuss and Suzie quickly plugged the bottle back into her mouth.

"She is a good little eater," Vinnie said fondly, then smiled brightly at Suzie. "She reminds me of our neighbor, Brooklyn."

Suzie laughed. "Another good eater."

"Hey, I like food."

"It is one of your finest qualities," Vinnie said.

"Thanks a lot," I said wryly, then gave a gentle tweak to Lily's cheek. "At least I'm in good company."

The rest of the day passed in a whirlwind. Everyone was excited about Grace's party and there was lots of speculation about the big surprise she planned to announce tonight. It felt as if a month had passed since she first mentioned her big announcement, but it had been only five days.

It was wild, really. Being at Grace's home was like being on another planet or something. Time seemed to move differently here. But now I was beginning to wonder what kind of announcement would be coming from Grace that night and what effect it would have on the gathered throng. She had already told us about the book she'd written. We knew why she had invited Stephen Fowler. So what was left? Suzie had been so worried that it would have something to do with her aunt changing her will. I was glad that that issue was off the table.

I really hoped that Grace's announcement would be a happy one. We could all use some upbeat news after the week we'd been through.

I dressed for the occasion in black palazzo pants and a short, shimmery silver jacket. Everyone else kicked their wardrobes up a notch, too. Both Peter and Harrison wore tuxedos, and Kiki glided in wearing a slinky red gown. It almost resembled an old movie set. Unfortunately, I couldn't forget that one of us was a murderer, and the old, suspicious Brooklyn peeked her head out for a quick look around at her fellow guests.

We had gathered for the birthday festivities in the elegant Gold Salon. The five members of Chef Tang's kitchen staff were dressed in tuxedos today in honor of Grace's special day. The bartender began popping champagne bottles and two waiters walked through the room with trays of flutes filled with the bubbly.

Harrison, Grace's always genial brother, shushed everyone so that he could make the first toast. He held up his glass and asked us all to do the same.

"To Grace," he said. "A beautiful eccentric, a freaking genius, a hell of a good tennis player, and the best sister a man ever had."

Everyone laughed and cheered, and Harrison finished by saying, "Happy birthday, sis. Here's wishing you many more years of health, wealth, and happiness."

"Aw," Grace said, as tears sprang to her eyes. "Thank you, Harry."

Even I got a little sniffly — big surprise. I dabbed at my eyes to keep the tears from actually falling and cursed the gene that had endowed me with such sympathetic tear ducts.

"Cheers!" Harrison shouted, and we all clinked glasses and drank to Grace's good health.

After a second round of champagne and several more toasts, Grace announced that Ruth had a new poem to read.

"I hear it's a doozy," Grace added.

I really liked Ruth a lot and seriously hoped she was everything she seemed to be. I didn't think Grace could take it if she found out her dearest friend was a killer. But what in the world had the woman been doing with that shovel the other day? Had she been digging up a dead bird? Or perhaps burying a cassava root?

I shooed suspicious Brooklyn away as we

all took our seats. Ruth stood alone in the center of the room, looking serious and dignified as she faced Grace. She cleared her throat, and began:

"There once was a lady from Tahoe,
Whose friends, when they saw her, cried,
  'Yaw-ho!'
She wrote a great book,
New York took a look,
And in lights her name is now all a-glow."

As groans and moans and laughter filled the room, Ruth smiled primly. She cleared her throat, then continued valiantly through four more silly, hilarious verses, each more groan-inducing than the one before. By the time she reached the final few lines, we were on our feet, hooting and cheering.

"Amazing how many words rhyme with Tahoe," Gabriel said. I turned to see him standing right next to my chair.

"*Chapeau* threw me," I admitted.

"What about *big toe?*"

I nodded. "That was a good one, too."

We smiled at each other. Finally I whispered, "I'll miss you."

He raised one eyebrow.

"When you leave for Antarctica." I chuckled as he did his best to ignore me. "Really?

Polar birds?"

His jaw moved back and forth as he continued to stare straight ahead. "I didn't want to hurt her."

I studied him for a long moment, then nodded. "That was good of you."

From the other side of the room, Kiki called out, "Aunt Grace, you have to do a reading from your manuscript!"

"Oh no," Grace demurred. "I already did. Nobody wants to hear more."

"Yes, we do," Suzie said loudly. "Read the sexy parts!"

Harrison laughed, and Nathan led the prompt "Read it, read it, read it, read it."

"Oh, all right. If you insist," she said modestly, then opened the drawer of the end table nearest her and pulled out her manuscript. "I just happen to have a copy at hand."

I smiled. "She's too much. Isn't she?"

"The best," Gabriel agreed.

Grace opened the manuscript to a page in the middle. "This scene happens after Greta and Paul have filed their papers of incorporation. They've gone back to the office and Paul opens a bottle of champagne."

I'd read that part already and knew how it ended, so I sat back in my chair and prepared to watch the reactions of some of the guests.

Grace cleared her throat and struck a dramatic pose. Then she began to read. " 'I never thought this day would come, Greta.' Paul handed her a delicate flute filled with bubbly golden liquid and said, 'Let's toast to the success of our new partnership.' "

Grace looked up at us and waved her hand in a circle to indicate she was skipping some words. "So they drink. And they drink some more. And they laugh and giggle and one thing leads to another, if you know what I mean. And I'll pick it up right here."

She flipped a few pages, then continued reading. " 'It's always been you, Greta. There's no one else. I want you. I've always wanted you. I'll want you until the day I die.' Greta stared at him in shock. She didn't dare give in to the happiness his words filled her with. 'Oh, Paul, I . . . we . . . it would be such a mistake. A glorious mistake, but still a mistake you would regret. Maybe not tonight, but someday. And if I ever had to see the look in your eyes that told me you had stopped loving me, I would die.' 'I could never regret wanting you, Greta. I could never stop loving you.' He kissed her then, and nothing in her life had ever felt so wonderful, so perfect, so *right,* before!"

Grace grinned at her guests, then took a sip of her own champagne. "This is getting good."

Several of us laughed as Grace turned the page and continued reading. "Then he swept her up in his arms. 'I want you, Greta. Tonight I'll have you.' He carried her into the bedroom and laid her on the —"

Without warning, a baseball flew across the room and smacked Grace in the side of the head.

Vinnie screamed.

Grace grunted, then slumped over the arm of the couch.

Someone gasped. It might have been me.

Ruth screeched, "No! Grace!"

Everyone dropped to the floor or scrambled away out of danger. Sybil had been sitting in the chair nearest Grace, but she was on her feet now, staring in horror at the unconscious woman.

"Damn you, Grace. Wake up!" Ruth sobbed as she tightened her grip on the woman who lay unconscious in her arms. Wild-eyed, Ruth looked from Suzie to the stunned faces of the guests. "Who did that? Who threw that ball?"

"Auntie Grace," Kiki cried. She ran toward Grace but Gabriel caught her around the waist.

"No," he said, his voice deadly serious. "Stay back. You could be hurt."

My gaze darted around the room as I tried frantically to spot the person who had thrown the ball. I had only seconds to figure out who was missing from the group before they could strike again. But with everyone either crouched on the floor or scurrying around the room, it was hard to nail everybody down.

The weapon was a baseball or something that looked like it. It had been thrown from the doorway that was now half closed, so I turned and headed that way.

Gabriel had come to the same conclusion. We reached the door at the same time. I grabbed the doorknob, but jumped back when I heard a woman out in the hall screaming. "Let me go!"

"Not bloody likely," a man said gruffly.

I nearly fainted. I knew that gruff voice.

Gabriel and I exchanged glances. We heard a scuffle; then the door was flung open. Derek Stone stood in the hall, wrestling with a squirming, angry Merrilee in his arms.

Chapter 15

Derek?

Gabriel grabbed me from behind as I started to slide, then pulled me close and whispered, "You're not really going to faint, are you?"

"Don't be silly," I insisted, though, okay, I was a little short of breath and for a second or two there, it had been a little iffy. And who could have blamed me? "I . . . I tripped on something."

"Nice try."

"Let me go." He steadied me and I took a quick step away from him. So maybe seeing Derek had been a shock. And maybe I'd felt a little light-headed, but I was fine now. Except for the fact that everything inside me was jumping up and down in exhilaration at the thrill of seeing him again. Naturally I was much too cool and controlled to let him know that. I sucked in a gulp of air, let it out, and prayed for composure. "Hello,

Derek. Fancy meeting you here."

"Hello, darling." His voice was tight because he was still struggling to contain Merrilee, who twisted and turned and whined and yelped, trying to escape his iron grasp.

Despite everything I'd imagined about him, despite my own emotional pendulum swings and psychotic-girlfriend moments over the past week, I couldn't do anything but soak in the loveliness of Derek. It was wonderful to see him again. He looked better than ever, if that was possible. Even though, on closer examination, I noticed that the man was kind of a mess. He needed a shave. His hair was spiky and unruly, as though he hadn't combed it in a while. He looked tired, too, and his shirt wasn't tucked in. Dear God, it wasn't even ironed.

He was the sweetest sight I'd ever seen.

Had he been in so much of a hurry to find me that he hadn't bothered to stop and freshen up, at least comb his hair and shave? Right at that moment, if I'd had the time to burst into tears I would have. Unfortunately, I was a little busy. And so was he. Crying would have to wait until the strange mystery of Merrilee was concluded.

"Bring her in here, would you?" I said to Derek, and shoved the door open all the way. "We need to have a little talk with her."

"Of course, darling," Derek said, and I could hear that familiar sardonic British lilt in his voice.

I ignored the warm shivers that tone brought to my skin and instead admired the way he easily lifted Merrilee off her feet and carried her into the room.

Yes, Derek was simply gorgeous and strong, a walking, talking advertisement for all that was Tall, Dark, and Dangerous. And I loved him. But that didn't mean I wasn't going to have a few words with him later about a certain Miss Thomasina Suck-wit and her unauthorized use of his cell phone. Not to mention the fact that he hadn't called me. Not once.

And while he was answering those questions, maybe he could also tell me what in the world he was doing here.

Later.

Grace was just lifting her head. Ruth still had a grip on her, but now she helped her rise and sit on the couch. Grace's eyes were crossed and foggy as she rubbed her temple. "What happened?"

"Merrilee tried to kill you!" Sybil shouted.

"I did not!" Merrilee snapped.

"Everyone saw you, Merrilee," Ruth said

quietly, though the pain in her voice rang out.

"Why did you do it, Merrilee?" I asked. "Why did you throw a baseball at Grace?"

"I didn't!"

"You did, and you almost killed her," Ruth pointed out, her own voice quavering. "Was that your intention? To kill this woman who gave you a home and a job and all the love in her heart?"

Merrilee slumped in Derek's grasp, that momentary show of spunk suddenly and completely gone. She swallowed. Stark fear showed on her face. "No."

"I'm afraid you can't deny it," Derek said. "I was right behind you in the hall. I saw you throw the ball."

Maybe I was still in shock from hearing Derek's voice. But I just couldn't work it out in my head why Grace's sweet, loyal housekeeper had tried to hurt her.

"It's just a bump on the head," Grace said, her voice shaky. "Let me stand up. It's my party and I . . . urrghh."

She collapsed onto the couch cushion and Ruth wrapped both arms around her waist. "You're not going anywhere."

Grace laid her head on Ruth's shoulder. "But Merrilee needs me."

"She needs you? Grace, she just threw a

baseball at your head!" Ruth was furious and glared at Merrilee. "What were you thinking? Explain yourself."

Merrilee started to cry. "I didn't mean to hit Grace. I'm so stupid. It's all my fault if she dies."

Derek frowned at me and I almost smiled. Naturally, he had quickly picked up on the incongruity of the situation. Merrilee didn't sound like a killer. She sounded like a scared young girl.

I said, "What do you mean, Merrilee?"

She wrung her hands in misery. "I know I'm as sharp as a marble, but I thought I could at least throw a ball! I can't even do *that* right. What's wrong with me?"

"Nothing's wrong with you, Merrilee," Nathan argued, his tone dutiful. He shoved Peter out of the way and stormed across the room, where he glared at Derek until he surrendered Merrilee willingly and took a few steps back.

Nathan moved in and grabbed her in a tight hug. "You can throw a ball straight, honey. You just need practice."

Derek's frown grew deeper as more confusion set in. He wasn't the only one. I'd lost the thread of this conversation as soon as Nathan had sprung into action.

"Nathan," I said. "What are you talking about?"

"No harm was done," Nathan insisted, then whipped around to address everyone in the room. "Look, Grace is fine. A little woozy, but fine. So stop picking on Merrilee, all of you."

"Picking on her!" Sybil shouted in astonishment. "She tried to kill Grace!"

But Nathan ignored her as he stared into Merrilee's eyes. "If you want to learn to throw straight, I'll teach you how. I'll do anything for you. I love you and I want to marry you."

Merrilee sputtered, "B-but —"

He put one finger over her lips, shushing her. "Please just say yes and make me the happiest man in the world."

Wow. I hadn't seen that coming. But looking at Nathan and seeing the flush of happiness on Merrilee's cheeks, I could only wonder how I'd missed it. Some detective I was.

"You can't marry her!" Sybil yelled, and stomped her foot on the thick carpet. "She should be dragged off to jail for attempted murder. In fact, she probably killed Bella. She's dangerous. Am I the only one who can see that?"

If anyone else had said that, I might've

gone along with them. Not for long, of course, since Merrilee clearly wasn't a murderer. But this was Sybil talking. Why was she so up in arms? She didn't give a rat's ass about Grace. She probably would've popped open more champagne to celebrate if Grace had been hurt any worse than she was. Actually, that was something Madge would do. Sybil would simply sit and read a magazine.

Or would she? I spent an extra moment or two watching the woman and her body language. And wondering.

Then I gazed over at Merrilee. I knew she had some reasoning difficulties, so I asked the question all over again. "Merrilee, can you tell us why you threw the ball at Grace?"

"I didn't," she said, repeating herself.

"But . . ."

Merrilee held up one shaky finger and pointed it at Madge. "I threw it at her."

Madge gasped.

"Whoa," Gabriel muttered.

"Me? I didn't do anything!"

Harrison stepped forward. "Madge, what did you do?"

"Shut up, Harry!" Her facial muscles were so taut, I was worried that they'd spring loose like the strings on a violin. "I didn't do a damn thing. She's insane."

Merrilee shook her head back and forth. "Not her. *Her.*"

Madge stepped aside, then turned and stared at Sybil. "You."

"Right," Merrilee said, still pointing. "Her."

Sybil's face turned white. "What do you mean, me? You were going to kill me? How dare you!"

"I wasn't trying to kill you." Merrilee gulped, nervous now, but not about to stop talking until she'd told us all what had happened. "I just wanted to hit you with the ball."

Nathan's arm came around Merrilee's shoulder and she seemed to stand taller, straighter. She was staring at Sybil and still pointing. "I saw you. I know what you were doing."

Sybil glanced around and laughed weakly. "What in the world is she blathering about? Can somebody please call the police? She should be in jail, or, better yet, in an insane asylum."

I took another step forward. "Should she, Sybil? Really? What did she see you doing that caused her to throw a baseball at you?"

"So you're interrogating me now?" She laughed harshly as she straightened her jacket. "What a joke. I'm leaving."

"But, Sybil," Peter said, "the police won't —"

"Oh, screw the police. I'm not going to sit around waiting for permission from them."

"You're not going anywhere," I said. "Tell me, what were you doing in my room last night?"

She flinched, but quickly covered it with a shake of her head. "Don't be ridiculous."

But I knew it was her. That gasp I'd heard when Leroy jumped down from the ceiling panel was Sybil's, reacting in shock and horror to Leroy pouncing on her. She hated cats.

"What were you doing there, Sybil? Were you going to poison me, too?"

"Shut up," she muttered.

"That's it? That's all you have to say?"

But Merrilee wasn't paying attention to the confrontation between me and Sybil. She just kept pointing at the woman. "She has a gun. She has a gun and she was going to shoot my mother."

Her *mother?*

Grace?

Now my mind was reeling from one thought to the next like a drunk trying to wind his way home down Lombard Street.

My gaze darted back to Sybil, who shook her head rapidly and raised her hands in the air. "I don't have a gun. She's insane, I tell you!"

I turned again to Merrilee. "Where did you see a gun, Merrilee?"

Merrilee hesitated, so Grace reached out and clutched her hand in support. "Go on, Merri. Tell us what you saw."

"She . . . she has it in her purse. I saw her take it out and hide it in her lap. But then she started to point it at my mom, so I ran next door to the game room and found something to throw at her. To stop her. I found the baseball from the pitch-ball game and I threw it."

"That was very resourceful of you," I said, casting a long look at Derek to see if he was keeping up. Had he seen Merrilee running back and forth from room to room? I knew he'd witnessed her throwing the ball, but could he corroborate her entire story?

But for the first time since I've known him, Derek was no help. Instead he shrugged as if to say, *I just got here and have no idea what's going on.*

Then Merrilee spoke again. "But I missed."

"It's okay," Nathan soothed. "You tried. It's okay."

As Merrilee was telling her story, I watched Gabriel moving subtly through the crowd until he came to a stop behind Sybil.

"This is absurd," Sybil said in a huff, and sat back down in the same chair she'd been using before. She noticed Gabriel then, and after sparing him a look of annoyance, she calmly raised her hands in the air again. "Look, Ma, no gun."

Merrilee frowned. "But she had one."

"Check my purse," the woman said, folding her arms across her chest. "Go ahead. See for yourself who's lying."

Gabriel picked up the extremely expensive designer purse that Sybil had placed on the floor by her chair. He opened it and searched around, then looked over at Derek and shook his head. No gun.

I sighed in disappointment. Sybil didn't have a gun. So what, exactly, had Merrilee seen?

"I told you," Sybil said, then added with a sneer, "I can't believe you took her word against mine." She waved her hand dismissively in Merrilee's direction. "Anyone can see that she's an imbecile."

Ruth gasped. With a loud harrumph, she stood up, walked over to Sybil, and slapped her face so hard, her hand recoiled painfully. "I am not a violent person, but I'm sick to death of people like you calling Merrilee names like that."

Sybil rubbed her cheek but didn't rise to the bait. "You bitch. Just a second ago you were shouting at her yourself."

"That's different," Ruth said with an apologetic glance at Merrilee. "We're family. And I was . . . upset." She glared at Sybil. "But *you* will apologize to her right now, or I'll make you sorry you ever said that word."

"Apologize?" Sybil said, incredulous. "Are you nuts?"

"Sybil, please," Peter said, his voice calm and reasonable.

Sybil glared at her husband. "You shut up. I've had it with you. You're a weak man, Peter. You make me sick, the way you leave yourself susceptible to every woman who walks by you."

"What? I've never cheated on you in my life."

"Oh, really?" she said, her voice taunting. "Exactly who were *Paul* and *Greta,* anyway? I read that stupid manuscript. I know what you were doing behind my back."

His forehead furrowed in disbelief. "It's fiction!"

"Not that part," she muttered.

He shook his head. "But . . . but that was twenty-five years ago. I barely knew you."

"You cheated on me!"

He looked both shocked and exhausted. "You and I weren't even dating yet. You had just joined the company."

"Oh. Well, fine," she sputtered. "You have an answer for everything. But what about last night, when you were flirting with that one?"

I looked around to see who she was talking about, then realized she was pointing at me. "Are you insane?"

"No, I'm not. But you're pathetic. Any woman who tries to steal a married man should be shot."

Despite knowing the woman was off her rocker, I was taken aback. "I don't want your husband. And you have a real problem if you think your husband was interested in me. He's friendly, that's all." I didn't add that Peter talked to other women in order to avoid talking to Sybil. That would be a low blow.

Disgusted now, she stood and faced her husband. "I'm sick of all the women, Peter. I won't take it anymore. I've filed for divorce and my papers make it clear that you're to blame for ruining my life. I intend to take you for every cent you've ever made."

Stephen Fowler cleared his throat. "Technically, California's no-fault policy won't get you a —"

"Oh, shut up!" Sybil shouted, then scowled at her husband. "It doesn't matter. I've got my own money now. I don't need yours."

Peter frowned. "What money?"

She was speechless for a split second, then finally spat out the words, "You're an idiot."

"Maybe I am," he said, watching her quietly. "Tell me what money you're talking about. Is it the company account? Are you the one who stole the money?"

"I didn't steal it," she claimed angrily. "It's mine as much as anyone else's."

"You stole it," he persisted. "Why? What were you planning to do with it?"

"If you can't figure that out, you're a bigger moron than I thought." She rolled her eyes. "God, what am I doing here?"

Spinning around, she started for the door, but Gabriel blocked her way. "You're not going anywhere. Sit down."

"No," she said evenly. "If you're going to take the word of a half-wit housekeeper, I'm leaving."

"No, you're not." He grabbed her arm and started to drag her back to her chair, but she yanked her arm away. "Don't touch me again." Then she whirled around, shaking with fury. "I've had it with all you people."

"Sit down, Sybil," Peter said with more

force than I'd heard him use all week.

"Fine," she said, and flounced down into the chair.

"Sybil, please," Grace pleaded. "Can't we talk about this?"

"Talk?" Sybil glared at Grace. "To you? You're the worst of them all."

"We can work this out," Grace continued. "If you need money . . ."

"Oh, for God's sake. Do you think I'd take a damn thing from you?" She slipped her hand down beside the chair cushion and whipped out a small handgun. Standing, she pointed the gun at Grace. "Now will you shut up?"

Ruth screamed.

"Sybil, no!" Peter yelled.

Suzie shouted, "Aunt Grace!"

Nathan grabbed Merrilee and pushed her out of danger, then huddled nearby, wide-eyed and watchful.

I couldn't breathe. Sybil's gun was aimed at Grace, but she'd just mentioned shooting me.

Suddenly she spun around and pointed the gun at each person in the room before turning back around to Grace.

Everything seemed to move in slow motion, except this wasn't a film. It was real. Merrilee had been right about Sybil. Now it looked as if Sybil might actually kill Grace in front of us all. I had to stop her.

I took one step forward and Derek grabbed me around the waist, forcing me back. "Don't even think about it."

"Let me go. We've got to help —"

Again Sybil swung the gun around in a wide arc, alternately aiming it at each of us. "Stay back, all of you."

"God." Peter groaned. "Don't do this, Sybil."

"Who's going to stop me?" She laughed. "You? That would take balls and you don't have any."

Ouch. I felt bad for Peter, but worse for Grace. I needed to do something to get that gun away from Sybil.

"I know you killed Bella," I said.

Derek's arm tightened around my waist and he whispered, "Don't do this."

"Why, Sybil?" Grace asked.

"I hate you," Sybil said. "I've always hated you. You and Peter were the perfect little partners, weren't you? Always in your own little world, with no room for anyone else. It didn't matter what we were doing. If you called, Peter dropped everything and ran off to be with you."

"It was just business," Grace whispered.

"Oh, really?" Sybil said, her voice dripping with scorn. "I know what kind of *business* you had in mind. I read that vile manuscript of yours. And I want you dead more than I want to take my next breath."

"Sybil, don't," Peter said.

"Oh, stop talking, Peter," she said wearily, then turned back to Grace. "I've tried to kill you three times now. But you're like that damn cat of yours." Her voice was deadly calm as her finger pushed against the trigger. "But that doesn't matter anymore because this time I won't miss."

"You pushed me down the stairs," Kiki snapped.

Sybil glanced at her sideways, then shrugged. "I was trying to get to Grace and you got in my way."

Blinking at the woman's callousness, Kiki said, "I hope you go straight to hell."

Go Kiki, I thought, admiring her spunk.

"I'll see all of you there first," Sybil said silkily.

Kiki had managed to distract Sybil for a few seconds, anyway. We would all have to keep doing that until someone could get that gun from her.

"How did you get Ruth to take the poisoned tea to Grace?" I asked, ignoring Derek's tug in favor of keeping Sybil talking. The more the woman talked, the less

390

chance any of us had of being shot. That was my theory, anyway.

Sybil sneered at me, but was willing to share her secret. "There's only one person who drinks that vile crap in this house. They keep a pitcher of it behind the bar. I just filled a glass, added a dollop of weed killer, and set it on top of the bar. It's not my fault that the old crow grabbed it." She waved her hand in Ruth's direction.

Ruth's face went pale. "Oh, my God. Oh, my God." She clutched Grace's hand. "I'm so sorry. It's all my fault that Bella's dead."

"No, it's not, Ruth," I insisted. "It's all Sybil's fault. She used you to get to Grace, but Bella got in the way."

Sybil sent me a withering look. "Oh, so high and mighty. Whatever."

I was sick of that word *whatever*. It was so dismissive. But I refused to be stopped from seeking answers. "You sent me the dead bird and the tarot card."

She gazed at me, her face now devoid of expression. "I'd forgotten about that. The tarot card was for spite, because you think you know so much."

I tried not to react. "What about the bird?"

"That bird was a good find," she said, nodding as she reminisced. "I saw Ruth burying something bloody in the snow, and when she went back to her house, I dug it up."

"You dug up that poor bird?" Ruth asked, shaking her head. "What's wrong with you?"

Sybil ignored her in favor of me. "I thought it would warn you off, but you're quite the stubborn wench. Aren't you?"

"Yeah, I am."

"Won't do you any good. And I'm through talking." She twisted around and pointed the gun at Grace again. "Bye, bitch."

"No!" Suzie shouted. "Gabriel, get the gun!"

Sybil swung and aimed the gun at Gabriel. "I don't think so."

Gabriel raised both hands slowly and stepped back.

But Suzie had caught Sybil's attention and now she pointed the gun right at her.

I heard Vinnie's soft shriek behind me.

Suzie clutched Lily tighter in her arms as Sybil considered her for a moment. She took a few steps closer. "Hand over the baby."

Suzie swallowed, then clenched her jaw. "Lady, you won't get this baby out of my arms in a million years."

"Just give me the kid."

"No."

"Hello? Gun?" Sybil waved the gun at her,

but Suzie didn't budge, so she added, "I'm not going to hurt her. I just need her as a shield until I get far enough away from here."

An unearthly roar arose from behind me. I turned and watched in horror as Vinnie charged forward like a tiny Amazon on steroids.

"Vinnie, no!" Derek shouted, and dashed after her.

Sybil spun around to see who was coming and Vinnie slammed into her like a freight train. They both went flying several feet backward while the gun was thrown off in another direction. Derek grabbed it.

The two women landed on the floor and Vinnie continued shouting and swearing in three different languages as she pummeled Sybil anywhere she could land a punch.

Suzie still clutched the baby, but looked ready to dive into the pile to protect Vinnie. After a quick moment of indecision, she stood and shouted to her cousin, "Kiki, the baby."

Kiki ran over. Suzie thrust Lily into Kiki's protective arms, then rushed into the fight. Kiki quickly moved back and out of range of any danger.

"Derek, help them," I said, moving in as close as I could get, itching to stop the melee, but powerless to do anything but watch.

Suzie tried to pull Vinnie off Sybil, but Vinnie was in a zone all her own. Suzie finally knelt down and grabbed hold of Sybil's arms to block the slaps and punches she was landing on Vinnie.

"Hold this." Derek thrust the gun at me. "And be careful, damn it." He maneuvered his way into the scuffle and patted Vinnie's shoulder, then pulled her back and off Sybil. "I think you've done her in, champ. Nice tackle."

Gabriel rushed in and yanked a still-swinging Sybil off the floor.

A second later, Ruth jumped up and shoved her elbow into Sybil's stomach.

That had to hurt.

Suzie wrapped both arms around Vinnie in an emotional hug, then led her over to Kiki, who stood against the wall, clutching the baby. They moved to a side sofa and all three women collapsed together on the cushions.

"You were awesome," Suzie said, then reached over to adjust Lily's blanket, mainly to assure herself that the baby was fine. Vinnie rested her head on Suzie's shoulder.

Meanwhile, Sybil wriggled in Gabriel's grip, but he looked unfazed. Glancing around, he asked, "Anyone got some duct tape?"

"I have some in the library," I said weakly. I handed the gun to Derek, then leaned against him, feeling exhausted. For once I'd done nothing but watch while everyone else tangled with a vicious killer, but I was still worn out.

"I'll get it," Nathan said, and ran from the room.

"Oh, my God," Grace whispered. She looked around. "Is everyone safe?"

"Are you?" Ruth asked, and rushed back to her side. Grace pulled her into a tight hug. A moment later, Grace gazed up at Merrilee and reached for her. Merrilee let out a little sob, took hold of her hand, and sat on the other side of her.

"You people make me sick," Sybil said through clenched teeth.

"Shut it," Gabriel said, jerking her enough to startle her into silence.

"Got it," Nathan called from the doorway, waving the duct tape. He ran over and handed it to Gabriel.

Within seconds, Sybil's wrists were sealed together behind her back. Defiant still, she shot hateful stares at anyone who glanced her way.

Ruth ignored Sybil and put her arm

around Grace. "How's that hard head of yours feeling?"

Grace glanced at Merrilee and smiled. "It's only a little sore. In fact, I can barely feel any pain anymore."

Merrilee's eyes were still wet with tears as she laid her head on Grace's shoulder and closed her eyes.

"I'm so proud of you for protecting me," Grace said fiercely, and squeezed Merrilee tight. Then she looked at Ruth and took her hand in her firm grip. "And you. You were a warrior princess. Thank you. All of you. You all saved my life."

The emotional strength behind those words hit Ruth and she burst into tears. Grace pulled her closer. After a moment Ruth used her blouse cuff to wipe the moisture from her eyes. Then she glanced around the room. She seemed to be searching for the right words and finally blurted, "Grace and I have been lovers for five years."

"Well, duh," Kiki said.

Madge gasped. "Grace! That's disgusting."

Suzie threw her aunt a world-weary look. "Seriously, Madge? You're going there? Now?"

"Shut the hell up, Mom," Kiki said, clearly

appalled by her mother. Then she turned back to Ruth and Grace. "That's so cool, you guys."

Suzie grinned and gave her cousin a thumbs-up.

"But, Aunt Grace, why did Merrilee call you her mother?" Kiki asked.

Grace flinched in shock. Her eyes grew big and she stared at Merrilee. "Did you call me that?"

Merrilee nodded and bit her bottom lip, but didn't say anything.

Grace was befuddled now. "Oh, my. Everything was happening so fast, I — I didn't realize." She turned to Ruth and shook her head. "Help me?"

Ruth's forehead furrowed in apprehension. "Are you sure?"

Grace's head bobbed as she nodded over and over. "Please."

"Okay, okay." She patted Grace's knee, then took a deep breath as she scanned the faces of everyone there. "It's just that, well, it's simple. Grace is Merrilee's mother."

Utter silence filled the room for a full thirty seconds. Derek's arms gave me a squeeze and I was really glad he was there.

"Wow, lots of secrets coming out," Harrison said finally. "And that's a real nice one." He walked over to the couch and bent down to give Merrilee a light kiss on the cheek. "Welcome to the family, sweetheart."

"Thank you," Merrilee whispered, "Uncle Harrison."

But Ruth wasn't finished yet, apparently. She took another deep breath and held it in her lungs as though she was considering her next words. Then she said in a rush, "And, Peter Brinker, you are Merrilee's father."

I watched Peter's face lose its color in an instant as he gaped at the three women on the couch. "I'm . . . what?"

"No!" Sybil screamed, and launched herself headfirst into Grace and Ruth.

"Stop it!" Grace cried, and tried to bat Sybil away, but the woman was unstoppable despite having her wrists bound behind her. She thrust her shoulders as hard as she could and managed to knock Ruth twice in the head before Gabriel yanked her back into her chair.

"Jeez, woman," Gabriel muttered, clutching the squirming woman's arm to hold her down.

Derek moved in. They got Sybil to stand up and turn around so Gabriel could rip the old duct tape off her bound wrists. Then Derek moved out of the way and Gabriel pushed her back into the chair. Both men wrestled to keep her arms steady against the arms of the chair. It wasn't easy; Sybil was a fighter. But finally Gabriel was able to wrap the duct tape around each of her wrists and the arm of the chair, binding her to the piece of furniture. She looked like a monster, seething with rage as she tried but failed to escape.

Gabriel looked at Grace and Ruth and shook his head. "Sorry. I really thought I'd subdued her. Guess not."

Ruth and Grace were both breathing heavily, gulping in air as Sybil continued to spit epithets at Grace and Merrilee. Then she turned on Peter. "You rotten son of a jackal. I should've killed you, too."

"God, Sybil," Peter said, shaking his head. "What's come over you?"

"I told you," she said, spitting the words out. "I read that stinking book she wrote." She struggled and writhed in the chair. "It made me sick, but I read every page. I knew you were in love with her. Have you been lovers all this time? You have, haven't you? You bastard! How could you sleep with her? She's a lesbian!"

Suzie hissed out a breath and clenched her fists, but said nothing.

"She wasn't when I knew her," Peter muttered in his own defense.

Sybil laughed wildly. "And now you're the

father of that idiot child of hers? Oh, that's rich."

Ruth bounded off the couch. Gabriel stopped her just in time, but she still managed to jab her finger at Sybil. "I told you not to call her names, you vile cow."

Sybil bared her teeth and looked ready to growl, but she caught a glimpse of Gabriel looming above her and said nothing.

Now that Sybil was securely constrained, Nathan approached Grace. "Since you're Merrilee's mother, I would like to ask you for the hand of your daughter in marriage."

Ruth sighed. Love was in the air. Well, love and murder, along with assault and attempted kidnapping and a few other crimes I'd already forgotten about.

"Looks as though I've missed quite the house party," Derek murmured in my ear.

His breath was warm and soft and nearly distracted me from the scene that was playing out before us.

"My mom doesn't think I should marry you," Merrilee said, cutting Grace off before she could answer Nathan.

"I didn't say that," Grace replied.

"Then what did you say?" Nathan lifted his chin as he faced Grace and said, "I'm in love with your daughter and she loves me, too."

"Is that true, Merri?" Grace asked the question quietly, her gaze fixed on her daughter.

"Yes," she said, then turned to face Nathan. "I do love you." Merrilee hesitated, then said, "It's just that when it comes to brains, I'm a few sandwiches short of a picnic."

Ruth bit back a rueful smile. "That's not true, Merrilee. You're a lovely, smart woman."

"But Nathan is a brilliant archivist," she insisted. "He'll get tired of me."

"Impossible," Nathan said, but his smile faltered at her adamant tone. "Grace, help me."

Grace reached for Merrilee's hand and kissed it, then touched it to her cheek. "You are a beautiful woman with a lovely heart, Merrilee. Any man would be lucky to have you."

"That's right," Nathan said.

"Do you really love him?" Grace asked her quietly.

She nodded. "Yes, Mom."

"Then marry him, baby. Don't give up this chance for happiness. Those chances don't come around that often."

Merrilee looked up at Nathan and began to smile. "Okay. If you're sure, then, yes, I'll

401

marry you, Nathan."

"Thank you," Nathan whispered, then reached his hand out. Merrilee took it and stood. And Nathan kissed her with all the love he had in his heart.

"Aw, sweet," Ruth whispered.

"They make a beautiful couple, don't they?" Grace murmured, dabbing at her tear-filled eyes.

I sniffled and then blinked to clear my bleary vision. Without a word, Derek passed his handkerchief to me and I blew my nose.

"You people are as stupid as she is," Sybil mocked.

"That's it," Gabriel said, and tore off a six-inch length of duct tape. He pressed it over Sybil's mouth and said, "You need to learn to quit while you're ahead, lady."

It looked like she was trying to shriek but no sound came out. Only blessed silence.

"I think this calls for some more champagne," Marko said, lifting the magnum up from the bar. "Who's with me?"

Grim-faced, Peter held his glass out immediately.

"You're gonna need it." Marko giggled as he filled Peter's glass to the brim. Then he moved on to the next glass.

Something occurred to me and I turned to Grace. "Does this mean that the story in your book was real? There really was a baby."

Grace glanced quickly at Peter, then said, "Yes, there really was."

"But you didn't give her up for adoption."

"I couldn't." She gazed up at Merrilee and took hold of her hand. "I was going to — I really was. But the moment I held you in my arms, I knew I couldn't give you away to strangers. You were so beautiful, so tiny. You needed me too much."

"But you never said a word," Peter said. "No one at work ever knew. Why?"

"I'm sorry." Grace stared at her hands. "I just couldn't tell anyone about her. I couldn't take the chance that someone might see her."

"Not even me." Regret colored Peter's voice, and Sybil's half-muted mutterings from behind a layer of duct tape was the only other sound in the room.

Grace smiled at her business partner. "We had a one-night stand, Peter. By the time Merrilee was born, you and Sybil were engaged to be married. I couldn't ruin that for you. And until the very end, I had honestly planned to give my baby up for adoption."

"But why couldn't you tell anyone?" Kiki asked.

"Times were different back then," Grace said. "We had advertisers that would have dropped us in a heartbeat if they knew I was an unwed mother. We had government contracts that would have been canceled if word got out. It's just the way things were in those days."

"You had government contracts back then, Aunt Grace?" Suzie asked.

"Yes. They were interested in our war game strategies," she explained absently.

"So what did you do about the baby, Auntie?" Kiki asked.

Sybil started kicking her heels against the chair, objecting to all of this in the only way left to her. I scowled at her and Gabriel held up the roll of duct tape, one eyebrow lifted as if to ask, *Want some more of this?*

She quieted down, but her eyes showed how livid she was.

Grace gazed at her nieces. "I had a wonderful housekeeper who took care of Merrilee in her home."

"Mrs. Bancroft," Merrilee said fondly.

"Yes," Grace said, patting her daughter's hand. "I stopped by the Bancrofts' home almost every night and rocked Merrilee to sleep. And when she started school, I sent her to the best boarding school in the country."

"I wasn't very good in school," Merrilee admitted. "But I was really good at making the beds in my dorm room and seeing that all my friends ate really well. I like taking care of people."

"You're still good at that," I said.

"I know. So when I graduated from high school, Mom wanted me to continue with school, but I knew I would be a lost cause in college. I convinced her that I could run her home smoothly and efficiently and she put me to the test."

"And you passed with flying colors," Grace said proudly. "You are perfect at your job."

"Mrs. Bancroft taught me everything she knew."

Grace smiled her love.

"And I love living here with you so much. And I love Ruth and Shelly and Ray and Chef Tang." Merrilee beamed, but her smile disappeared abruptly and she turned to Nathan. "Oh, no. I didn't ask. Would you be willing to move in here and live with my family?"

He didn't hesitate. "Absolutely, yes."

They kissed again and Grace clapped her hands with joy. Ruth chuckled. "Looks like we'll have more babies in the old house one day soon!"

I was just happy that someone would be watching out for Grace's books from now on.

"I suppose we should call the police," Grace said, casting a glance at Sybil, who scowled back with her eyes.

"Wait," I said. "Now we know that the part about the baby was real. But, Grace, was there really ever a corporate thief stealing your ideas?"

Grace opened her mouth to answer, but Nathan stepped forward and jutted his hand out to stop her. "Oh yes," he assured me. "There really was a corporate thief."

"How would you know?" Marko said.

Nathan's steely gaze took in Marko, then circled to Peter, and finally zeroed in on Grace. "I know, because the thief was my father."

I gaped at him. Seriously, this was the best house party ever. But now what was going on?

"Who the hell are you?" Peter said, studying Nathan more closely.

Grace drew in a sharp breath. "I don't understand," she said, staring at Nathan. "What are you saying? The thief was never found, Nathan."

"Because he was hiding in plain sight all along," Nathan said, then spun around and fixed his gaze on Marko. "Isn't that right, *Dad?*"

CHAPTER 16

Marko stared dumbfounded at Nathan. He studied the younger man for a long moment; then his eyes narrowed and he said, "Marky?"

"Marky. Right. Nice try, *Dad*." Nathan stared at the older man with naked contempt. "My name is Nathan. When Mom walked out on you, she ran as far away from you as she could get. Then she changed our names. She didn't want to have anything to do with you, your name, or your sleazy lifestyle choices."

Nathan used air quotes for those last two words.

How odd. Now that Nathan had revealed himself to be Marko's son, I could see the resemblance as clear as day. Why hadn't I seen it before? Nathan was a taller, sturdier, blonder, healthier, younger version of Marko.

Grace was clearly stunned by the revelation. She stared back and forth at the two men as though she were attending a tennis tournament.

Finally, after a quick glimpse at Peter, who looked equally dumbfounded, Grace settled her gaze on Marko. "Marko? Why?"

"Why what?" Marko asked, sounding like the twelve-year-old jerky kid again.

Grace's eyes were damp, but she sniffed proudly and pounded her fist against the sofa arm. "I want to know why you did it. How could you? How could you steal from us? We gave you everything. Money. Fame. An ownership interest in the company. For God's sake, the company was practically your home. Even before your wife left you, we had become your family."

Marko blinked and looked around nervously. Derek and Gabriel and even Peter had shifted their stances, leaving him no way out. But it didn't look like Marko was ready to go anywhere. He continued to say nothing, just swallowed apprehensively as he seemed to consider his shrinking options.

"Dad appears to be tongue-tied," Nathan said easily, "so let me answer that for him. He did it because it was the easy way to get money. He's a cheap, lazy bastard who'd rather do anything than work for a living."

Nathan paced in a leisurely circle around

his father as he spoke. "Back in the good old days Marko was never home. In fact, I wasn't sure I'd recognize him, since I barely remember him being around. And when we moved, Mom tore up all her photos of him. Anyway, back then he worked all the time, around the clock, creating new video and arcade games for the company. And why did he do it? Because he was addicted to money. He was a greedy bastard. He made a ton of money but it was never enough."

Marko said nothing to defend himself. He just kept staring at Nathan with a half smile on his face, almost as if he were *proud* of him. Bizarre.

Nathan stopped and glared at his father. "It was never enough. Was it, Marko? You could never have enough to satisfy your own greed. You always wanted more. And what did you do with all that money, Marko? Did you buy your family a nice home? Did you take your wife out to dinner once in a while? Buy her pretty clothes to wear? What about your six-year-old son? Did you buy him a toy now and then? Take him to see a movie?"

Nathan had worked himself up until his face was contorted with anger. He seemed to realize it and took a moment to straighten his posture and calm himself. He glanced briefly at Merrilee and her soft smile seemed to instill in him a sort of peace. His shoulders relaxed; the lines around his mouth and eyes smoothed. He began to stroll back and forth again, one hand in his pocket as though he didn't have a care in the world.

Just when I thought he wasn't going to say another word, Nathan whirled around and shouted at Marko, "No!"

I jolted. Nathan was a regular Perry Mason with Marko on the witness stand, about to go down in flames.

"He hoarded the money. We saw none of it." Nathan continued aiming an accusing finger at his father. "You never gave us a single dime more than what it took to feed us scraps. You socked your ill-gotten fortune away in some offshore bank. You were a miser, a skinflint, a miserable jerk who made his money by stealing other people's ideas and selling them to the competition. You disgust me."

Silence reigned.

Wow. Impressive. Nathan had been living in this house with this man all week and I hadn't had an inkling of his feelings or an inkling of the kind of man Marko really was.

This might've explained Nathan's bad mood last night, but I had a sneaking feeling that the grumpiness had more to do with Merrilee than with him having to deal with his father.

But it must have been difficult all week. Had he known how he was going to reveal the truth? Or had he been coasting, waiting for the exact right moment? How could he have socialized all week with the man who had ruined his and his mother's lives all those years ago?

I glanced at Derek to get his reaction. He looked back at me with one eyebrow raised as if to say, *Interesting people you've been hanging out with.*

Oh, he had no idea. I couldn't wait to tell him everything.

Merrilee walked over to Nathan and wrapped her arms around his waist. For a moment he stood rigid; then he almost collapsed into her arms.

Grace finally spoke up. "Well, Marko, what do you have to say for yourself?"

Marko's jaw shifted and his eyes zeroed down to squinty pinholes. Was he thinking up some lame excuses? With his face scrunched up, he looked sort of like a tall, spiky-haired, trapped rat.

But suddenly he threw his hands up and began to laugh. "Damn, you got me! I'm busted."

The room was completely quiet as we all stared at him in amazement.

"That's it?" Grace said finally. "That's all you've got to say for yourself?"

He shrugged. "What am I supposed to say? The boy's right. I know you won't believe me, Marky, but I'm proud of you, son. You've made something of yourself."

"You're proud of me?" Nathan shook his head in disgust. "This isn't a family reunion, Pop. I intend to make sure you fry in jail for what you did."

Marko snickered nervously. "Pretty sure there's a statute of limitations out there somewhere, boy. But good luck with that." He turned to Grace. "I'll pay back the company if that'll help."

"It will," she said. "Tell me, Marko: did Bella know that you stole our ideas and sold them to the highest bidder?"

He hesitated, then frowned. "I couldn't tell her. I wanted to, but she was too damned honest. I didn't think she could keep the secret."

"Good. I'm glad she had nothing to do with it. I can't believe she ever had anything to do with you at all."

"She never did," he admitted, scowling. "Not yet, anyway. I was hoping to close the deal this week, but she kept putting me off."

"Then she was even smarter than I gave her credit for." Grace stood then and looked

413

him in the eye. "So that's it. You'll pay back the money, Marko. And you're fired."

"You — you can't fire me," he blustered. "You need me, especially now with Bella gone."

"You're so wrong, Marko," Grace said evenly. "If you think my company won't survive without you, then you're an even bigger fool than I thought you were."

Marko's pride faltered. He looked around for someone to latch onto, someone to talk to or commiserate with. But everyone ignored him and he was left to stand alone in the middle of the room, a pitiful shell.

I was glad to see that Grace had gotten her spine back. I'd worried that Sybil's attack followed by Marko's betrayal might have crushed some of Grace's spirit, much like Greta's spirit was crushed after she gave away her baby.

Okay, that was fiction. *This* was real.

It made sense that Marko wouldn't bother to defend himself, though. I'd thought from the start that he personified the term *slacker.* So why would he exert any energy in his own defense? It was too much trouble for a laid-back dude like himself. And that was the thing I found most pathetic about Marko Huntley.

■ ■ ■ ■

Grace insisted that Marko be arrested. But until the police arrived he would have to be detained somehow. Derek and Gabriel agreed with her, so Gabriel worked his magic with duct tape while Merrilee called the police.

Now Marko faced Sybil, duct taped to his very own chair in the Gold Salon. As a precaution Gabriel decided to rip the tape off Sybil's mouth so she wouldn't suffocate. Of course, that meant we all had to put up with her howls of pain for a few minutes.

Tired of her caterwauling, Gabriel got up close to her and said, "Look, I didn't want you to choke to death on your own rage before we had a chance to bring you to trial. But I'll cover that foul mouth of yours in a heartbeat if you don't shut up right now."

She huffed in response but said nothing, so we all headed for the door, intent on salvaging Grace's birthday party in another room.

"Wait!" Sybil cried. "Don't leave me here with that filthy creature!"

"Screw you, lady," Marko groused.

"Not you, you idiot," she shot back. "The cat. I'm allergic."

"It's Leroy," I said. "I'll get him."

"Don't you want to leave him here to taunt her?" Suzie said.

"I would," I said, "but that would be cruel to Leroy." I moved to pick him up, but Leroy had his own agenda. He sauntered over to Sybil and sniffed around her ankles. She tried to kick him, but before she could strike, Leroy reached out and clawed her leg, ripping her nylon stockings.

Sybil screamed. "Get him out of here! I'm going to puff up."

"She doesn't even like the cat," Ruth said, shaking her head.

Grace nodded. "Looks like the feeling is mutual."

I really did have to wrestle with the urge to leave Leroy in the room to torment Sybil. But in the end, I knew it wouldn't be fair to the nice kitty. So I knelt and scooped him up. I started to push myself up off the floor but noticed something under Sybil's chair near her designer bag. I took a closer look. It was another lost book.

"Vinnie, can you take the cat?"

"Of course," she said, reaching for Leroy. "And I'm going to have Merrilee order him fresh tuna for the rest of his life."

"He deserves it." I crawled a few more feet to see what had caught my eye.

"Get away from me," Sybil barked, and tried to kick me with her pointy-toed shoes.

"Oh, shut up," I muttered. Before I could slap her foot away, Gabriel warned her to stop. It worked. She was still for the moment, so I crawled around the side, stretched my arm underneath the chair, and snagged the book. Kneeling, I took one look at the dappled brown cover and knew what I had. "*Gulliver's Travels,* volume one!"

"Good job, Brooklyn," Nathan said, knowing what it meant to find the first volume.

Derek reached down to lend me his hand. Once I was back on my feet he chuckled. "One thing's for sure: with you, my life will never be boring."

I blinked in surprise, then slipped my arm through his. "You have no idea how sweet those words are to me."

I glanced at Grace and waved the book. She gave me a quick nod that I interpreted as approval of my taking the books. I was glad I wouldn't have to argue with her, because, frankly, after the week I'd had, there was no way I was leaving this house without my rapidly growing cache of rare books for the Covington Library.

We left Marko and Sybil stewing in the Gold Salon while the rest of us adjourned to the game room next door. The men agreed to take turns checking on the captives.

The fact that we'd discovered who Bella's murderer was gave us another reason to celebrate. Of course, Sybil had helped by exposing herself. But who was quibbling?

After the champagne was poured, Grace insisted that Nathan explain how the son of Marko Huntley had come to be working for her in her own home.

He told her that he'd been keeping tabs on everyone in Grace's company for years. As a computer whiz — a skill he refused to admit came from his father — he'd gained access to and knowledge of the most extensive online search programs. He had recently heard about Grace's book being shopped around New York City, and he devised a plan.

Grace played into his hands around that same time by advertising online for a librarian to catalog her books. When Nathan took the job, his only goal was to try to get a look at her manuscript. He wanted to see if Grace would name names. Wanted to see if she had ever discovered that his father was the thief who had cost her company millions of dollars.

"But then I got here and I fell in love with

Merrilee," he said, and had to clench his jaw to keep from becoming too emotional. "I fell in love with you, too, Grace. And you, Ruth, and this bizarre house and everyone who lives here. I'm sorry I lied to you. I can only hope that someday you'll look at me as someone other than the son of the man who stole from you."

"I already do, dear," Grace murmured.

"Thank you for that," he said, closing his eyes for a moment. He opened them and added, "And if you can find room in your heart to forgive me for deceiving you, I'll be eternally grateful."

Merrilee's hand was shaking, she was gripping his so tightly. She had been staring into Nathan's eyes, but now she turned and gave her mother a beseeching look.

Grace smiled at them both. "Of course I forgive you. As long as you promise to bring some order to the chaos that is my library."

Nathan hesitated, then frowned. "But I told you I'm not a librarian."

"But you're good with a computer," she insisted. "You said so yourself. Can't you just buy a program and learn how to work it?"

"Sure, I can do that." He scratched his jaw in embarrassment as he finally made eye contact with me. "That's why I could never show you my catalog program."

"I figured that out," I said drily. "It's okay. I know of a few good ones I can recommend to you."

"Then it's settled," Grace said. "So let's stop all this serious talk and get back to partying."

"I'll drink to that," Harrison said, and downed his champagne in one gulp.

I watched Grace mingle and worried for her. Her attitude was a little too glib and I wondered when she would take some time to mourn the loss of her former friend Marko, as well as poor Bella. They had all worked together and collaborated creatively for so many years. It had to be a tremendous blow to her confidence and well-being.

But on the other hand, she had faced down a jealous, raging, gun-toting maniac and lived to tell the tale. So maybe she could call things even. Either way, none of it was probably what she'd had in mind when she began to plan her fiftieth birthday party.

Happily, she had good friends and family who would help her get through it.

Peter Brinker, still clearly flummoxed, wasn't quite ready to party. "Grace, please help me understand why you never told me or anyone else about Merrilee. You didn't have to go through it all by yourself. We could've supported you during that time. I could've contributed to Merrilee's upbringing."

Grace gave him a sad smile. "My only excuse, once Merrilee was born, was that I knew Sybil better than you did. There was never a doubt in my mind that if she suspected Merrilee was your daughter, she would've made your life miserable. You'd probably be forced to quit the company." Grace squeezed his hand affectionately. "I couldn't afford to lose you, Peter. And I don't mean that in the monetary sense."

He was in shock. I felt sorry for the poor guy. He'd missed out on Grace and Merrilee and had spent his entire life with Sybil. Nobody deserved that.

It took Peter a moment, but he finally nodded and gave Grace a sad smile filled with regret for the years lost and opportunities wasted. Then he walked over to Merrilee and held out his hand. "Hello there, young lady. I'm your father."

Merrilee's eyes filled up with tears and she threw her arms around him. After a few seconds, she pulled back. "I always wanted a dad, but I'll understand if that scares you. Maybe we can just start out being friends."

"I would like that," Peter said, then turned

to Grace. "For two smart people, you and I have been kind of dumb all these years."

She accepted the comment with good grace and slipped her arms around Peter and Merrilee. "Let's try to be smarter from now on."

As if in agreement, Lily began to wail. Vinnie laughed, completely charmed. She picked up the baby and bounced her in her arms.

Derek gaped at the two of them. "I saw the baby, but didn't realize . . . it's Vinnie's?"

"Long story," I told him.

As Suzie went to join Vinnie and their daughter, catching them both up in a tight hug, Derek smiled and murmured, "Can't wait to hear it."

A loud banging stopped all conversations.

"What in the world?" Grace said.

"It's the front door," Merrilee whispered. "I'll get it."

"We have to get that doorbell fixed," Grace said.

"Probably the police," I muttered. "Just in time to spoil the party."

It was indeed the police, but they stayed long enough only to formally arrest Sybil and to take Marko in for questioning. It was Derek who convinced Detective Pentley that it would be better to come back the next day, when everyone was sober and able to give full statements.

Maybe it was Derek's British accent or the fact that he pulled the British Intelligence card, but the detectives retreated quickly with a promise to return the next day.

"Wait just a minute," Stephen Fowler demanded. "I refuse to stay in this hellhole one more minute. I'll follow you back to the station and give my statement. Then I'm going home."

Detective Pentley watched the entire room burst into applause, which caused Fowler's face to turn red with rage. He used every vile word in his vocabulary, damning us all to Hades before finally storming out of the room.

"Good riddance," Ruth said.

Grace sighed. "I'm going to need a new lawyer."

The party was back in full swing shortly after that. Everyone seemed to be having a good time and I turned to Derek. "We need to talk."

He skimmed my hair off my cheek with the backs of his fingers. "Yes, we do."

I caught his hand in mine and, oh, it felt good to have him beside me again. Still, I had to ask. "Don't take this the wrong way,

Derek, but what are you doing here?"

He gave a swift glance around the room. "I came here to save your life, as usual."

I stared at him, unable to look away. "You're late."

His lips twisted in a half smile. "I got here as quickly as I could."

"But why?"

He sighed and ran his hands up and down my arms, causing goose bumps to rise everywhere he touched.

"I know Thomasina answered my phone when you called," he said, watching my reaction. "She confessed to it after I had her arrested."

"Seems a little harsh to have her arrested just for being a snarky bitch. I mean, it's not like she actually lied. She just made me feel like crap."

He smiled. "Darling, she was arrested for being in cahoots with her own stalker. They were trying to embezzle money out of her financier father."

"More embezzlers?" I shook my head. "You've got to be kidding."

He raised one eyebrow. "I never kid."

"No, you don't," I murmured. "But it's still shocking."

"I assure you it's true. I saw that you had called, but I thought you had merely let it ring, then hung up. I had no idea she had answered the phone and given you cause to worry."

"Oh, I wasn't worried," I said breezily. "Why would I worry?"

"Why indeed?" He took hold of my arm and walked me over to a bay window that looked out on the lake. "It's beautiful here."

"Yes, it is," I said lightly. "I've been having a marvelous time."

He gazed down at me. "The truth is, once I realized what Thomasina had done to you and then traced the rest of her lies, I went a little berserk. I couldn't get home fast enough. And you weren't there. I'd forgotten you were coming here for the week, but remembered as soon as I walked into our home and called out your name. So I tried your cell but you weren't answering your phone and I thought . . . well, never mind what I thought."

"The phones must have been out because of the storm." A warm curl of delight started in the pit of my stomach and spread out, head to toe. *Derek* had been worried about *me*. Always nice to know.

"Right," he said, shoving one hand through his perfect hair. "But that wasn't my first thought. I figured I'd angered you so much that you weren't taking my calls.

Then I realized you were in the mountains and the lines might be down. I raced here, drove as far as I could get by car. They were only allowing SUVs and trucks through the pass, so I rented a snowmobile and came by land the rest of the way."

"You got here by snowmobile?" *My hero,* I thought with a happy sigh.

"And where do I find you?" he asked, and laughed. "In the middle of a murder scene. Naturally." He shook his head, laughed again, pulled me into his arms, and held me there. "Damn it, Brooklyn. I missed you. I was beside myself trying to get here to tell you . . ."

"To tell me what?"

"That I'll never stop trying to prove how much I love you."

"Oh." And there went the tears again. *Gee whiz. Is there some kind of surgical procedure to get rid of the damn things?*

"Darling Brooklyn, look at me," he said. Tilting his head, he saw my wet face. "Ah, you're sweet."

"I'm a sap," I muttered.

He ignored that. "After turning Thomasina over to the authorities and while racing back to you like a man possessed, it occurred to me that I'd never really made a clear commitment to you."

"Commitment? Of course you have. You —"

He pressed his finger over my lips. "No, don't say anything. Let me speak. When I came back to town a while ago to open my new offices, you were there for me. You were always there for me. You took me into your home and shared your life and your family with me."

"Well, of course," I said, gazing at him, unsure where he was going with this.

"Yes, it's that simple for you. Isn't it? I value that about you, Brooklyn. I've told you that I love you, but I've never had to work for your love and affection. You've always made it easy for me, accepting me into your life, always trusting me no matter what. Always so loving."

I swallowed, but couldn't speak. I really didn't want to ruin his homage to my trusting nature with tales of how worried I'd been about him and the thieving Thomasina.

He continued. "So when I finally realized that I might have allowed that trust to be broken, I was frantic to see you. I rushed back to assure you that I needed your trust back. Needed it more than I'd ever needed anything in my life. And I needed to let you know that I trusted you completely with my life and with my heart."

"Oh, Derek, of course I trust you. I missed you. I love you."

"I missed you enormously. I cherish you and I love you."

He kissed me then, and all my silly fears melted away. Someday I would regale him with what I'd gone through while I was here and maybe I'd tell him what a psycho girlfriend I'd been, but not today. And probably not tomorrow. It would take me a while to get to that place, but I would get there.

He pressed his forehead to mine. "Are we good?"

"Oh yeah," I said with a big smile.

"You guys are the greatest," Suzie said, wiping away a tear.

"Oh! You have to meet Lily," I said, taking Derek by the hand and walking him over to Vinnie, who carried the baby close to her chest. I introduced Derek to the little angel and explained everything that had happened.

"Congratulations," Derek said, and kissed Vinnie's cheek. "She couldn't have two more wonderful, generous, loving parents than the two of you."

"You are such a lovely man," Vinnie said. "Thank you."

"Damn it," Suzie said, wiping away more

tears. "What is up with the waterworks?"

"I feel your pain, sister," I said, and handed her a tissue.

Vinnie touched Derek's arm. "You have missed quite a bit of excitement this week. Why don't you two come over for dinner next week and we'll bring you up to date?"

"I wouldn't miss it." He glanced at me, then said, "We'll be there."

"Would you like to hold the baby?" Vinnie asked.

Derek grinned. "I was hoping you'd let me."

She passed Lily over to Derek, who laid her on his chest. He closed his eyes and smiled as he rocked slightly on his heels. His hand moved gently up and down the baby's pink-pajama-clad back.

I could feel my heart breaking, it was such a precious sight. Then he looked at me and smiled. "Pretty special, huh?"

I nodded, unable to speak.

"Oh, my God, Brooklyn," Suzie whispered. "He needs one of those."

Oh, boy. I fumbled for my tissue before I drowned in these darn tears.

Next to me, Kiki sighed. "Isn't that the sweetest thing you've seen all day?"

"Pretty much," I whispered, trying to swallow around the lump in my throat.

"Oh, hey," Suzie said, and looked at Grace. "You were supposed to make a big announcement tonight."

Grace rolled her eyes, then wrapped her arm around Ruth's waist. "My big announcement. Well, I was finally going to come out of the closet in front of my family and friends, but Ruth decided to push me out instead."

Ruth blushed. "I've got a big mouth."

Everyone laughed and Suzie gave her aunt a tight hug. "Welcome to my side of the closet."

"You were my inspiration, sweetie," Grace said softly. "You live your life with no apologies and no excuses, and I admire you more than anyone I've ever known."

"Oh no," Suzie wailed, and began to cry. "Damn it! There I go again."

I silently handed her another tissue and she blew her nose.

"You're such a girl," Vinnie said to Suzie, and hugged her.

"I think it's time for birthday cake and ice cream," Grace announced.

Merrilee was already on it. She ran to open the door for Chef Tang, who walked in pushing a kitchen cart holding a beautifully decorated sheet cake with blazing candles.

We sang "Happy Birthday," then the chef cut and plated the pieces of cake. Merrilee and Ruth walked around, handing a plate to each guest. I noticed that Grace wasn't eating any.

"Aren't you having any cake?" I asked. "It's delicious."

"I'll have some tomorrow," she said. "But tonight I get my favorite dessert. Once a year Tang bakes me a special treat. It's an old family recipe his mother and his grandmother used to make. He brought it with him from his remote village in Thailand."

Tang walked back into the room, carrying a large parfait glass filled with an elaborate concoction topped with huge swirls of whipped cream.

"What is that?" I asked.

"Mm," Grace said, licking her lips. "It's Tang's specialty. The best tapioca pudding in the world, made completely from scratch."

ABOUT THE AUTHOR

A native Californian, award-winning writer **Kate Carlisle** worked in television for many years before turning to writing. A lifelong fascination with the art and craft of bookbinding led her to write the Bibliophile Mysteries featuring Brooklyn Wainwright, whose bookbinding and restoration skills invariably uncover old secrets, treachery, and murder.

CPSIA information can be obtained
at www.ICGtesting.com
Printed in the USA
FFOW041535180213
889FF